Tabula

Rasa

J.S. Morton

First published in the UK in 2022 by
Dystopic Publishing Ltd
71-75 Shelton Street
Covent Garden
WC2H 9JQ
ISBN 978-1-3999-2101-5

All rights reserved. No part of this publication may be reproduced, stored in a retrieval system, or transmitted, in any form, or by any means (electronic, mechanical, photocopying, recording or otherwise) without the publisher's prior written permission.

www.dystopicpublishing.com
www.facebook.com/dystopicpublishing
www.instagram.com/dystopicpublishing

"Everyone is a moon, and has a dark side which he never shows to anybody."
Mark Twain

1

"Hold up, hold up, Karan!" Ray yelled. He stood with one arm propped against a building in the cold alleyway as he took a sip from the lukewarm lager. "Dude, stop a second, will ya? I gotta take a leak," he said.

"Ray, no!" Karan jerked around, scowling. "Come on, not here. Not now! You're better than pissing in alleyways!"

"I'm not. I'm really not." Ray shrugged. "Especially when it's a matter of life or death."

Karan shook his head. "Come on—I said we'd be there at eight!"

Ray's hand moved from the wall and his frozen fingers grasped his zipper. "As if Zeke's ever been on time for anything in his life? He probably doesn't even know what time it is!" He let his trousers slide down and drop to his ankles and continued to drink stale beer as urine trickled. Then the dam burst, and his desperation was relieved. "Ahhh!"

Karan stared at the vintage watch on his wrist. "Dude, hurry up! I swear, five minutes, and we'll be at Zeke's, and you can piss all over his toilet seats."

"Calm down, Tonto. You'll see the new place soon. Just hold your horses, will you?

With his bare bottom exposed, the light caught Karan's attention, and he shifted his gaze. Starting at the zip, he slowly raised his eyes. As they ascended, he got the briefest glimpse of Ray's crown jewels, but it was taboo, so he looked away. Ray continued to pee as he drank. Karan turned his back and let out an indulgent 'sigh'. He should have been frustrated, but he knew his buddy all too well.

A few feet away, Ray lingered in limbo. As the liquid vacated him like a powerful hose tossed on a lawn.

There was a splatter as warm urine hit the ground, like blood coursing from an artery. Ray was emptying himself one way or another. Urine or blood? It could be either.

The golden, beery respite released like furious demons desperately fleeing hell; it was one of life's most fundamental tasks yet such a simple pleasure!

Karan paused in the dark with his back turned to refrain from the lure of another glimpse of Ray's manhood. He glanced up at the night sky and took in the scene. The alley was cobbled, reminiscent of a German market town, but it wasn't Germany; it was the South of England in September, and the weather had grown particularly torrid. The ferocious wind howled down the stark stone walls that served only to funnel its fury like a pack of tortured wolves ringing into Karan's ears. He shuddered. The sound was unnerving.

Karan strolled to the end of the tunnel and noticed a vehicle mirror, and he paused to look becoming trapped alone in a bubble of his noise. Stuck in his reflection. He looked at it and saw Ray in the background, forcing him to juxtapose the two of them. They were of similar age, both mid-forties, but if you had to guess, Ray was the one who looked it!

Ray was destined to be bald from birth, and his metabolism had long since abandoned ship. A hedonistic lifestyle of sausage rolls, pork pies, and ale was catching up with him, but somehow it worked. His height, bulk, and rugged good looks had given him a *stocky* appearance. People naturally assumed he was a *hard* man and wouldn't trifle him. He wasn't ill-intentioned, but a lifetime of losing meant he revelled in his newfound glory.

Ray was a knowledgeable chemist, and no idiot, but fidelity and diplomacy were skills that sorely eluded him. He was the owner of many failed relationships. Yet, despite his detractors, something about his mid-forties 'man' look aided him in his quest to sleep his way through the local population of youthful females.

In contrast, Karan was boyish in complexion, tall, and lean. His parents had emigrated from India as betrothed children, and he had a naturally darker skin tone. A reason oft used by Ray when it came to explanations as to why Karan looked so much younger. A sentiment Karan would repeatedly do his best to ignore, given its wild cultural unacceptability. The truth was he did look younger. But it had everything to do with their difference in lifestyles and body maintenance and absolutely nothing to do with his ancestry.

Karan and his husband, Ivan, both ate, drank, and socialised vigorously. But when they weren't, they were dedicated to living a holistic lifestyle that included gym, swim, spa, massages, and spin classes. In comparison, Ray spent his free time eating, drinking, fucking, or watching the *History Channel*. Karan's only tell-tale sign of his age was the greying of his otherwise exceptionally black hair. But it consolidated his look, and there was little to suggest that he wasn't closer to twenty than fifty.

After an eternity of piss Ray finally finished, pulled his clothes back up and opened his mouth as he closed his zip.

"Remind me again why we're going?"

"We are going to see *our* friend," chastened Karan.

"Hmmm," a noise by way of reply. "More your friend than mine."

"Shut up! We've known Zeke almost as long."

"Knowing someone doesn't make them my friend," said Ray. "Were it not for you, I don't think I'd see him at all!"

"Oh, now that's just the beer talking. How many have you had?"

"Speaking of knowing him, does anyone know Zeke? I mean, do you? Really?" Ray continued as he waved his arms wildly in the air.

"What are you talking about?"

"Zeke," replied Ray. "He's in there, but he isn't! I stare into those eyes, and I see nothing. It's just a blank slate that stares back at me. The guy's pathological."

"If by 'pathological' you mean he calls you on your shit?" replied Karan. "Then you're right!

"Anyway, you love telling the blank slate story."

"*Tabula rasa*? Yeah, that's because it's weird!" Ray replied. "Ha-ha, anyway don't get me started on that evening. That was the night you made me meet him!"

"Hey, you brought up blank slates! Anyway, the guy is perfectly normal, happily married, child on the way."

"Happily married," muttered Ray. He shook his head towards Karan's platitude. A movement laced with cynicism and perhaps a nod towards his failed marriages.

"If anyone's weird, it's you," Karan said, facing him. "You're pathologically incapable of being happy."

"I'm just saying," continued Ray. "If your gut tells you something is off, it is! Do you know how many prescriptions I fill with that man's name?"

"You're drunk. Zeke's cool, man, and you know it! When you dislike someone, you usually dislike the part that doesn't resonate with yourself."

"Save the psychobabble for school!" Words uttered, Ray, caught up with his friend, snuck up on him and barged into his side playfully.

"Well, we're waiting on you now," Ray joked as he turned about and ruffled Karan's hair as he walked away. Head ruffled; Karan glanced up at his scalp.

"Eww."

Oblivious to his friends' protests, Ray walked, talked, and drank. Warm beer dripped onto his t-shirt and fell towards the floor, a beery tear that fell like blood and smashed and broke on the cold concrete.

"Anyway, he says weird thimgs!" The mispronounced words fell out of Ray's mouth as he oafishly multitasked.

"Well, if he does, at least he can pronounce the word 'things'," Karan replied as he caught up to his buddy. "Anyway, Zeke is complicated. You would be too if you'd been through as much trauma as he has! Cheer up, you grouch. We're off to see friends, drink—" Karan's own words trailed off as he snatched the lager from Ray's hand and stole a sip before his friend could protest. "Eugh, that's warm," Karan proclaimed, shuddering as he let the lukewarm liquid glide past his lips.

"Well, it's yours now," Ray beamed with a bullish smile.

They turned left at the end and disappeared into the darkness, their voices now just an echo that danced into the night. In the background, Ray's warm urine pooled like blood as it trickled down the cold stone towards the drain.

Stood at the perimeter gate, the duo huddled side by side. The journey (time that included Ray's pit stop) had taken forty-five minutes.

"Fifteen minutes." Ray had said as they left his house on foot. They were cold, shivery, and keen to escape the elements. Yet as they entered the gate, they stopped and turned to each other, both sets of eyes aghast as they took in the vision.

"Woah," said Ray.

"Fucking Woah, you mean?" It reminded Karan of a secret hideaway an eccentric Bond villain would own.

"What did you say Zeke did for a living?" asked an unusually speechless Ray.

"Erm, art dealer?" Karan answered.

Ray eyed up the converted barn before he replied, "Arms dealer more like."

Karan laughed, still barely able to believe his senses. He had seen some of the renovations but had little interest in visiting the Olsen's construction site/fuck den. Outside of social occasions, he hadn't seen much of them since they bought the land. No one really had. Sometimes, it annoyed him, but he knew he was probably jealous of their marital bliss.

To Ray, marriage was a disaster and to Karan a vacancy. His husband Ivan ran a pharmaceutical company and travelled regularly, often, frequently, usually, mostly. There were many ways to phrase it, but Ivan was typically in absentia.

"We should enter," Karan said to Ray. His words were laced with a tinge of anxiety. They'd been stood for an excessive amount of time, and the silence had only grown louder.

The main building loomed before them. A behemoth, incandescent before their eyes. It was no longer the dilapidated, small, ancient barn. It had come a long way.

The day after they'd purchased it, Zeke had insisted that Karan came to see it. He'd told him all about it, their plans, and what they would do with it. Zeke even made Karan go inside. He itched every time the memory was recollected in his brain, forever scattered across his mind. He was scared of what it could have been, but now he feared what it was. It was irrational. But isn't that what fear is? Irrational?

Karan had dreaded an evening in a small, dirty barn. This, however, was not that! It was a stunning duplex, contemporary and old, stylish, and shabby. It was both modern chic and intimidatingly cool. Karan knew Zeke made good money, but this was something else.

They had kept a few of the original wooden beams and filled them with humongous windows. Panes that featured hefty metal shutters, primed and ready to slide across. They stood on duty like an executioner, hovering over the axe. LED lights shone out from behind the windows like a lighthouse. Karan looked at the shutters once more and felt uneasy. Could they keep people out? Or trap them inside?

The compound contained the main house, a garage, and an annexe. Beyond that, there was only land for miles, an open field that met a tall electric fence. It had once seemed like a never-ending project. But now it was complete. It was almost incomprehensible.

They reached the front door and hovered in darkness for too long until Karan stepped forward and pressed the doorbell. The circular button illuminated at the edges and changed colour as it spun. It reminded him of a Catherine wheel, but the light came without sound as he stood captivated. They were trapped in a bubble, waiting, had the doorbell rung? Did anyone know they were here? Ray stepped forward and prepared to wrap his fists against the robust metal door. But as he balled his hand and readied for an attack, the door creaked before swinging open like a safe vault. They remained lifeless as their senses were assaulted by lights, sights, smells, and sounds. The visceral, sensual attack on their wits landed mere moments apart. It left their brains attempting to decipher and take it all in at once. From complete silence and relative darkness, they found themselves momentarily stunned.

Zeke's figure appeared like a mirage as the door rolled open. His intimidating frame loomed and hung in the entrance. He was of average height but muscular in build, dressed in shorts, a vest, and flip-flops, which showed large chunks of his tattooed body. He registered the pair and ran his hands through his jet-black hair. His bright blue eyes glared at them menacingly before a smile appeared and etched itself slowly over his face.

"Guysss," he said excitedly as he stretched out his muscular frame to accommodate a double hug.

Keen to enter the Elysium but unable to avoid the clutches of the outstretched armed giant, they entered awkwardly in unison, immediately finding themselves trapped in a bear-like hug.

"Karan, Ray," Zeke exclaimed excitedly.

After almost having the life physically squeezed out of them, they were set down by Zeke, who addressed them individually. He took Karan first and grabbed him firmly by the shoulders.

"Karan," he asked. "How's Ivan?"

"He's good, Zeke, he's good."

"And how are you?"

"I'm—"

Zeke immediately turned his attention to Ray and lunged toward him. He clutched at his arms in a movement that almost physically raised him.

"And Ray," he said, "you smell like beer."

"Brought one for the road," Ray replied.

"Naturally, who doesn't? That must have been some journey!" Zeke then stared at him inquisitively. "But the real question is do you smell too much like beer or not enough?"

"Never enough, buddy, never enough," Ray answered. He snuck past his host and sauntered away. Having made his escape, he turned back towards Karan. Their eyes connected just long enough for Ray to spin his finger around his ear and mouth the words 'crazy' while pointing at Zeke.

Karan chuckled and rolled his eyes simultaneously before stepping in and disrobing.

"Ray being Ray?" Zeke asked.

Karan nodded. "You know how he is after a few?"

"Absolutely," replied Zeke. "Still, we can't have a housewarming party without his brand of charm, can we?"

"He does have a certain je ne sais quoi!" replied Karan. Having entered and prised himself from the long grey trench coat, Karan found a nearby hook and hung it neatly inside the front door.

"Digging the place," Karan said, turning towards his host. Zeke grinned.

"It's cool, isn't it?"

"Buddy, cool doesn't even cut it. I love the garage."

"Wait until you see what's inside it."

"You got the GTA?" Zeke smiled some more.

"Among others."

"Dude, I gotta see! Those things cost a fortune. Do you remember looking them up online years ago?" he asked rhetorically.

"All in good time, my friend. Come, let me show you around."

"How's Cassie?" Karan asked as they walked.

"At her mother's," replied Zeke.

"Oh!"

"Ah, it's nothing. I'm away in the morning."

"But it's your housewarming! It's unlike Cassie to miss a soirée."

"She's pregnant. And you're welcome!" he said, hitting Karan playfully on the arm. "You're not missing out. It's mood swing city! Anyway, take a deep breath, and look around you. It's like a scene from *Scarface* in here. I know it's still inside of her, but this is no place for my baby."

Karan laughed, "Duh, of course. Although presumably less blood and machine guns?"

"For now," Zeke replied, winking at him.

"The funny thing is, I wouldn't put it past you." Karan laughed. "Zeke Olsen, the man who can get you anything."

"Cheers to that," replied Zeke.

Karan paused before moving the conversation along, "New York, right?"

Zeke clicked his fingers in Karan's direction. "That's the one!"

"What is it you do when you're out there again?"

"The magic is in the art, my friend."

Karan cocked an eyebrow and looked at Zeke. "Come on!"

"I've told you a thousand times, buddy! Anyway," he said, placing his arm around Karan's shoulder, "Let's not talk about work now, it's playtime. Let's go upstairs. You two were the last to arrive."

2

Zeke closed his eyes and took a deep breath as he stood alone in the field. The cool air rushed in and inflated his lungs like balloons. With his eyes closed, he imagined himself back in Norway. His paternal grandparents hailed from just outside Lillestrom, and although it had been years since he'd visited, it appeared to him like a recent dream. He remembered the feeling of the winters and their harsh chill. He could taste the nearby fjords and the crisp mountain air with every sip. The space and the emptiness filled him up. It gave him the feeling of being surrounded but utterly alone, insanely lost, curiously found. The void forced the reminiscence upon him, and he realised how far away that life now seemed.

But this would be his space here, he imagined as the cool summer breeze fluttered through his neatly arranged long hair. A plucky gust dislodged strands that stretched back across his otherwise shaved head. The darkness fell over his eyes, tainting his vision. Zeke removed his hands from his pockets and combed them through his hair. His fingers brushed over his head before returning to his side slightly too late.

A lone figure entered the field and had taken advantage of his moment of hesitancy. A gut feeling alerted him to the danger, but he was too slow. Two arms appeared and wrapped themselves around his middle, clutched at him, jolted, heaved, and wrestled him to the floor.

"If I were an assassin, you'd be dead!" she spoke.

"I can think of worse ways to die!" he replied as he eyed up his attacker. "Death by sexy virago?"

"Hey," she said, "I'm not bad-tempered."

"Okay," he replied antagonistically.

Cassie knelt over him, pushed her weight down on his arms, and pinned him. Blonde hair dangled from her brow and tickled his face in the wind. Her breasts heaved in and out and pushed into his chest with every deep exhale. Their eyes made contact and she gave him a look, one just for him.

Zeke took it in for as long as he could. He studied; he remembered the moment's perfection and drank it in. Then out of her line of sight, he manoeuvred his hands and reached upwards. His arms moved into position; once there, he pushed Cassie's limbs out at the elbow, and she fell face-first into him. Their heads collided with a solid 'thud' as she landed in a chaotic collision. She rolled from him and lay side by side on the grass.

"You're an idiot," she said. "You know this is yours?" Cassie shoved her bloody finger into Zeke's chest and wiped it clean. The impact had drawn a small amount of blood from his nose. It trickled down his palette and onto his chin. He turned towards her and licked the blood from his face as their eyes met.

"What do you think?"

"I think you're gross."

"You knew that already," he replied. "I meant about the place." Cassie tilted her head back and looked hard across the field. The old wooden shed appeared transposed in her view.

"I'm picturing it with snow," she said.

"And...?"

"I love it!"

"Really?"

"Yeah, but it's tiny! I have no idea where you're gonna sleep."

Zeke moved and jumped up suddenly. He grabbed Cassie by the arms in the same motion and hauled her from the floor.

"Raze it from the ground," he proclaimed. The movement exuded an excited *yelp* as Cassie was hoisted to her feet. "As the phoenix rises from the ashes, we'll start anew, me and you. We can rebuild it bigger and better than before."

"Zeke Olsen," she replied, "you're still an idiot. I don't know how many clichés you've just ripped through!"

"Not enough," he said in a grandiose voice. "You see, where you find your fear, there is your tas—" Cassie kissed him before saying anything else. As she removed her lips from his, she said,

"You know I'm a psychologist, right?"

"And I am an artist."

"Are you high?"

"High on you," he replied casually. "Anyway, don't see it for what it is. Think of what it could be! A haven, paradise, bliss, ambrosia, Valhal—"

"If you say Valhalla, I'm going to punch—"

"Woah, Woah! Wait, think for a minute! We could have space, noise, light, parties, cars, offices, and children?"

"You had me at cars and noise," she chuckled. But seriously, can we afford it?"

"Of course, we can!" he replied. But of course, they couldn't. "You're an Olsen now. We are Vikings, and we must have land."

"You're a lunatic, Zeke Olsen."

"A lunatic and an idiot? Then you, my dear, hit the jackpot!"

"But your savings, I thought we'd spent most of it on the wedding and honeymoon?"

"Well," he said, "I have enough for the land, then we'll sell the flat. That covers most of it."

"But the—"

"You trust me, don't you?"

"Always, and forever," she'd replied earnestly.

"Then don't worry about the money!"

They'd stood side by side in the field, separated only by breath. Zeke held both her hands softly, and as he opened his mouth to speak, he remembered her once more in fond amazement. He studied every inch of her, the tip of her toes to the top of her head. As he reached the summit, he saw the moisture and detected the water accumulating atop her eyeballs like a glass pond—Cassie's inner woman appeared as she broke into tears. Yet, as he surveyed the inches of her face, he noticed that the lines and the harshness of age had softened somehow. Like a portrait of *Dorian Grey*, she looked younger, smoother, and more innocent. But then she would! Because this was just a memory. Six, maybe, seven years had passed since this moment.

"It's so secluded. We can make as much of a racket as we want!" Zeke remembered her saying.

"No one will hear you scream; you mean?" he'd replied. Managing to pull off confident and jovial rather than creepy and insidious.

She'd shrieked and jumped into his arms, and the two fell haplessly into the brush once more. As they lay on the floor, he swept the blonde hair away from her moist eyes and held her head between his hands. He recalled the warmth of her skin as it met his palms, remembered those beautiful, bursting brown eyes returning his gaze. Life made sense when they were together, the moon had no shadows, and his pain was lifted. It was precisely the moment he could live in forever.

Zeke relinquished himself from her gaze and studied Cassie's rakish perfection. She was resplendent. Elegant yet dishevelled, lean in figure, but full all the same. Cassie was always fighting fit. Could life ever be as perfect as it is right now? Could she? An idle thought was finding its way into his memory. The happiest you've ever been was not necessarily the happiest you'll ever be! Or was it? He was happy, but could he have been happier?

A cool breeze washed through his thoughts and projected onto them. Cassie nestled deep into his side and set her chin down on his chest. Her head moved up and down awkwardly with each breath, but it did not bother her.

"Hmmm," was the noise that oozed out from within her. "This is lovely. Can we just stay here forever?"

"Sure," he replied as his head drooped and his eyes drifted back. He remembered fixating on the darkening evening sky and felt his mind move to oblivion. "Sure," he said again, a word of conviction, an assurance as much to himself as to her.

"Sure," he'd repeated as though the reinforcement would somehow make it come true. "Sure!"

3

"Mr Olsen, excuse me, Mr Olsen! Sir!"

A sweet sound stirred his senses, echoed around his eardrums, and pervaded his consciousness. The serene, almost tranquilising words were accompanied by a gentle tap on his shoulder, contact that slowly dragged him back to life.

Zeke's hung-over, semi-open eyes were greeted by a uniformed female flight attendant who was hunched over next to him. With his gaze fixated at her feet for a few moments, he began moving his eyeballs all the way up the length of her figure. Just as he was savouring every bit of that succour-inducing sight, his senses were suffused with an exotic perfume. It was an intricate, intoxicating scent. It permeated his nostrils and stirred his soul.

"Mr Olsen?" she repeated. "We're preparing for landing. I must ask you to stow your tray table, turn off your electronic devices, and open your blind?"

Zeke furiously blinked away at the medicated void of sleep and reaccustomed himself to his surroundings. He sat forward and emitted a slight grunt as he did.

The party had lasted until the early hours of the morning. Finding himself alone, Zeke moved to the study, sat in the dark, and glared out at the dawn.

Everything was so peaceful at night. You could literally see, hear, and smell *it all*. He noticed their home still emitted a *new house* smell, and he was amiss to leave so soon. Despite taking an inordinate amount of time to complete, the fact remained that this project meant a lot to him. But now that it was finished, he felt a strange conflict. Inexorably, the expected relief was accompanied by a hefty dose of *now what?*

Having sat pensively in the study for too long, he was impelled to rush when the taxi approached. He shoved the rest of his things in a bag and made for the front door. It was just after four in the morning, and the traffic should have been light. But somewhere between forgetting, drinking, and not wanting to leave, he'd left it very late.

The taxi arrived, and he jumped in hastily. The car pulled through the gates and onto the main road; he'd spotted Cassie's car returning to the compound as it did. That she was coming home at that time was inexplicable, but it was *her* house. He didn't have the time to stop. Instead, he'd drunkenly thrust his head from the window and yelled,

"I'll call you as soon as I land! Love you!" His voice started loud before it petered out into the twilight. Maybe she did hear and wave back as their vehicles parted or perhaps she didn't notice at all?

"Mr Olsen?"

The sobering sound hit him. Zeke looked up and met the gaze of the flight attendant. He somehow got his head to nod and offer up some form of audible confirmation.

"Thank you, sir," she said before righting herself and returning toward the cockpit. Zeke allowed his mind to wander with her, conjuring some rather salacious thoughts. A mere moment of prurience. He shook his head, purged the thoughts, and shifted his attention to the tasks.

Zeke shut his laptop before leaning over to stash it away carefully in his carry-on bag. As he moved, he caught the eye of an elderly gentleman sitting across from him. It was as though the older man had sensed his thoughts through some form of subconscious male carnal frequency. Their gaze met, and the man winked at him, then nodded towards the recently departed. As their eyes locked, the man raised his glass and tipped it towards him. He had been holding a drink at the start of the flight! Either he was a very fast or extremely slow drinker.

Zeke returned a cursory, slightly awkward nod and then turned away quickly. He reached across the empty seat and slid up the silky shutter keeping the patient light at bay.

"Always with the blinds," he thought to himself. As he yanked it upward, light leaked into the plane. He remembered reading something about it being to do with emergency planning. They didn't want passengers blinded by the daylight when the doors opened in a crash landing. That was the reason! Zeke loathed aeroplanes! If humans belonged in the sky, they would all have wings, which hadn't gone too well for Icarus!

The shutter rose, and the outside world revealed itself to him—body, wing, engine, clouds, and finally—the bright lights of America. New York was vast and unerringly impressive, given the great height. He felt like a child looking down at a model village as he beheld the titan below him.

The plane circled, and he peeled his gaze from the window. A glimmer of light from above reflected off his right hand and back into his brain. The distraction was welcome, and he smiled as he looked down at the ring on his finger. It sat in place of his wedding band, which was currently in his bedside drawer. So terrible was he with his belongings that Cassie would make him leave valuable ones at home whenever he went abroad. The band had worn away at the tattoos on the finger, and the generations of *Olsen* fingers had eaten away the band. Zeke was not a fan of jewellery, but something about the monogrammed ring kept it in place. He wondered what stories it could tell. He remembered so little of his grandfather, who first bore it. And he wondered how it had survived the fury of fire when his father had faded?

Zeke's grandfather was also named Ezequiel Olsen, but he used his full name, unlike Zeke. Norwegian-born, he'd married an English woman and much like the Vikings before him, he'd split himself between the two countries—an actual Christian name mixed with pagan heritage. The print on the ring had initially read *ES*. The lettering had almost faded, and the band was failing, that couldn't happen! Zeke made a mental note to get it repaired when he got home.

The name *Ezequiel* was biblical in origin, meaning God strengthens, or God is strong. Zeke's school was a Christian one, and he was well versed in the chapters. It was something he'd never really embraced nor wholly dismissed.

The plane banked as the nose started to dip. The movement forced Zeke back to reality and a small knot formed in his stomach.

"Cabin crew, take your seats for landing, please."

The plane rolled sharply to the right before beginning its descent. It had been many years since Zeke had been to New York, and it was one of the last trips he remembered taking with his parents that hadn't ended in tragedy. As he shook away the memories of dearly departed, the plane trembled, and so did he.

The ungainly tube with wings bobbled and waved as it dipped over the rooftops, swaying in the crosswinds as the outside world slowly got bigger and bigger until finally, the wheels thudded as they made a connection with the tarmac. Terra firma, thank God they were down!

4

Zeke stared across at Cassie; he watched her as she watched him. It was about two in the morning. He looked deeper and surveyed her bloodshot but gorgeous brown eyes. They reflected his image as they gazed generously back at him. Behind the browns, he saw wonder, generosity, patience, and kindness. He wondered what she might find beneath his brilliant blues. Does she see what he wanted her to, or could she see the true horrors? If anyone looked too deep, they would find a thinly veiled disguise. This was the face he showed to the public, but Cassie wasn't just anyone.

Zeke had experienced things no teenager should. There was pain, and then there was pain. Zeke knew the latter. No living soul should ever witness the sight of their parents burning right before their very eyes. But knowing and showing are two different things entirely.

The world is filled with destitution, greed, poverty, and tragedy. Terrible things happen every day, yet few are ever exposed to them. Those who are find themselves conditioned, forced to learn how to smile, mask the pain, and appear normal. Because there is no place in polite society for pain. It is a showreel for life's best bits, nothing more.

Cassie was probably the only one who knew the real him. She knew of his horrors and pain, but she couldn't feel them.

Zeke replays the moment in his head. The pair stood alone, chaotically entwined in the street. The rustic village pub had made them leave about an hour before.

"Go home, you crazy love birds!" the barman had yelled playfully as he slammed the door. It had been a long, scenic stumble home.

It was summertime, and the air was sultry. The duo sat by the river in the twilight. Zeke examined the waterway as the moon's glow reflected off the water and into Cassie's pupils. To him, it was like staring directly into another galaxy; these eyes held a gloss, a desire within them. One that somehow existed just for him.

They had owned the field with the barn for six months, and the renovations were far from plan or budget, but it didn't matter. They had each other, warm weather, and a large tent. He'd watched on as he poured money deeper into it. They had begged, borrowed, and barely survived. They'd woken hungover on the floor only to go to work and come home to construction. It was less than ideal, and his back hurt constantly. But it had been simple, fun, and honest. When you live in chaos, you reach a point where it doesn't matter if life isn't perfect or if things don't go to plan. Everything is wrong, and therefore nothing is.

Life had been working, building, redecorating, drinking, painting, drinking, fucking, dancing—late mornings were followed by early nights. And somehow, between the two of them (and a small amount of help), the garage went up, followed shortly after by the rest.

Their budgetary constraints even meant that Cassie allowed Zeke to keep the much-loathed chest freezer. He'd found it on a street corner many years ago, dragged it back to his flat, and restored it almost to life. It was over six feet long and three wide, rusted, bashed and stickered. Cassie had branded it "the budget morgue." It was gross, but it was roomy and free. It worked and could simultaneously freeze kilo upon kilo of reduced meat and rapidly chill beer. Having tagged along, it now resided in the garage.

They would go on to complete construction in time for Cassie to finish her PhD, and they would contrive to conceive a life together. It had been confusing, dirty, and messy. Zeke had everything he'd been looking for, everything he needed, and yet life had begun to wane before it had waxed.

They'd sat beside the rosy river until the sun poked its head from the horizon. It was light when they stumbled hand in hand along the country lane, back to their land. He remembered, dreamt it as though it were yesterday. They had a skip in their step as they arrived home. Zeke hopped the fence and entered their property, letting go of Cassie's hand for the briefest of moments while he vaulted the old wooden barrier. Once over, he turned back around and stretched a hand toward his lady. But when he spun, he came face-to-face with nothing. Just a blank space where Cassie had once been.

Zeke looked around in panic. He was alone in the field, and he stared into an abyss. It was like an empty canvas, a snow globe bereft of snow. This isn't how he remembered it; this isn't what happened! Cassie would never just disappear!

Zeke thought he'd already been to perdition. He knew its taste and its smell. But this was different. Actual hell, it seemed, was an absence of people you loved.

"Cassie!" he yelled in panic, begging for her as he called out in the dark. "Cassie, Cassie, Cass…"

5

Zeke opened his eyes and bolted upright in terror. The room was pitch black aside from a small ray of light that trickled in from under the door. A cold, stale blanket of sweat lay drenched across his lean, muscular frame. He'd landed, departed the airport, fought for a taxi, and survived the Brooklyn concrete jungle.

Upon entering the room, the neon glow of Times Square had peeked through the hotel room blind, almost burning itself onto his retinas. He'd arrived, closed the door, and slumped down on the chair next to the window. A digital hum had seeped through the noiseless glass and willed him into sedation. The city had been electric, eclectic, and eternal. Inside, he was jaded, jet-lagged, and joyless. He'd closed his eyes gently and fell into a slumber.

Zeke shook off the panic and glanced at his watch. The digital numbers flickered away, and his brain deduced that it was one in the morning.

"Shit!"

Cassie, he thought to himself. Cassie! It would be about six a.m. back home.

"I'll call you!" he'd said. But he couldn't call, not now. It once was the first thing he'd do upon landing. She'd stay up and listen attentively as he described the flight, the people, the sights. Now it all flashed by as a drugged, drunken haze.

The taxi ride had seemed never-ending. It was a Friday evening in New York. The air was thick, and the traffic was deceptively dense. Zeke slipped in and out of consciousness as the driver burbled away. Something to do with muggings. Perhaps it was gang-related? Gangs of New York? His internal monologue yelled out as the driver moaned away. He was incessant, never stopping to wait for a reply. His words could have been some great awakening, but it was all noise to Zeke. He was off to a room in his mind where no one could find him. A dwelling deep inside where only thoughts existed.

Zeke raised himself from the chair and stood. He removed his charger and adapter from his carry-on, then knelt and fiddled away, desperate to get the alien socket into the wall. Power coursed through the cable, and the screen burst to life. He would likely have numerous missed calls, texts, and countless communications from the two, maybe three, people for whom he cared.

Zeke considered his unborn daughter. In little under four months, they would produce a child—oh, the marvel of birth! It was a scant miracle. People conceived because they were bored or because society deemed it necessary. These desires were enabled by modern medicine. Gone were the days when you might have to choose between descendants or losing your paramour to childbirth.

His body settled down to relax once more as he forgot all about the charging phone. But his mind kept going. Should people have to pass some form of test before conceiving? Ought they be judged on their merits and reasoning rather than whims?

After they'd announced their new arrival, the excitement from everyone around them was palpable. Friends and family alike would enquire daily about the unborn lump. Cassie would update them on its comparative size and weight. Did anyone really care? Zygotes progress, and babies grow. As much as he loved Cassie, Zeke didn't understand some of the things she thrived on. It was just procreation—a primary human function. He wondered if giraffes, lions, or elephants got as excited as humans during gestation.

With his mind busier than a racetrack on race day, Zeke sat back up. He'd lost an hour, maybe more. His brain was unwilling to switch off despite the long day, and when he finally glanced at his phone, there were a thousand notifications, all of which he ignored. His return flight was in less than thirty-six hours. What a whirlwind this was going to be.

Giving up on sleep, Zeke raised himself and stumbled across the room to the minibar, then cracked one of the small bottles and raised it to his lips. Zeke took a short, sharp swig of the cold, acrid liquid.

"Ugh."

Of course, he'd grabbed the whisky. He lowered the bottle to his waist as his other hand moved a handful of painkillers in the opposite direction. He took another sip from the miniature bottle to wash them down. His back pain always tripled after many hours doubled over in airports. The discomfort originated from scar tissue and worked in tandem with his chronic inability to sleep—the two evil twins that regularly kept him away from the land of rest, restoration, and sanity.

Zeke had struggled with hurt, pain, and trauma for over twenty years, and his mind had turned him into a sleepless ghost. People would offer sympathy and medical professionals a short-term solution. But it was one of those things you just don't get unless you do. It had been so long since he'd slept sober that he'd forgotten how. Something once so intrinsic had become a solution-less puzzle.

Zeke lay back down on the bed, shut his eyes, and willed for the darkness to come for him; it shouldn't be long now. As he drifted off, he thought about Cassie, Karan, and his parents, but when he closed his eyes, he couldn't picture any of them. On the inside, there was only a dark, empty canvas of thoughts racing the other—a competition to see which stupid idea would keep him awake the longest.

With the cocktail struggling to take effect, he opened his eyes and stared down the ceiling. He watched as the possibly fictional ceiling fan spun round and round, round and round. With his eyes open, he could see something that probably wasn't there. But when he closed them, he saw nothing. He watched the fan rotate like a propellor blade, the chopping noise soothing his whirling brain.

Keep an eye on the fan.
Whirrrrrrrr.
Keep watching the fan.
Whirrrrrrrr.
Focus on the fan.
Whirrrrrrrr.

6

A noise from the corridor shot underneath the door frame and rattled around his skull. The fragile nap was shattered and gone forever. Zeke doubled over in a panic and grabbed his phone.

Thankfully, it was only five a.m. there was no way he could afford to oversleep. The relative time meant that Zeke only had four and a half hours until he was due at the gallery. He'd attempted sleep three times and got almost halfway there, but there was zero chance of returning. He stirred and made a cold coffee to flush down more pills to kill the pain.

Zeke stepped away from the side and threw back the curtain. The hotel was on New York's doorstep. He should make the most of his spare time.

A tired trawl of Times Square at sunrise had been sufficiently surreal. Not many cities sleep, but New York was in perpetual motion. It was five-thirty in the morning, and the whole place was alive. Zeke had walked, talked, and eaten. A constant chorus in an all-night saloon.

The early excursion left him with less than two hours until he had to be at the art gallery. Early morning meetings were hell, given that he rarely slept, and even if he could, he seldom wanted to. There was so much lost time in sleeping.

He would get to the gallery just before or after nine. It would be a simple exchange. Zeke was at his best when he didn't stop or think. So, he casually strolled back to the hotel, showered, dressed, and corrected himself before stepping back into the world.

He had been hired predominantly for these moments. Beyond that, he did little actual work for Marguerite. It was a good arrangement. When he wasn't travelling, he wasn't needed for much, and it afforded him the ability to put maximum effort into small moments.

It was Saturday morning in New York, which apparently meant absolutely nothing. The masses were just as fierce as any other day. Getting on a train was a real fight as he pushed through the square and down to the underground.

The subway early on a Saturday was madness. It didn't help that he'd barely seen sleep or sobriety in the last two days. The noise was vivid, the sights were loud, and the seats were old and shabby. When he finally found a chair, it was uncomfortable and stained. It made him wonder how much of the grime was either blood or semen. Sitting on the crowded, dirty bench, he sensed a familiar pain creeping in as his dark friend appeared. Alone with his thoughts was sometimes the worse place to be. There was a discomfort no one could see or feel except for him. People would be kind if he had a knife protruding from his back. They would run to his aid, offer him help, or at least their seats. But his pain was completely invisible, and sometimes it made him question whether it was ever really there. Always in pain, never in pain, is there a difference?

Zeke climbed out of his head and into the world around him. He was in a long line of pipes, tubes filled with people squashed together like Pringles in a can. Everyone was in such a hurry to get where they needed to go. Every morning on repeat, another day, another tube, another job. He remembered the life, minimum wage work, never knowing where his next meal would come from, or not being sure if he had the money to see out the month, underpaid for overtime, desperate to get by. It seemed like an odd thing to miss, but it would elicit a feeling, a fear that kept things honest. Zeke worried that his lack of problems might cause him to go looking for some.

People blurred past Zeke as he remained motionless in his seat. Suited in black wearing a pale face, he waited, watched, waited, watched. The train finally stopped for him, and Zeke surveyed his feet as they moved from carriage to carriageway, under to overground. He hit the surface and upped his pace. The digital map deciphered what was essentially the Minotaur's maze, and he broke a sweat as he rounded the last corner. Some steam poured from a grate in the ground as a yellow cab hovered over it. Was it a priceless scene or an overpriced canvas? Zeke slipped some tablets gently under his tongue, rocked his head back and forth to swallow, and then moved through the park and towards the gallery.

The building was in the centre of the Bronx, oddly out of place, fancy yet downtrodden. Like a street beggar with a top hat and monocle. It had no business being there. The irony was that he had no place being there either.

Marguerite had plucked him from his weary, dreary life behind a bar in Chichester. She'd seen a man who'd never fit in but didn't stand out. He could be anything and nothing. His only real talent was being like an *Etch A Sketch*, able to draw anything on his face. He wasn't fake. He'd just figured out how to successfully navigate a world in which he didn't belong. It was rare that his energy didn't bring people towards him, Ray being perhaps the only exception, he couldn't be like Zeke, and he disliked him for it.

The building's silhouette shone out over the river like the shadow that lurks behind you. It caused Zeke to shudder as he arrived and grabbed the glass door. Zeke carefully removed his headphones, tangled them up in his bag, and prepared himself before pulling them open. He stepped into the lobby, raised his grin, and put out his hand. His palm met another, and they shook. Zeke noticed the outline of a clock on the wall, except the partition was glass, and all he could see was the reverse.

Zeke moved through the lobby, through some more glass doors, until he found himself on the right side of the timepiece. It was nine-fifteen, and he had roughly twenty-two hours until his return flight. It would be a long and hectic day.

He stood patiently at reception, almost staring at the courteous, blond lady who approached him. She smiled, took him by the hand and led him through the lobby. Dressed in red, she was beautiful and lustrous, a sight that reminded him of Cassie at their wedding. She took his hand and kept a hold of it as she walked, and they sunk further down the rabbit hole. The grip on his hand was firm but sensual, and he could feel her heart beating as she led him through the glass maze.

He did his best to focus and listen, but somewhere between her accent and the red dress, he lost himself. Zeke thought again about Cassie, then back to the woman whose hand he now held. How would she look in ten years' time? It was a question he always asked to keep himself honest. It was redundant as ever, because he was here now, not in ten years.

As he moved, he thought about love to remind himself of his. Everyone who was in the early stages of it had it written all over their faces. When they were done showing you, they would tell you. In-person, via text messages, or on social media. Hashtag love! But who's version of love was the real one? People stole for love, killed for love, or even sacrificed for it. A million different interpretations existed for one word. He and Cassie were carnal, and they had a connection; maybe that was their love?

Zeke continued through transparent hallways, transitioning from the visitor side to the business one and thankfully, the glass walls ended.

Zeke's job was to act as a buyer. But really, all he did was smile, nod, and make people laugh. He had done it dozens of times in various countries across the world. He would leave home with an expense account and return with some form of art. Today he was here to facilitate the purchase of a very expensive sculpture made by a hot new artist from the Bronx. He would meet the creator, get them to like him, tell them how and where their art would be displayed across the globe, smile, nod, smile some more, and then leave. For this, he would get a free trip, and a handsome commission provided he got the job done, which he always did.

Zeke didn't ask any questions, as with most things he did for the gallery and Marguerite. Something didn't quite add up, his pay was disproportionate to what he did, but the mystery satisfied his curiosity, for as long as he didn't know it could be anything.

Today's purchase was a sculpture. Where the 'sculpting' came into it, Zeke wasn't sure. The statue was of Planet Earth. Bulky and three-dimensional, basically a giant globe. Instead of a traditional fulcrum, an enormous fist crashed through from the South pole and exited through the North! It was highly ham-fisted.

He remembered looking at the brochure before he left home. His gaze split between the pamphlet and the view from the study. He could see miles across the fields sat against the backdrop of the Meon Valley. He'd been reading up on the artist but had become more bored than usual. The image of it had been enough, yet somehow it was even more garish in person.

With the piece standing before him, Zeke took a sideways glance at the sculpture to get another perspective. What did it mean? What was it representing? Was it symbolic? Maybe there was a deeper connotation? Destruction of the planet at the hands of man?

The artist and his art were branded as edgy and intelligent, the first word in new art. The reality was some idiosyncratic piece of work. If he had to guess, it was made by some spoilt rich kid, one whose daddy had told him he could be an artist. It was brash, and it would spend its first six months outside his office in Chichester. He figured if he had it moved closer to Lara's office, it would at least give him grounds to stop and stare!

Lara was to be Zeke's new understudy, he'd had a few now, and he still wasn't sure what they were supposed to learn from him. Most of them had been lifeless sycophants, and although he'd yet to meet Lara, a twenty-minute search of her social media had taught him most of what he needed to know. Lara was adventurous and intelligent, she had character, and she was beautiful. This one should at least be interesting.

7

"Hey, Cassie, Cass!" Karan's words bounced off the kitchen walls and back into his ears. "Are you in there, Cassie? It's me, Karan, don't be alarmed!"

Cassie squinted upwards towards the noise. She sat in a trance surrounded by books. She appeared to catch sight of her teacup that sat on the kitchen table before she focussed on the words coming from the door. With her attention back in the room, she spotted Karan, who was standing casually in the kitchen doorway.

"Ahh, it's Karan! What a fright you gave me!" she said sarcastically.

"Hey," replied Karan. "If I was an intruder?" he said, darting into the room towards her. Cassie shrugged, laughed, and then raised herself using her hands on the table so that she was close enough to whisper to him.

"Well then," she murmured in a low tone, "you'd need to ask yourself if I'm stuck in here with you. Or are you trapped in here with me?" As the letter *e* ghosted into Karan's ear, Cassie banged the underside of the table with her knee. The thud made the teacup jump in its saucer, and the double bang made Karan almost physically leap from his skin.

"Not funny!" he yelled in shock as he grabbed a newspaper from the countertop. He rolled it up and began to make swatting motions.

"Uh, uh, uh. Can't attack the pregnant lady," she said as he menaced his way over.

"Hmm," he replied as he gently set the rolled-up paper down on the tabletop. Karan crouched so that he was close to her bump. He stooped and then muttered, "You can't hide in there forever," to Cassie's mid-drift. Standing back upright again, he said, "It's rare anyone gets the drop on Cassie Olsen! Is everything okay?"

"Oh Karan, just pregnant, that's all. Didn't sleep much last night. Don't sleep much any night at the moment."

"Yeah, I bet! At least you and Zeke have that in common now?"

Karan took a seat at the table next to Cassie. He placed his arm on her shoulder and squeezed it kindly as he sat. "Speaking of. Have you heard from Zeke?" he asked. "That was some party the other night. I assume he made it?"

Cassie shook her head. "No, Karan, but he's your best friend."

"Your husband," he mumbled as he reached into the jar on the table, removed a cookie and shoved it between his lips. He munched for a moment as he considered his thoughts.

The house was rarely locked during the day. With it being so remote, the pair had an open-door policy for friends, family, and random neighbours. Cassie loved people. She treasured the ambience of noise and activity, especially when people dropped in and out. Zeke claimed to hate it. He played on the 'misanthrope' archetype. But they were a popular couple, and Zeke was always secretly happy when they had gatherings. To Zeke, there was an art to socialising. It had to be his way; he was like an internal combustion engine. One that required a perfect mix of solitude and socialising. Too much of either would affect his performance.

Karan had no work that morning and as usual, Ivan was away. He'd driven across to check in on Cassie and see if she'd had better luck contacting Zeke.

The three of them had known each other for years. The trio met at the university. Initially, they were both friends of friends. Or they attended a lecture or mutual party, overlapping constantly but never quite coming together until they did. Cassie was known to wonder who loved Zeke more, her or Karan?

"Maybe, but I don't live with him," Karan went on. "He is also soon to be the father to your child! Shouldn't you know how he is?"

"Oh, I'm aware," she said, holding her hands aloft. "You're just miffed because your friend hasn't texted you!"

"Your friend hasn't texted you," Karan replied, mimicking her. "Also, I'm pretty sure he hasn't messaged you either."

"Oh, Karan! You know him just as well as I do. He's in New York for what thirty-six hours? That man will be completely off his fucking tits!"

"Cassie!" Karan exclaimed as he put his hand over her bump to cover her ears. Cassie turned to look at him rolling her eyes as she did so.

"Come on. You know what Zeke is like unsupervised. As long as he can still smile, nod, and walk, he'll do whatever he wants. I mean, he's probably over there with some half-baked notion that I don't know he buys cigarettes every time he leaves the country. He'll smoke about three packs and come back looking like he's just run a marathon! And that's just the cigarettes! I'd think yourself lucky you don't have to deal with him when he gets back! I'm like a detox nanny!" Karan looked at Cassie, then up at the ceiling.

"You are probably right; he's been a bit of a live wire recently. Maybe I should pick Zeke up when he returns?" Karan pondered.

"You do what you want, buddy." Karan paused in thought for a moment and scratched at his chin. Keen to stop the behaviour, Cassie poked her leg out and kicked Karan's shin. "How's Ivan?"

"Oh, you know Ivan!" Karan lamented, "Work, work, work."

"Not everyone has as much free time as you, Karan," she quipped. "Maybe you need a hobby?"

"Pfft," he remarked. "I've got plenty of hobbies. I'd just rather do them with my husband. The company runs itself, but he always has to be so hands-on."

"Aw," Cassie replied unsympathetically. "Do you wish he'd put his hands on you a bit more?" Karan glared at her.

"Okay, I will let that slide since you're pregnant. But yes, actually, yes, I would!"

"Gross?" Cassie retorted as she pushed back her chair. It squeaked against the linoleum as it moved. She put her hands on the arms and went to stand awkwardly. Karan motioned to help, but she refused.

"I got it," she said. "I've another four months of this! It's only going to get worse. Anyway, look around you, K. Look at this modern, sharp, open, un-baby friendly place we've built. Everything is pointy. I have enough problems.

"I've got to get this house ready for a baby, I've got to get a vacant man-child prepared for a baby, and I have to get equipped for a baby. You realise I have to push it out! I'm afraid your boring husband is your problem.

"Actually, you know what? I'll swap. I'll take Ivan. You have Zeke!" Karan chuckled; Cassie stood and met his gaze. "I'm fucking serious!"

"Oh, Cass," replied Karan, "you crack me up. Anyway, you two got a name yet?" he asked, changing the subject. Cassie said nothing. Instead, she just continued her stare.

"For real?" she joked. "You're gonna ask me that?"

"Is that a no?"

"My husband is somewhere in New York doing whatever it is he does, fuelled by a cocktail of alcohol, drugs, and insomnia. I'm here trying to babyproof a house we just completed building, finish up my handover notes for work and then somehow find a girl's name that we both like that isn't also the name of some woman Zeke's slept with."

"Yikes," said Karan standing and flicking on the kettle. "Another tea?" he asked.

"Tea, fucking tea! Where's my beer, my tequila? Why must I go through all of this sober? Cassie can't have a glass of wine, can she?"

"Crikey," replied Karan before continuing. "You make me laugh, Cass," he spoke again as he stretched for a mug. "What about Julie?"

Out of sight of Karan, Cassie had moved to within a whisker of him. She reached out with her hand and flicked the back of his ear as he switched on the kettle. Her finger connected with his ear, and the sound of the letter *e* almost squeaked from his mouth.

"Now, who'd be dead?" she whispered into his assaulted ear.

"*Ow!*" Karan said playfully. He rubbed at the back of his ear and laughed, shaking off his lost pride. "You…" he said, pointing his finger towards her. "…you are sneaky."

"Julie? Really Julie? Please tell me you remember crazy fucking Julie?"

"Oh my God," he said hysterically. "The one with the knives? Crazy Julie, I'd forgotten all about her."

"Well then," replied Cassie as she lumbered out of the Kitchen. "Unless you have any more useless suggestions. I've got work to do."

"Mind if I stay for a bit, I can chop some wood if you like?" Cassie reached the bottom of the stairs, paused, and looked back at her friend.

"You do whatever you need to do with your wood, buddy. I'll be upstairs. If Zeke does ever call, I'll tell him you were worried."

Karan laughed again, "Love you, Cass," he called as she mounted the stairs.

"Right back atcha, buddy."

Alone with just his thoughts, nursing a throbbing ear and wounded pride, Karan sipped gently at his piping hot cup of tea. He looked at the stacks of books, they ranged from psychological profiling, to what to expect when expecting. He shuddered at the thought of it all before he stepped to the kitchen door, opened the door, and closed it behind him. The door shut softly and sealed the silence once more. From the kitchen, Karan could be seen moving across to the woodpile. Once there, he grabbed the axe from the stump and raised it above his head before silently, swiftly swinging it down.

8

Zeke had smiled more times today than he could count. He was surrounded by people that he would never recognise again. His cheeks hurt from all the grinning, and he'd shaken a million hands. He'd nodded, said *uh-huh* and *oh really* more times than he could remember. He'd signed some paperwork, told a joke, initialled some more forms, smiled again, touched a few more hands, said *best wishes*, *we'll connect soon*, laughed, and then finally fled the scene.

The nearest unguarded exit he found was in the gift shop, and he bolted straight for it. The sign declared that an alarm would sound should anyone open it. It was worth the risk.

Zeke pressed down hard on the cold metal handle and braced himself for an alarm that never came. He paused for sound, but the only one that arrived was the pounding intensity of New York. He snuck through quickly, lest he be caught, shutting it silently behind him. The door closed and signalled a point of no return. The tranquillity of the glass hall and fountain fuckery that was the Gallery was shattered by the smouldering intensity of the city. New York was big, loud, and packed a powerful aroma. Zeke around and found himself in an alleyway, it was non-descript but oddly unique. Everything looked dirty, and he could almost smell each bin he looked at. Anything to be out of there.

Zeke reached into his bag, removed, and reattached himself to his MP3 player. He then entered the bag once more, pulled out the lighter and pack of cigarettes he'd bought at a kiosk, and put a cigarette between his lips. Zeke turned towards the door with music in his ears and wind in his hair. He huddled under his jacket and cupped his cold hands, sheltering the flame. He closed his eyes to avoid seeing the bright dancing fire, lit the cigarette and breathed it in deep. He tilted his head upwards and exhaled into the darkening sky.

Zeke lowered his head, bringing his eyes back level with the alley. Out of nowhere, three men appeared through his haze and approached him with speed. Zeke realised that one of them was moving their lips. So, he quickly raised his hands to remove the headphones from his ears, but they approached faster than he could react. An arm reached through the smoke like a sheeted ghost and grabbed him by the lapel. The movement forced him back, and his head hit the metal door as his feet left the floor. There was confusion, a feeling of stumbling, falling, and a desperate attempt to reach out and steady himself. But his equilibrium departed, panic set in, and he had the same feeling he'd had moments after the car crash. He remembered the fear and the lack of control. His cigarette fell to the floor, and the scent of a man replaced the smoke in his lungs. Another blow, and then everything went black.

9

Zeke sat and fidgeted as he twiddled his thumbs. He was pensive, impatient, and bored. Staring down the linoleum hallway only brought him so much joy. He beheld the corridor and then the notice board. Then he looked back and finally met the gaze of his beautiful wife sitting across from him.

Cassie was less than two feet away. She was calm, calculated, and relaxed. Always so fucking cool.

"Fuck me. You're fidgety!" Cassie said. Zeke is, or at least he was! He nodded without replying, stood, and moved to the notice board. Once in situ, he reached out and plucked at one of the brochures.

"Lyme disease, Cassie? Fucking Lyme disease. We've not even made a baby yet. What if she gets Lyme's disease?"

"Aww," she replied. "You want a girl."

"What? Maybe! Anyway, why are there never any happy brochures?" he asked as he tossed the pamphlet down on the tatty wooden table. Cassie chuckled.

"Come here, stupid." Cassie took him by the hand and said, "Everything will be fine." The warmth of her fingers cooled him once more, and he settled back down.

"How are you not scared?" he asked her.

"Why are you?" she replied jokingly. "I didn't think you wanted a child."

"Yes, no, yes. I changed my mind."

"Ah, so you don't like not having control?"

"Do you?"

"Not really," she replied. "But look, it isn't up to us. So, getting worked up about it won't change the situation. Either we can have a child, or we can't. We'll cross that bridge if and when we get there."

"You're right. You're always right!" Zeke said as he began to bang his feet on the floor. "But this appointment," he said, tapping at the watch on his wrist. "This appointment was supposed to start *twenty-five minutes ago!"*

Zeke's elevated voice did little other than raise a few eyebrows from those sitting down the hallway. A few restless children jostled near a set of automatic doors. Their movement made the entrances open and close, allowing Zeke to see through. He saw nurses gathered at their station. One of them looked up, and their eyes met before the doors closed, severing their connection. Zeke tried to stand again, but his hand was still attached to Cassie's. Their eyes met. She smiled and pulled him toward her, and he sat.

The sliding door opened once again, and then, after aeons of waiting, Zeke's ears picked up the squelch of plastic safety shoes bearing down the sterile hallway toward them. He looked up as a scrubbed-up nurse arrived.

"The doctor will see you now," he said.

A gust of air filled the surrounding space as Cassie exhaled. The only tell-tale sign that she might have been anything less than composed. They stood in unison and nervously followed the man down the hallway. He ushered them to a room, and they were seated once more.

The lady doctor arrived with news that there was no news. The proverb would tell you that it's a good thing. But they had been contriving to conceive for over three months now. No news was terrible! They were both healthy, fertile, and pro-procreation. There was no medical reason for their struggles.

"Is there anything we can do to help facilitate this?" Zeke heard Cassie ask. Her choice of words was excellent, as always. She had a PhD of her own, yet she was at a loss. Not for words, though, never for words.

"Well, there are certain foods you can try, and stay away from stress, but otherwise, there's no medical reason you aren't conceiving." The doctor smiled at them, as though this was welcome. It wasn't!

The three stood, joined hands, and exchanged pleasantries. Cassie had leaned on a colleague to get the appointment, and here they were. Back to the drawing board. Zeke hoped she could deal with her mental vexation, as well as his. The ride home would be quiet.

The silence continued as they remained in the car on the driveway. Cassie was the first to get out. Zeke remained in his seat, drifting into the warm leather behind him until someone knocked on the window and dared to enter his dream.

"Mr Olsen, excuse me. Mr Olsen, sir!"

10

"Excuse me, sir! Mr Olsen!" The words somehow entered his dream and snuck into his brain. Undisturbed, Zeke remained motionless until an arm grabbed his shoulder firmly. The limb was relentless, shaking him softly but with purpose until he awoke.

Zeke bolted forward and reached out in panic. "Cassie?" The steward shaking him had taken a step backwards but was otherwise unfazed.

"No, sir, it's Phil! We're coming in for landing. I need you to put your chair in the upright position for me, please."

Zeke looked around him. This wasn't his car! Where was he? He took a moment to steady himself, and his panic faded quickly when he saw the familiar sight of first-class. They were coming into land! He hated landings. If there were an emergency, he'd rather be asleep.

"Would you like me to get you another Band-Aid, sir?"

"Another what?" Zeke replied, confused.

"A Band-Aid, a plaster, sir. Would you like another one? Your head is bleeding again."

Zeke raised his eyebrow at the comment, an action that caused a degree of pain. He reached upward and dabbed his finger at it. The steward didn't wait for a reply, and by the time Zeke realised what was happening, he was already on his way back, armed with a stack of plasters. Zeke awkwardly took the items from him and said, "Thank you!"

"Uh-huh," was the man's reply.

Plasters in hand, Zeke looked up and noticed that the seatbelt sign was on. He had no idea why anyone would remove it when travelling over four hundred miles per hour.

Nevertheless, Zeke undid his belt and snuck out of his seat with caution.

He moved down the aisle, grabbing headrests until he reached the bathroom. Once inside, he ran the tap for hot and took a seat to pee.

As the yellow urine left his body, he caught sight of his hands, the right was swollen, and he noticed a speck of dried blood under his ring. Zeke reached out and ran his hand under the tap, the hot water shifted the blood, and it circled the drain, a bloody whirlpool before it disappeared forever. Zeke grabbed some paper towels, then having flushed, he stood back up and caught sight of himself in the mirror. Using the towel and hot water, Zeke rubbed away at the blood that trickled down his face. Then he removed the old plaster and surveyed his appearance. There was a fair-sized cut above his right eye, the surrounding socket was swollen, and the cheek was starting to bruise. Whatever happened would leave a scar, but so far, no memory.

Zeke shrugged at himself in the mirror as he tipped some painkillers into his hand. His painful cheek took some focus away from his back, but that didn't stop it from hurting. He strained his memory back to the alley as he swallowed the pills dry.

"Sir!"

The knock at the door startled him, forcing Zeke to accept that he was jumpier than usual. "I must ask you to return to your seat."

Zeke left the bathroom, holding on tight to each seat once more as he passed by. He arrived back at his chair, sat, and belted back up. There were no memories in his head after leaving the gallery! He'd been back to the hotel and got changed. That much was obvious. He wouldn't be on the flight without his passport, and upon checking the contents of his bag. He found everything he'd had on him before the alley was still there, including the cigarettes. The plane began to dip and as it did, he wondered what might greet him when he opened his hold luggage?

Total memory loss was a first, even for him. Could it be due to his medicating? The plane banked as the nose dropped. As it turned, he saw the welcome sight of land, of home. Zeke gripped the armrests tightly and braced himself for impact.

Zeke waited until the carousel was almost empty before giving up and heading to the information desk. The delay was mildly inconvenient, but he was glad not to find his suitcase. His head contained visions of a blood-stained bag appearing through the flaps, then going round and round unclaimed. The news was that the bag was lost, and he happily accepted the compensation offered. He had confirmation that the pack had been checked in, yet no case came out! The airline gave him two hundred pounds and promised to call if it showed up.

The delay had caused him to miss his original train, and as he stared at the departures on his phone, he considered getting a taxi or maybe even a room for the night. With a decision to be made, he was about to make his way to one of Heathrow's various bars until he heard his name uttered by a familiar voice.

"Zeke! Zeke! Over here!"

There were many voices Zeke wouldn't recognise, especially in a crowded room. Karan's was not one of them. He'd known it was him the second he'd heard it, and he smiled as he turned and saw his buddy.

"Karan," Zeke said with a degree of surprise. "Come on. The airline gave me two hundred quid. Let's go to the bar!"

"No, can't!" Karan said with a sense of urgency. "Ivan is outside. We've been waiting for you forever."

"Airline lost my bag!" replied Zeke as he shrugged. "Plus, you're not a train. I didn't know you were coming."

"Surprise!" said Karan. "Maybe if you'd replied to a single message, you would? Now get in the fucking car! Ivan is doing my head in."

"Hey," replied Zeke, "you wanted to spend more time with him."

"Yes, well, I'd forgotten it was like driving with Miss Daisy!"

"Miss Daisy's driver," replied Zeke.

"You what?"

"Miss Daisy," said Zeke. "She didn't drive. Her driver did. That's why it's called *Driving Miss Daisy*, not Miss Daisy Drives!"

"Thanks, Quentin. Can we go now?"

Zeke chucked his bag towards Karan and walked off towards the exit. "Waiting on you now."

Karan shook his head and took off after Zeke. He caught up with him and put his arm around his friend's shoulders.

"Good to see you remembered to wash off the cigarettes!" he said, sniffing at Zeke.

"Oh, she knows."

"Yes, she does, but you used to care about these things."

"I'll shower before she gets home. I promise mum."

"So, Zeke! Are we going to talk about your head?"

Ivan's Bentley pulled up to the pick-up zone, and Zeke jumped in the back.

"Hey Ivan," Zeke said as he sprawled out across the backseat and strapped himself in hastily. Zeke studied Ivan as he waited for Karan to join them. It had been a while since he'd seen him, and while he was as well presented as ever, his immaculate suit was bulging in the middle, and the waistcoat touched where it fit. Ivan was well over six foot, so he wore it well, but Zeke couldn't help but notice his hair was a shade browner than normal which was perhaps an attempt to compensate for the deterioration of his physical condition.

"Hey, Zeke!" Ivan replied. Then the passenger door opened, and Karan climbed in.

"Finally," Ivan said.

"Well, we're waiting on you now," Karan replied, tapping the dashboard. Zeke lay in the back and grinned. He set his head down on his bag and closed his eyes. He drifted in and out as the car pulled away. The hum of the motor sang to him and sedated him softly. The ambient noise of Karan and Ivan's bickering filled his brain. He watched their arms gesticulate wildly from his position in the back as his eyes shut again. A fond nostalgia swept across his mind. The last ever journey he'd taken with his parents had started just like this.

11

Zeke couldn't remember the exact moment both his parents died. The minutes just before and the seconds afterwards would be forever ingrained in his memory. But the moments between were still missing.

He recalled getting in the rental car at the airport, putting in his headphones, and the long, hot, tedious car journey, and he remembered the huge roundabout.

Zeke had a vivid memory of the shoeless boy selling watermelons, of his parent's bickering because they were lost. He remembered his mother moving. But the moments after that seemed not to exist. His mum undid her seatbelt and reached behind her to grab the map before squeezing his leg kindly. But her touch had startled him, he was annoyed that she had disturbed his slumber, and he shot her a scowl. Sometimes, he wished he could return, just for a moment and replace it with a smile. It would be the last touch and final look they ever exchanged.

Instead, Zeke had looked away in disgust, annoyed that he'd been brought back to the reality of the sticky, tedious car journey. He'd looked out of the window, and the next thing he knew, he was lifeless and cold on the hot tarmac.

He'd watch on in horror from the roadside as the car and everything in it melted and turned to dust before his very eyes. Red hot flames danced from the wreck, licking its lips at the edges of the metal chassis, satisfaction at the meal it had just consumed. The sight, the sounds, and the chaos would all have been fascinating for a bystander. But not today. Today, he looked on not as a spectator but as an unwilling participant. His whole life changed within minutes. The fire was just twenty feet away, but the heat was immense; he could have been in hell.

The car no longer resembled a vehicle or anything for that matter. It was grey, with splashes of orange. The backseat was empty, and the front featured two blackened silhouettes, just a burning, hollow husk, the hire car, and his parents. The flames appeared so brightly, vivid, rising higher as they extinguished life, hardening some things and softening others.

Zeke's parents had both been diplomats; that was their life. They had Zeke and placed him in boarding school aged five, knowing that they would be retired within six years, he would be out, and so would they.

They had carved out a relatively prosperous life in the Middle East and moved around frequently. Zeke had no home and craved the day it would all change. They were in the UAE that day for a farewell dinner. The day they died was supposed to be their last in the country, not their last on the planet.

With early retirement on the horizon, his parents were due to sign off with a bang, albeit not the one they expected. They would holiday for a week in Dubai after their farewell, going out in style. Zeke's father even upgraded the rental car to something fast, an unprecedented move for him, ultimately fatal. It was a bold move for a typically conservative man, who was far from adept at handling powerful vehicles. Unusually for the part of the world, the car came with a manual gearbox and most of the car's power was wasted in a wheel spin or stalling, but his father persevered.

They'd sat at the edge of the fast-moving roundabout for about ten minutes. Zeke had taken it in with amazement upon approach. There were so many lanes, and everyone was driving like a maniac. But traffic gets boring very quickly for a young boy, and he'd drifted off to music before his mother had woken him with the leg squeeze.

Then, with amazement, he'd met the eyes of a boy in the street, walking up and down the central reservation selling bits of watermelon. The boy was dirty and shoeless. He'd smiled when their eyes met, and the boy's kind eyes made Zeke reach into his pocket to retrieve a banknote. As he went to open the window, the car lurched forward, and he saw the boy's eyes widen in terror as he hurdled the barrier and sped off. A few moments later, Zeke's head rebounded off the window as the car's tail hit the barrier, and the glass shattered. What transpired in the prevailing moments, he could only guess.

He could put some of the pieces together from what he had been told and the small bits he remembered. It had happened something like this.

The tailback behind them grew restless, horns honked, and tempers tempered. The argument boiled over, and the impatient traffic had seen his father make an impulse move in the fast car. Their vehicle nosed into the roundabout only to be hit by a large truck. The impact threw his mother, who had yet to strap herself back in, across the car and into her husband. Zeke's head hit the rear window, and luckily it broke, rendering him unconscious. The shoeless watermelon seller and his father saw it happen from a distance, and they ran to Zeke's aid, hauling him out through the broken space. They managed to drag him out and over the central reservation before the fire broke out. As fate would have it, their car collided with a gasoline tanker, and it was an inferno within minutes.

He was later told that the impact had likely killed his parents instantly. But knowing that his mother had, in all probability, killed his father did little to ease the memory of watching them burn from across the street.

The crash's impact, coupled with being dragged through a window, had caused severe damage to Zeke's lower back, fracturing one of his vertebrae. Given the risk posed to his spinal cord, he needed not to be moved more than necessary, this left Zeke alone for months in a Middle Eastern hospital. The next few months were life-changing for Zeke. The pain, the lack of companionship, the memories, the heartache, and the inability to express how he felt turned a happy young soul into a cold, lifeless being. Days rolled by, turning to night, and with it came the darkness. Zeke cried for weeks until the tears finally ran out. The same boiling water that softens the potato hardens the egg. One day he finally found out what he was made of. The day the tears stopped, so did the emotions that rolled out with them.

Zeke's only surviving relative was his mother's aunt, June. But June was not only mid-seventies. She was also terrified of flying, and despite his condition, could not make the trip out to visit him.

She took him in as her own when he was finally able to return to the UK, but as much as she loved him, he no longer had a home, family, friends, or feelings.

12

The issue with anything chronic is that it's chronic. When something refuses to go away, you must accept it as your new normal. Your old life, in essence, dies, and a new one starts budding. But as with any loss, it's a process, and you have to deal with the accumulated grief. The stages follow next. There's denial, anger, bargaining, and depression to deal with before you get anywhere near acceptance. For a young boy, coping with the actual loss of his family and an injury he would retain forever was a long and challenging process. But your mind retains memories of the halcyon days. The life you had before this happened to you, and as much as you can accept the change. There are times when it still becomes overwhelming. You can't simply switch off your feelings and become numb to the world around you.

In Zeke's case, he had no idea how he would have turned out had the throes of life not thrown him into a world of anguish as a teenager. The car crash caused a ripple effect and turned a spoilt posh child who knew nothing of tragedy into a cold, borderline sociopath. He reasoned that it could have been worse, but the what-if scenario always intrigued him. Who would he be had it not happened?

When you live in pain, whether emotional, physical or both, you learn to deal with it. Humans are incredibly adaptable. One constant since the beginning of time is change; it comes and goes like a tide, often unbearable at first until you finally learn to live with it. The brain struggles to distinguish between intense emotional or physical pain. Each one presents itself to the mind as an intolerable amount of suffering. Until the roundabout moment, Zeke never knew how intense pain could be, not really. Yet as he lay crumbled, crippled, crying, cold on the hot tarmac, breathing in fumes that contained chemicals and particles of his recently cooked parents, he felt his lungs giving out with each silent scream that escaped from his mouth. The two types of pain came for him hard, all at once, creating a ripple. People aren't born to be one thing or another; it is usually an effect of circumstances accumulated along the way.

The demise of his parents left him a healthy sum of money, entrusted to June until he came of age. With June being his only living relative, she became his sole guardian.

June was both kindly and hardy. She and her late husband never bore children, and she accepted Zeke wholeheartedly. But she wasn't equipped to raise a teenager full-time at her age. Leaving Zeke's soon-to-end tenure at boarding school to become a permanent fixture, and the rest of his adolescence was split between school and June. The money left to him handled his school and tuition expenses. Then with June's inevitable death, it became his inheritance.

Zeke's schooling saw him live in long dormitories with zero privacy and his home life in the company of an elderly lady. He ate at long wooden benches or in high-backed chairs and was either never or constantly alone. It was one extreme to the other, and the notion of *home* was utterly lost on him. The security and the warmth of belonging had long parted ways with him. He had no one and nothing to look forward to. He missed his mom's cooking, he longed for his dad's hugs and those Christmas dinners where they would all eat fancy cuisines in merriment.

When one is forced to cohabit with people one would otherwise not choose to associate with, you learn to cooperate, get along with, and communicate to get through.

When the news came that June had passed shortly before the end of his final term at school, it washed off his back like water from a duck. People and places were temporary, and the pain was inevitable. It was of no shock to him. June's death didn't feel like a loss to him and so he hardly mourned as people expected him to. He carried out his usual routine as he attended all his classes and even performed decently by his standards in the end-of-term exams. August came by in a rush and he graduated from school without much clue about what to do next.

With money in his pocket and no place to call home, Zeke left school, picked a spot, bought a flat, and settled down to begin a new life. He cut the small ties from his former ones and set about his rebirth.

The University of Chichester came calling, and he took the offer with both hands. But his brain, as efficient as it was, didn't blend well with academic deadlines and study. He'd yet to experience freedom or fun and owning his own flat during the first year had been an excellent way to explore both.

Having tried and failed at politics, art, and psychology, he accepted what he assumed to be his limitations and took up employment in a local bar. The money came in, the fun continued, and the deadlines of academia faded away. He was free to do what he wanted, but living a life devoid of meaning and guidance, set him down the path of exploring pleasure. He became reckless, living in the moment without growing any attachments. He would come home late at night drunk, switch on his television and flick through the channels. It was a part of his impassive routine. Every day was basically the same.

Despite earning the role of duty manager, it didn't take long for the monotony of bar work to take its toll. Zeke had experienced so many highs since leaving school, but he fast became jaded. Everything was fleeting, another shift, another party, another girl, and his life began to pass him. As the days wore on, he considered that his life was destined to be more than it was, or at least it should be, but it is hard to find a tree when woods surround you.

Zeke was outside thinking one night after work—something he would often do. It was warm, the wind was still, the city was peaceful at night, and it was a great place to think. Zeke's twenty-fifth was fast approaching, and he found himself listless. The joy of buying a small home in town had now become his anchor. Should he sell it, move, or start over again? The thoughts stacked up and invaded his brain, he should go home, but he knew they would only grow louder in the darkness of bed.

Zeke took one last look at the cathedral in the distance and shifted his butt. He stood and started the short walk home. It was just after one, and he had work again in less than eleven hours. Surely this couldn't be life.

The walk home, although short, would take him past the bar. It was unavoidable without a massive detour. Zeke turned the corner and took in the deserted street. It was a Monday evening, and the exams had begun. Most places had been deserted, meaning work was obnoxiously slow. A life often filled with excitement was now at an impasse, and he kept his head low to avoid making eye contact with a place he was beginning to loathe.

Yet as he neared it, he spotted a lone woman banging on the shutters. They would have closed up after he left shortly after eleven. No one would be inside; rattling the locked door would be futile.

"We don't keep any cash there overnight, just drinks," he said as he ghosted past her. "But there must be easier ways to get a nightcap?"

The woman looked up, surprised, seemingly caught out by the presence of another. Zeke continued his walk but made it just a few paces past her before hearing.

"Hey, hey."

Zeke made out the words over the sound of heels on the cobblestones and stopped. The noise of footsteps followed him, so he paused, intrigued, and waited to see what transpired.

"Hey," she said, approaching from behind and tapping him on the shoulder. "I know you."

Zeke felt the tap and turned to see who it was. It might make the night at least vaguely exciting. His eyes met hers, and he recognized her immediately.

"I know you," she repeated. The words left her mouth, and she placed her hands on either side of Zeke's shoulders. "Wait, don't tell me!" Zeke watched in amazement as he felt the warmth of her hands against his skin. "You're the guy who owns the flat? Aren't you?" He nodded. "No way," she said. "I never forget a face. You know I came to one of your parties once?"

"I might remember," he replied casually.

She smiled, removed her arms from his shoulders, and offered him a hand. "Cassie Slater," she said.

"Zeke Olsen," he replied, extending his hand to meet hers.

A streetlamp shone down on them from above, illuminating their faces, and for a moment, everything else stopped. Clocks around the world were motionless, and for a while, nothing and no one else mattered.

"So, the bad news is the bar is closed," Zeke broke the silence. "But if you're desperate, I know a twenty-four-hour garage not far from here."

"No," Cassie chuckled. "It is not what you think! Come." she took him by the hand and led him toward the window. "You see that?" she asked.

The slack in his arm gave, and Zeke was whisked toward the glass. The contact recharged him, and he never wanted it to end. Zeke followed her to the shopfront and looked through the shutters, the sticky glass, and at the object on the floor. The moon's light aided his vision as he squinted through the bar's window. He could just about make out a flash drive on the floor.

"You see that? It's mine."

"Well," replied Zeke, "I'd be out rattling shutters too if I'd have misplaced a butterfly USB stick."

"It has my dissertation on it," she replied glumly. "This is beyond the butterflies. Come on, help me?" She took his hand once more and moved it to the window. "If we both knock," she said manically. "We might draw more attention."

Zeke chuckled. "Hey," he said, moving his hand away from the glass. "If we keep this up, the only attention we will attract will be unwanted!"

"Eugh," she said as she turned and slumped to the floor. "It's due in by nine a.m. tomorrow. It's hopeless. Three years wasted."

"I might have an easier solution," he said, reaching into his pocket and taking out a set of keys.

"Wait!" she said, jumping from the ground. "You work here? I thought you were studying?"

Zeke didn't reply. Instead, he put the key in the lock and started to turn it. Cassie threw her arms around him as he did, and he almost had to drag her with him inside as he opened the door.

"You had keys all along?" she said as Zeke moved to the panel and deactivated the alarm. "You could have said something!"

"And miss out on all the histrionics? Are you kidding?"

She slapped his arm playfully and ran toward her flash drive, collecting it gladly and clutching it with both arms. She embraced the device and dashed toward him, catching him off guard. She threw herself around him in another giant hug.

"You're a lifesaver."

As she hung from him, he placed his arm around her waist. Her scent drifted into his nostrils and cast a deep spell on him. Her perfume, the coconut in her hair, and the feel of her breast pushed up against him was almost too much to handle, and he removed her gently.

"Drink?" he asked. As Cassie considered the proposition, he stared down at her. The movement of the hugs had opened a small gap in her blouse, and he caught sight of her red undergarment. He wondered if it was a matching set, unaware that he would get his answers in the small hours of the morning.

After a few drinks, Cassie stood and declared, "Mr Olsen, I must use your restroom."

"Sure, go ahead. It's upstairs and to the left."

Stood by himself in the empty bar, Zeke poured himself another shot before wearily looking at his watch. The time was either just before or just after three, but he was having difficulty distinguishing which. He must have been staring for a while because when he looked back up Cassie had reappeared unnoticed, and she stood before him. Zeke peeled his eyes from the watch he'd been fixed on and noticed that her appearance had changed slightly. Her hair was now up, showing off beautiful cheekbones, the intoxicating scent had been renewed, and unless he was mistaken, some more of the buttons on her blouse had come undone.

They'd had one more drink before closing back up. Cassie had insisted that she *walk him home*, and the tension only increased as they strolled. The journey was short, but that night it appeared very long. When they finally reached his flat, his shirt was off before they'd opened the door, and it became a race to see who could get each other's clothes off the fastest. Zeke was almost nude by the time he shut the front door before Cassie grabbed him before they collided like waves bursting from the ocean.

They'd fucked hard, passionately, long into the early hours of the morning. Starting in the living room, then into the kitchen before taking it upstairs. The sweaty, loud writhing continued until seven a.m. and was only halted by Cassie standing abruptly to leave.

"I gotta hand this in," she said, waving the flash drive at him. She hurriedly dressed, kissed him on the head, and bolted out of the door.

Knowing he started work at noon meant it would be a long day for Zeke. He smiled to himself before he settled back in bed. The following seventeen hours would be the only moments of uncertainty he would ever have when it came to Cassie.

With a hangover and little sleep, the shift was as long and unpleasant as expected. The memory of the night before, fresh in his brain, kept him going. But there was the odd pang, a fear that he might never see her again. They hadn't swapped numbers, and he didn't know where she lived or what she did beyond a course that was soon to end.

When the shift finished, Zeke went about his routine before moving toward the door; much to his delight, a lone figure waited patiently on the doorstep. Instead of stepping out and locking the door behind him, he'd opened it, grabbed her, and done the opposite. His relief at seeing her was quickly overtaken by innate carnal desires. She'd taken straight to his arms, and they'd repeated the previous night's antics, desecrating most of the bar.

Life changed very quickly after that, Cassie stayed on after her undergrad, and it wasn't long before she became a permanent fixture in his life. As for Zeke, he wasn't destined to tend the soiled bar for much longer. A few weeks later, he would meet Marguerite, and life would get even stranger.

13

Zeke stood alone in the crowded bar waiting for Karan to arrive. The atmosphere was lively, yet he was sombre and felt surrounded. It was a day that had long been on the cards, but he was generally anxious about making new friends and something about that Ray character had prompted him to put off that particular encounter.

The day had arrived, and he'd promised Karan—an unbreakable commitment that he'd regretted almost immediately.

The pub was a typical upper-class country inn. The drinks were overpriced and either craft or from some local microbrewery he'd never heard of. He sipped at his expensive lager and used it to wash down some painkillers. The pain in his back often made him more anxious in social situations, like an anchor that would drag him down, away from the conversation. It was hard to attempt small talk while drowning.

Zeke looked around at both the pub and the clientele. Like it or not, he would have to get used to it. His offer on the land had been accepted, and that was the "local." It was, of course, oxymoronic. Zeke moved from the city to retire away from people. Yet there he was in the new locale, being introduced to others, people who no doubt knew everyone's secrets. In a city, he was surrounded but anonymous. In the countryside, he was isolated but identifiable.

As he surveyed the scene, the wealth, or at least its illusion, was plain to see. The noise of ambient conversation comforted him. Surrounded and isolated, indeed.

Outside the doors of the remote inn, the weather raged. Inside, it was warm, clammy, and loud. The breath from inside met the cold glass and condensed instantly. Chatter echoed elegantly off the ceiling and into Zeke's ears. So many conversation snippets, so much being said about so little, yet this was normal. How could vanity, greed, ignorance, shallowness, gossip, and hubris be ordinary?

Suddenly, a hand appeared from nowhere and crashed through his daze like the abrupt onset of a storm. The open palm startled him, "Zeke. Hey, Zeke. Are you in there?"

Zeke followed the hand down the length of the arm and up to the face of its owner.

"Hey, Karan," he replied, recognizing him immediately. "How are you doing, my friend?"

"Seriously?" Karan shook his head in fond exasperation. "Just like that? I've been shouting to you from across the room for like five minutes." He ordered two drinks and shot Zeke an impatient glance over his shoulder. "Come on. I left Ray over there. Let's go."

Zeke slowly slid down from his stool and followed Karan's lead, pleased that his friend blazed a trail so he didn't have to fight through the noisy ensemble himself. Karan looked over his shoulder periodically and spoke as loud as possible without yelling.

"So, this guy Ray I've been telling you about lives in the village. Nice guy, a bit of a live wire." Zeke nodded but didn't say anything. Karan stopped and turned back to him in the crowd. "Hey, I never know when you are or aren't listening."

"It's a billion decibels in here." Zeke laughed.

"Granted. Either way, just stay away from the topic of marriage. I can't deal with any more sanctimonious lectures." Zeke nodded in affirmation before Karan turned around and continued moving.

"Ray," Karan exclaimed as they reached the booth and sat. "Meet Zeke. Zeke, meet Ray."

With a broad grin, Ray outstretched his hand, which Zeke grasped limply and released as soon as it was polite. Barreling past his discomfort, he joined Karan in the booth and said, "So, what are we talking about?"

When last orders rang out, Ray leapt to his feet and grabbed another drink before sitting back down.

"Ray," exclaimed Karan.

"What? I'll be quick. You're driving, remember?"

"Yes," replied Karan, "but for once, Ivan is home, and I'd like to join him!"

"Is he still busy?" Zeke asked.

Karan nodded.

"Told you that you shouldn't have gotten married!" Ray beamed.

"You were married three times!" Karan retorted, biting too quickly. "Anyway," he said, raising his hands in surrender,

"I'm not getting into this now. I'm taking a leak." Once on his feet, he gave his companions a stern look. "When I get back, we're leaving."

Not wishing to find himself alone with his new acquaintance, Zeke stacked the empty glasses and carted them to the bar. Having set them down, he turned to find himself face to face with Ray, literally within a breath.

"It was good to finally meet you, Olsen," Ray said.

"Likewise," returned Zeke.

"Although, to be honest, with the amount Karan talks about you, I did feel as though we'd already met." Zeke laughed as Ray's rum-laced words hit his face.

"Probably could have stayed home tonight then?"

Ray lumbered closer to him. He moved with the gait of a man who had drunk to excess, which certainly hadn't happened while they were out. "That's the thing," Ray said, putting his arm around Zeke's shoulder. "I thought I knew everything about you, but now I feel like it's nothing."

"Well, what's life without a little mystery?" replied Zeke, looking at the unwelcome arm awkwardly.

"Hmm," replied Ray. "The thing is, I'm good at reading people. But you! You, I can't get a thing. You're just a blank slate."

"Well, we all are at some point," Zeke replied.

"Whatchya mean?

"*Tabula rasa?*" Zeke offered. "Are you familiar with the school of thought?"

Ray shook his head. "Sounds made up!"

"Everything's made up!" replied Zeke. "Anyway, it's Latin, meaning clean slate. It's essentially the idea that we're born without an inbuilt mental concept. We all start as blank slates, and the way we turn out is dependent on our experiences."

"Okay." Ray stretched out the word into an entire monologue's worth of scepticism.

"I mean, who were you before the world told you what you needed to be?"

"I don't listen to the world!"

"Okay, but take psychopaths, for example. They can seem normal, even though they have a complete moral disregard. But they weren't born that way. Plus, one in every hundred people you meet is a psychopath. You may well have encountered one today!"

"Tell me about it," Ray mocked.

"Anyway, just think about it. Are you true to yourself, to those around you, or are you living the life you've been told to? The one people are supposed to see."

Ray considered it for a minute before replying, "I've changed my mind. I have figured you out!"

"You have?" replied Zeke.

"Yeah, you're weird!"

Zeke turned to him and smiled. "I'll drink to that," he said. Karan returned as they finished up, and the three of them departed.

"How are you getting back?" Karan asked Zeke as they said their goodbyes.

"Cassie."

"Tell her I said hi?"

"Will do."

The two friends embraced before Karan turned and started after Ray, who was already stumbling off into the distance.

"Zeke's weird, isn't he?" Ray said as they walked away from the pub toward the parked cars.

"He's different, I suppose. But then, so are you."

"That's one way to put it."

"You know, I thought you two would get along. I'm surprised you don't know each other through one of your secret alpha male groups." Ray shoved his friend playfully.

"Really? That guy? Do I also give off the 'I string up dead cats at home' vibe?"

Karan chuckled, "Kinda."

Ray scoffed. "Oh, and the first rule of 'alpha male' club is we hunt down and kill all those who mock alpha male club."

Karan laughed. "Well," he said, "Zeke and his girlfriend just bought the empty patch down past Johnson's yard."

"Fuck me," replied Ray. "He really is crazy!"

"It's a lot of work; that I'll admit. He'll grow on you. Plus, the man throws the best parties. I've never known you to turn down a party under any circumstance."

"Like a moth to a flame," Ray conceded. "Just don't let him talk to me about psychopaths again?"

"I find the topic fascinating!"

"Yes, Karan, but you teach psychology."

Time and occasion failed to soften Ray's views on Zeke. He was not one known for capriciousness. Indeed, once Ray made up his mind about a topic, changing it would take a cataclysmic event.

Despite Ray's many character flaws, his reading of people was more often right than wrong. His gut told him there was something odd about Zeke—he should have listened. Ultimately, ignoring his instincts would cost him his life.

14

"Oh my God, Ray, did you see what happened to Zeke in New York? Truly awful business." Karan asked as he sat back down on the corner of the sofa. He took a healthy sip from the wine glass he'd just poured before handing the second off to Ray.

"Finally," he moaned in reference to the drink. "And yes, I did. Just a scratch." He took a large gulp. "Frankly, I'm surprised someone hadn't taken a swing at him sooner."

"Ray," Karan chastened, slapping at his arm.

"I'm just saying, the way he is sometimes," said Ray. "I can see him rubbing someone the wrong way, especially in New York."

"Bollocks," replied Karan, "Zeke is good at what he does."

"What does he do? Either way, are you sure? He was going at it pretty hard the night of the party."

"Right, first off, if you died, every microbrewery in Hampshire would go out of business. Secondly, that was his housewarming. You know how long it took them to build that?"

"I'm just saying I'm amazed he even made his flight."

"Hmm."

"Okay, we've both known him a long time. Has he or has he not been hitting it pretty hard recently?"

"Okay, I'll concede. He has been unusually spacey. But, you know, it's been a tough time."

Ray finished his wine and then asked, "Speaking of absence, where's Ivan? I thought you two went up to the airport together?"

"Eugh, don't remind me!" Karan gasped. "That was the longest journey of my life. Something came up at work. He had to leave."

"Your man is at work a lot."

"So?"

"Sure he's at work?"

"Hey, just because your marriages were all failures doesn't mean you can poke holes in mine. Ivan's got a company to run."

"Alright, you don't need to explain it to me."

"It was a nasty cut on Zeke's head, though."

"Can we not talk about Zeke?" replied Ray. "I didn't come here to do that."

"Fine, I won't talk about Zeke, you won't attack my marriage," replied Karan. "Anyway, seeing someone you know getting attacked makes it real. I mean, it could happen to any of us. It makes you appreciate how short life is."

"Attacked?" laughed Ray. "Please. It's just a scratch. He probably blacked out and banged his head. That or he said something stupid. To be honest, he had it coming."

"He had it coming? What does that even mean? You sound like you're reading from the alpha male playbook! Is that where you're off to later? Do you have a meeting to add new laddish phrases to the manifesto?"

Ray laughed, grabbed a scatter cushion from the sofa, and whacked Karan playfully. Having done so, he looked at the pillow in his hand. "Why is there a picture of a dog on here? You two don't even have a dog?"

"I'm just planting the idea."

"Don't. The only thing that will change is you'll be alone with a dog to look after."

"Well, it's better than nothing. Do you want another drink?" Karan asked as he stood and made his way into the kitchen. The house was modern and spacious, empty in both senses of the word. Karan looked at the various images on the fridge door as he pulled it open, of all the pictures they had the one of him, Zeke, and Cassie from the university days was the most poignant. Karan looked down at the empty cup and the soulless house, both of which resonated deep within him.

"No thanks," Ray called back. "I gotta get going soon."

Karan reached into the fridge, grabbed a bottle of wine, and refreshed his glass. "He had it coming," he muttered in a gruff voice.

"I heard that," shouted Ray.

"Good."

"I'm just saying. You have to admit Zeke is a bit weird. Not everyone finds him as charming as you do. Plus, who knows what he does on these business trips. He and that lady owner are like two weird peas in a pod. I wouldn't be surprised if they were mixed up with something dodgy."

Karan returned and sat back down. "You need to stop watching those shows about conspiracy theories."

"Oh, come on. You're thinking it too. I mean, look at the man's house. It's an annexe of one of Liberace's dreams. No way anyone makes that much money selling just art!"

"You're just envious."

"Envious?" replied Ray. He stood and grabbed the wine glass from Karan's hand. He took a sip before he could protest and set the cup down on the fireplace.

"You know, I feel sorry for your ex-wives!" said Karan, as he rose and immediately moved the cup onto a coaster.

Ray threw on his coat and removed his keys from his pocket. "Gotta go," he said.

"Already?"

"Some of us still have a life."
"Who is she?"
"New."
Ray stepped toward Karan and ruffled his hair.
"See you later, buddy."
"You're not driving, are you?"
"Yeah, I'll be fine."

Ray departed and stumbled down the stairs to the front door. Once there, he stopped and fumbled in the light to find his car key. The wind was sobering, and he closed his eyes and breathed it in. Key in hand, he stepped into the road between some parked cars and opened his eyes just in time to see a bus race past. One more step and that would have been it. He ought to be more careful.

15

The trip to New York had been mentally and physically exhausting. The gap where his memory should have been troubled him, as did the mystery assault. Having been dropped home, Zeke had crawled into the house, onto the sofa, and dozed off, only to be awoken by Cassie. She'd aroused him gently with a coffee and looked at his head before shaking hers.

"Get some ice on that," she said quietly. "And do be careful. She kissed him lightly on the other side. "I gotta go. I love you." He'd burbled some form of reply before dozing back off.

Whenever Zeke did something stupid, he would expect Cassie to get mad. Yet since he'd known here, he'd completed a catalogue of asinine deeds, fifteen to be precise, and most weren't minor faux pas. Then just when he thought he might have gone too far, there she'd be. By his side, no matter what, the degree of sympathy would drop on occasion, but the *thick and thin* part of their marriage worked well, even if it was a rather one-way street. Zeke had ruined many a decent relationship by acting out and doing something stupid as a youth. But with Cassie, things were different. Even now.

They had only crossed paths briefly since his return, and no doubt she would have further questions at the right time. The fact remained, though. Cassie never got mad! It was unlikely that she wouldn't be the least bit scared, regardless of what he told her. There were a million women who would go running if you told them, you may have been the cause of your own downfall, one which could have got you killed. Not Cassie, though!

The story he told Karan was that he'd been attacked. An account that was as true as it could be. He was telling no lies, bar the omission that he didn't remember what happened. There was a significant gap between the end of the meeting and his return flight. There were hours that he couldn't account for, blood that wasn't his, and a missing suitcase.

When he finally recovered, Zeke stood from the sofa and stretched. He checked the time. It was late morning, and he had the a.m. off after his trip. Zeke moved into the kitchen, yawned, poured a coffee from the pot, and took a long savouring gulp of the warm liquid! As he took his vitamins, Zeke paused and considered the unanswered questions. What happened to him, where was his suitcase, and what had he done in the unknown hours? Why didn't he know? The pain in his back loomed large, but he was hesitant to do anything about it. For the first time in a long time, he realised that anything could have happened to him. He wasn't invincible, and he ought to be more careful. There was more to his life than just him.

Zeke climbed the stairs, coffee in hand. He entered the bedroom and into the en suite. Once there, he set the cup down next to the sink and waved his hand under the sensor to activate the walk-in shower. The powerful chime of the doorbell drifted up the stairs and filled his ears. Switching the shower off, he sighed, fetched his coffee up and walked into the bedroom, peeling back the curtain. A lone, unfamiliar car sat on the otherwise empty drive. The bell rang once more, signalling an impatience. Zeke downed the remains of his drink, donned a robe, and went downstairs to the front door.

"Zeke Olsen?"

Zeke almost gawked at the unfamiliar man standing in his doorway. The village was small, and the appearance of an outsider was curious, if not insidious. He looked official, and his suit was well worn in both senses of the word.

"Mr Olsen?" he repeated. The words circled his brain as it attempted to decipher the unusual accent.

Zeke offered a nod, as he had been standing in silence for longer than was socially acceptable. The man reached into his breast pocket, removed, and unfolded an ID badge that dangled mesmerisingly in front of Zeke's face.

"Mr Olsen, my name's Agent Jones. I'm with Interpol."

The words *agent* and *Interpol* wrestled in Zeke's mind. Neither came out on top or made any sense.

"Mr Olsen," he said, putting his badge away. "Do you mind if I come in?"

"What's this about?" Zeke asked, finally offering up some words. He then glanced at his watch, the universal sign that indicates time is of the essence.

"Sir, I just have a few questions about your last business trip," Jones continued. "Please, it's awfully cold, may I?" Zeke acquiesced and opened the door for the agent to enter. The man accepted the gesture and brushed passed him and into the house. Zeke ushered him to the sofa, and the two men sat opposite one another.

The stare-off was short-lived. Zeke gauged little from the man other than that he was frank and probably not someone who was readily invited out for a drink. Jones made his living in cheap suits, and the accent Zeke was doing his best to place featured hints of American littered with French.

Zeke glanced at his watch once more, "Is this going to take long? I have to be at work soon?"

"Of course, Mr Olsen. I will do my best not to keep you. I just have to ask you a few questions about your trip to New York."

"The words *New York* leapt from the Agent's throat and attempted to suffocate him. Zeke swallowed loudly; a function he was sure could be heard all over the world. He composed himself and spoke. "You have ten minutes, Mr Jones."

Dominance reasserted. Zeke sat back and crossed one leg over the other. "This all seems highly irregular, Mr Jones. I thought Interpol only really existed in the movies! What is it you think I can help you with?"

"Agent Jones!" he replied, leaning towards him, "And we get that a lot.

"Say, that's a nasty-looking cut on your head, Mr Olsen!"

"Just a scratch. Anyway, I assume there is a point here?"

"My apologies, Mr Olsen. My work is tackling organised crime. I've been tracking a group based in New York with ties here in Europe. The case had almost gone cold. That was until three known members of the group turned up dead!

"The bodies of the men in question, Mr Olsen, were found in an alleyway outside an art gallery. So, if you don't mind, Mr Olsen, what did you say happened to your head?"

"I didn't!"

A long torturous pause ensued as though the man was allowing him to consider what he said. Agent Jones reached into his bag and pulled out three photos, setting them down on the coffee table as the silence lingered.

"So, what happened after you left the gallery? You were at the gallery, weren't you?"

"Yes, and I don't really remember!"

"I must remind you, Mr Olsen, that withholding information pertinent to a crime is a criminal offence."

Zeke glanced down at the photos briefly, then back up at Jones. "I'm afraid I can't be much help. My memory of the occasion is muddled."

"Well then," said Jones, "tell me what you do know, and look at these pictures. Maybe they will jog your memory."

"Should I have a lawyer?"

"Well, that depends, Mr Olsen," he said as he tapped at the pictures. "Do you think you need a lawyer?"

Zeke took a deep breath. This was this man's life. They did this to everyone, pressure tactics. When he thought about it, he wasn't even sure why he was nervous.

"Look, Mr Jones, I had a business meeting. I stepped out the back for a cigarette and put some music on. I see some guy coming for me in the corner of my eye. Next thing I know, I wake up on the floor with a sore head."

"And that's it? Zeke nodded. "What did you do then, Mr Olsen?"

"Erm, well, it's a bit hazy. You have to remember there was a lot of travelling involved. I got up, returned to the hotel, cleaned up, got a drink, and then waited for my return flight."

"So, you were assaulted?"

"I guess so."

"Why didn't you get medical help or go to the police?"

"Where are you from, Agent Jones?"

"Boston originally."

"Okay, and in your experience, what would the NYPD do about an attack where the victim saw nothing? I had a flight to catch, remember. I also wasn't sure if my insurance covered medical. From what I hear, the bill for treating a wound like this would potentially have many zeros attached to it. Plus, it's nothing.

"I'm giving you my statement now, but I'm afraid I didn't see anything, nor was I aware that anything untoward happened after I left."

Agent Jones nodded, "I hear you, Mr Olsen, but would you please just take a look at the pictures?" Zeke begrudgingly looked down at the photos on his coffee table, three mangled corpses stared back at him, and the sight was quite unsettling. He studied them briefly before saying,

"No, Agent, I'm sorry, they don't look familiar."

"Please, Mr Olsen, take your time. These men were found dead meters from where you were attacked. For all we know, you might have crossed paths with their killer?" The words tugged at his conscience, and he picked them up for a better look. Two of them were strangers, there was something about the one with the goatee that sparked a wave in his mind, but he had no idea what. Zeke stacked the photos together and held them out to Jones.

"I'm sorry," he said, "but I doubt I'd even recognise myself if I were in that condition."

"Very well," said Jones as he took the images and reinserted them carefully in his case. As they exchanged the pictures, his hands met Zeke's, and he glanced down at his wrist. "That's a lovely ring you have there!"

"Thanks," replied Zeke. "Family heirloom. It's a signet ring."

"Well," replied Jones, "you certainly don't see many of them anymore!"

Jones stood and reorganised his possessions. He reached into his pocket and removed a small card, stretching out his arm and offering it to Zeke. "Just in case you remember anything else, Mr Olsen."

"Thanks," replied Zeke taking the card and placing it on the mantelpiece.

They shook hands before Zeke showed him to the door. Jones said his goodbyes and crunched across the gravel towards his car. He stopped short before getting in and turned towards Zeke, who was about to close the door.

"Mr Olsen?"

"Yes," replied Zeke stopping hesitantly in his doorway.

"You are potentially a key witness in a murder investigation. We may have a few more questions for you. So, please, don't leave the country!"

16

Day-to-day work for Zeke took place at the gallery in Chichester. The chain itself was rather eponymously named *Marguerite's*. The journey to work for Zeke was roughly twenty-five minutes. He was a buyer and seller. He was technically the gallery director when he wasn't, but it was largely ceremonial. His job was to find and buy art from up-and-coming artists and have it exhibited in one of her galleries for a time. Marguerite's exclusivity meant that the work on display there would drive the price up exponentially to be sold to a collector for a higher price eventually.

His daily duties were limited when Marguerite wasn't in attendance and even less so when she was. She was an enigmatic character, one not many people said no to; she was cold, calculated, and borderline scary. She came from old money and now had six galleries, not including this one. He knew a lot about her, and nothing at all, but again it was a mystery he was happy to let his mind wander with.

Zeke's morning had far from gone to plan, and he was running late, but then who does plan on speaking to an Interpol agent in the morning? Interpol? He still couldn't quite believe it! Despite his casual nature, the visit spooked him. In his mind, he'd done nothing wrong, but it is hard to be confident about anything that you don't remember! Three men were found dead in the same place he was attacked. Given that he knew nothing, that was troubling news. There were so many questions and possibilities and nowhere near enough answers. Had he been minutes away from death, could he have witnessed it, or worse, had he been part of it? Had he watched on scared, being neutral in the face of evil makes you complicit. No one finds out whether they are a coward or a hero until it is forced upon them. Could he have had a hand in their death? But even to him, the latter assumption was absurd, he hadn't thrown a punch since year ten, yet there was a possibility.

He drank coffee and stewed at home for far too long after the agent left before realising he was late. Speeding out of the door, he jumped into the car and made swiftly for work.

He pushed the car as hard as possible, desperate to outrun his thoughts and leave them in his dust as he sped away. But it was eating him. Why couldn't he remember? What other surprises were lurking around the corner? As exciting as it all was, he no longer felt in control. The agent could show up later with cuffs and take him away for all he knew. How do you defend what you don't know? He was in the alley and then on the plane; it was completely mental! Of all the insane things he'd ever experienced, losing entire hours whilst still functioning was a horrible feeling. Whatever had transpired, he couldn't account for his whereabouts, meaning that he had no choice but to lie for now.

Zeke pulled up to work late, looked in the mirror at the bruise on his face and did his best to paint a smile upon it. As he prised himself from the leather seat, he realised he had latent muscle pain in his upper body. He dismissed it as flight stiffness before strolling into the building.

Zeke managed just ten minutes sat in his office before the phone on his desk buzzed, and he was summoned. Marguerite needed to see him. Whether it was good or bad, there was an Olympics taking place in his head, and it was a welcome distraction.

Zeke had a good relationship with Marguerite, bordering on friendship, they went back a long way. Regardless, she was not a woman you let down. He'd seen her wrath and had no intention of having that ire directed towards him. Her galleries were in the middle of a rapid expansion, she was opening sites in chic spots across Europe and wanted nothing to stand in her way. After the last three days he'd had, he hoped she would be off-site, and as he walked towards her door, a feeling of dread sunk over him. Did she know? Had Interpol been in touch with her? If not, should he tell her? How does one even broach a situation like this?

"Oh, hey Marguerite, blacked out in New York. Three men died, and an Interpol agent followed me home! Otherwise, the trip was a resounding success!"

He shook his head at the notion as he grabbed the handle to her office door. His version of the truth would have to do for now.

"Ah, there he is, at last, the prodigal son returns. I take it all went smoothly?" Zeke nodded.

"Well, now we'll have that vile piece of work from that little shit. That damn gallery keeps upping their prices; it's us that does them a favour."

"It was as low as I could get them to go."

"Well, maybe they'll lose some of their gloss when the community finds out they have thugs operating in their midst."

"Worse things have happened," he replied. "Anyway, how did you kno—"

"That wife of yours gave me an earful. I can see why you like her. When is the baby due?"

"Soon," was Zeke's response.

"Anyway, well done on New York. The real reason I asked you here was to meet your new protégé.

"Young man, I would like you to meet Lara Richards." Zeke turned around and noted a smartly dressed young lady who was sitting in the corner. He hadn't noticed her when he entered, and her movement almost startled him. Zeke regained his composure as she stood and made her way over to him.

Zeke was, of course, already aware of the impending arrival of Ms Richards. He had perused her online profile multiple times for professional reasons, it's only natural to do one's research. But seeing her in the flesh was something else. Lara was tall, tanned, long-legged, and had the shiniest dark hair. She wore a nose ring, and if you looked hard enough, there were a few well-concealed tattoos. She wore elegance with grit, and he knew her to be intelligent and well-educated. To Zeke, a woman like Lara was the equivalent of offering heroin to an ex-addict. He was a changed man since he met Cassie. But Lara was still a danger, one he would do well to avoid. Aside from that, the change was welcome; when he wasn't travelling, very little happened in the gallery. There was only a small number of staff and not much excitement.

Marguerite wanted Lara to operate out of her Paris site. It was a smart move. From the looks of it, she could probably sell the Louvre back to the French government. She would be assigned to Zeke for the next few months and would follow him closely.

Zeke put his brain into gear as she moved toward him. He stuck out his hand courteously and said,

"Miss Richards, it's a pleasure to meet you."

"Oh, please," she said as her hand met his. "Call me Lara."

"Okay, well, it's a pleasure to meet you, Lara."

His repetition came from an unusual loss of words. Awestruck as they held hands, it felt as though their souls connected for a mere moment, intertwining for an instant before he pulled his hand away. No amount of paperwork or profiling stacked up; Lara Richards was a work of art.

"Miss Richards is your understudy Mr Olsen. I need her to be as adept at this as you are, teach and show her every trick from that brain of yours. But I want her in Paris as soon as possible, understand?"

Zeke nodded he understood loud and clear, Lara was probably not someone he wanted in his life for longer than necessary. "I hear Paris is nice…well, always."

A moment of silence fell over the glass office; Marguerite placed her glasses on her nose, looked at Zeke's head once more and said,

"How's the head?"

"Ice helps," replied Zeke.

"Good, well, let's hope it clears up before your next trip. We can't send you back to New York looking like that?"

"New York? Back?"

"Yes, Mr Olsen, the gallery heard what happened to you. They felt so bad about it, they've invited you out to one of their charity galas."

"Oh, well, that's not necessary," he said. As his brain panicked, still desperately trying to figure out what happened the day before.

"Nonsense, young man, you shall go to the ball! Anyway, make the most of it. Once that baby of yours arrives, you'll be glad I sent you."

"Aw, you're having a baby?" Lara chimed in. Her smooth words filled Zeke's head, and he turned back toward her. He'd almost managed to push her out of his mind, and there she was, there she would be, side by side, possibly for months.

"Take Ms Richards with you," said Marguerite.

"Ahhh," screamed Zeke's mind. It was almost as though she'd read his thoughts like this was some kind of test.

"There will be some big players in the art world there. Get her straight in the mix."

Returning to New York, taking Lara, ignoring the words of Agent Jones, and still not knowing what happened mixed in his skull like a smoothie made with foul ingredients.

"Young man! Are you with us? Zeke?" The silence had probably been palpable. He had no idea, awash in a sea of thoughts.

"Sure," he replied confidently. He seemingly had no other choice. He could admit that he might be losing his mind or carry on regardless. A slight panic crept over him as he felt the sweat begin to ooze from every gland in his body. He turned and nodded dutifully to Marguerite and Lara before promptly leaving the room. New York could hold answers or bring back memories. He wasn't sure if he wanted either.

Zeke was out the door and downstairs faster than the speed of light and he headed straight for the water cooler. It felt like all the sweat had come from his salivary glands, and his mouth felt like it had been stuffed with the world's most absorbent sponge. Making it drier than tinder. He filled cup after triangle cup from the fountain, downing them like a madman. As water returned to his brain, the awareness of others cruised back through him. He could hear the pong of the table tennis table in the back, the chatter of guests, the gossip of employees. The ordinarily serene gallery was a crescendo of noise. Did anyone else hear this?

A hand reached through his fog and touched him on the shoulder, like a tug pulling a stranded ship back to shore. He turned and looked at Lara, who faced him. Her arrival quietened the clamour, and she looked at him inquisitively,

"Was there no water to drink in New York?" she asked as she watched him pour cup after cup down his throat. Zeke motioned to the small paper cup,

"Too many other things to drink. That's the problem!" She chuckled.

"It's nice to finally meet you," she said with a smile. "Marguerite has told me so much, but there's nothing quite like putting a name to a face." He wondered if she, too, had looked him up as she spoke. After all, it's prudent in the digital age in which we live, is it not? Does everyone do it? Or just him?

"Well," he replied finally, "I'm sure I'm far less interesting in person."

"I highly doubt that, but hey, I guess we're going to a party. So, I suppose I'll find out!" A sly grin formed on her lips. They were going to a gala in New York together. The thought both terrified and excited him. But after what he'd just experienced, there was no way it could be any worse than the last trip?

Lara must have picked up on the silence as Zeke mused amongst himself and moved the conversation along, "So, you're having a baby?"

"We are indeed," replied Zeke. The thought of his unborn daughter brought a smile across his face despite the banality of the conversation.

"How is it going?"

"Well," he replied, "it's a breeze for me. But from what I gather, this is the easy part."

"Do you have any kids?" he asked, knowing full well she didn't.

"Oh gosh, no," she replied. "Far too young for that, plus I'm missing the other half of the ingredients."

They stood for a moment. It was neither awkward nor comfortable. There was an edge to Lara, one he liked, one he would like to discover, but it was more than that. She made him feel different about himself somehow. She reached out with her arm and touched him gently on his.

"I'd better get back to work. God is watching!" she said, motioning to the figure of Marguerite looming in a window above.

"Better act busy," he said.

"You two got a name yet?" she said, turning to depart. Zeke shook his head. "God, no."

"Then we'll have an excellent flight," she said teasingly as she walked away.

The smell of food greeted Zeke's senses when he walked through the door. It was after nine, and he remembered they had agreed to cook dinner together. All of which had completely slipped his mind. He'd taken a long drive after work, found an anonymous bar and had an even longer drink.

Life with Cassie had been a work in progress since the day they met. The progress had progressed. After ten arduous years, they had facilitated their plan, this was everything they'd worked for, yet suddenly there were twists and turns abounds. His story of the attack and the events in New York had served to mollify Cassie and just about everyone else. Realistically everyone in England assumes every alleyway in New York is a place you get mugged. But something was eating at him; should he tell her? She was his wife, and she was qualified, but he was afraid.

Cassie was rarely concerned about whatever he did, so long as he came home to her in one piece. Would opening his mouth spring a can of worms, potentially unnecessarily so. He decided that he would keep what he didn't know to himself for now.

"Hey, sweetie," she said as she heard the door close, "I ordered pizza, but I've eaten already."

"Hey," he said. He dropped his bag near the door and set his keys on the table. She was in the kitchen when he arrived. The sight of her sitting at the table surrounded by piles of failed attempts at knitting was everything he needed after an erratic day. He looked at her and laughed at her paltry attempts.

"Hey!" she said. "Come here. You, do it? The game is rigged. I don't think anyone knits. It's all produced by machines in old ladies' garages, and it's fucking impossible!"

"I believe you," he said. "You never see something being knit. Not really. You see people clacking away with two sticks and some yarn, then two weeks later, it's a jumper. Where's the process?" Zeke moved towards the fridge, opened it, and grabbed two slices of pizza and as many beers before sitting at the table next to Cassie. He removed a cap from one of the bottles and finished it in seconds.

"Everything okay?"

"Marguerite wants me back in New York?"

"When?"

"Soon."

"Well, providing you avoid fistfights and alleys, what's wrong with that? I'd make the most of it. Once this lady appears, you won't be going anywhere for a while."

"You won't be," he replied jokingly. His words made the joke, but his voice carried some tension.

"There's more to it, isn't there?" Zeke nodded. Cassie was the polygraph for polygraphs. If something was off, she knew.

"Hey," she said, reaching out with her hand, and wrapping it around his. "Talk to me; what's going on?"

"You won't believe me."

"Zeke Olsen, you are many things. A liar isn't one of them."

Zeke nodded, paused, took a deep breath, and then said. "An Interpol agent came to see me this morning."

"Uh-huh!" replied Cassie, "Often happens in sleepy Hampshire villages."

"Ha," Zeke laughed nervously. "See? I still don't understand it myself!"

"What did he want?"

"To ask some questions about New York!"

"Well, he can join the fucking queue," she laughed.

Zeke paused, then looked at her solemnly, "Cass," he began, "he was asking about some murders near where I was attacked."

"Shit Zeke, are you serious?" The slow movement of his head confirmed that he was. "But it has nothing to do with you, does it?"

"I don't remember anything after being hit, other than getting up and going back to the hotel. But Cass, this guy, came to the house. Told me I was a key witness, not to leave the country."

"Zeke sweetie, you are many crazy things. But you are not violent, okay? This has nothing to do with you. He's just doing his job."

"What about going back to New York?"

"Fuck him," said Cassie. "I mean, it's bad enough that he comes around here. He can't stop you from doing your job. If he had anything at all, you wouldn't be here. When has Zeke Olsen ever done anything someone told him to do? It will all blow over soon enough, trust me!"

"Thanks," he said. Their talk made him feel slightly better. She was, of course, right, unless she was wrong. He wasn't violent. He didn't even think he had it in him. In the case of fight or flight, he always assumed it would be the latter. As much as she assuaged his fears, she didn't have the full story, and it wasn't in him to tell her. The photos he'd been shown were firmly engrained onto a usually blank mind, and there was something about them that had painted themselves into his subconscious, like puzzles that needed solving. Had he seen something in them?

"So, I should go then?"

"It's not the best idea, Zeke! But like I said, you can't let him interfere with your life."

"You're right. You always are."

"Plus," she said, "if this Jones guy bothers you, he'll have me to deal with!" Cassie stood. She took Zeke's hand and placed it on her bump before kissing him on the head. "Well, I have an early start. Get some rest!"

"I will soon," he promised, "I will soon."

17

The rest of the week dissipated into a blur. Zeke was as easily distracted as he was able to become fixated. Work was tedious, and the wound on his head only served to fuel his anxiety. With head wounds, people tend to either ask, judge or speculate. The judgement and speculation annoyed him, but he could at least deal with them, the questions less so. Because he had no answer!

"What happened to your head?"

Even laced with concern, the questions troubled him because he didn't have a fucking clue. Lara was a distraction, but it was at least welcome. As uneasy as he was about returning to New York, he would at least have her company. Zeke was a paradox in that he could be both gregarious and misanthropic. His mixed upbringing had seen him spend time with people he didn't like. Now that he had the decision, he was selective. It wasn't that he disliked people. He just didn't like many of them and would always take no company over lousy company. But he had already seen enough to know that Lara was one of the exceptions, it had been some time since he'd made a new friend. It was rare that he met people that lived at his level.

The days rolled around slowly, and as his wound started to heal, so did his anxiety. The past trip became a distant haze, the cracks surrounding his lost memory healing along with those in his skull. He'd had no more dealings with Interpol and assumed it to be routine as Cassie had implied.

The anxious blur rolled around until finally, it was time to return to New York, and before he knew it, the pre-arranged taxi was at his door waiting to pick him up.

The festive season was almost upon them, and it was the first in their new house. Keen to celebrate it, Zeke had already eagerly hung ribbons of fairy lights all around the yard.

As he stood in the garden waiting, case in hand, he watched them blink away as the taxi pulled into his drive. The car already contained Lara, who sat in the back, beaming at him like a child at Christmas.

After the events of his last excursion, he'd tapered back slightly on his drug and alcohol use. It didn't aid his pain, but the reality was he wasn't a kid anymore; he clearly couldn't afford to push his body as hard as he had been. The relative sobriety had improved his organisational skills, and despite the early taxi at the even earlier hour, he was prepared and even mildly excited.

As he got into the car, he realised it had been a while since he'd had fun, surely this trip would be better than the last, they would attend a party, maybe meet some celebrities, and catch a little more culture. For the first time in years, he was leaving the country for something that wasn't exclusively a work trip. They were there to have fun, he had intriguing company, no responsibility, and he imagined Christmas time in New York to be like a fairy tale.

As the taxi drove through the early morning, Lara chattered at him incessantly, she was funny, interesting, and exciting. But he was anxious, in pain and wasn't quite in the mood. Meaning as much as he appreciated the company, he was relieved when the hour finally took its toll on her, and she went from an open mouth to closed eyes in less than five minutes, how he envied people who could sleep anywhere at any time. The car then turned sharply onto a slip road, and Lara fell towards him. The movement didn't wake her; instead, she nestled into his side and proceeded to snore. He nudged her lightly at first in an attempt to shift her, but the girl was sound asleep and waking her seemed unfair. As she lay against him, her hair fell against his face, and he could feel her warmth and scent, a potent unescapable concoction. The journey would proceed to take three whole hours. He was trapped.

Zeke watched in admiration as Lara slept for longer than he should have. In his defence, there wasn't much for him to do, he'd met the eye of the driver in the rear-view mirror on occasions, and each time he'd smiled adoringly at them.

When they finally arrived at the airport, Zeke stirred and successfully navigated Lara through security. She then appeared to come alive and insisted they hit up numerous bars and drink away their time in the terminal.

"When in places, you can fly to Rome," she'd said. Who was he to argue?

When their time came, the pair staggered drunkenly towards the gate. Once onboard, Lara demanded the window seat, sat, and promptly fell asleep. Their seats were side by side, and it wasn't long before he found her head on his shoulder again. Zeke inserted his headphones, keen to find some escapism in music, only to be disturbed soon after.

"Excuse me, sir," came the voice from the female flight attendant. "Can I please ask you to remove your headphones during take-off?"

Zeke looked up and saw the woman's motions through his noise. She gesticulated in a manner that could only mean one thing, so he reluctantly took them out.

"Thank you, sir," she said pleasantly. But before she disappeared, she looked at them both adoringly and said. "Don't worry. I won't wake your wife."

"She's no—" Zeke began, but the woman had already set off down the corridor.

The plane started to move, and Zeke immediately reinserted his headphones, washed down some painkillers with the rest of his vodka and closed his eyes.

The flight was an hour late to depart but landed precisely on time. The time relative to them was about eight a.m. and the airport was hectic as they hovered hazily through it.

The monotony broke when Lara spotted a chauffeur holding a placard that contained their names. She shrieked at the sight of them printed on a plastic card and rushed over to give the bewildered driver a warm hug. The courteous limo driver loaded their belongings into the car and pulled away smoothly.

The journey to the hotel was short and very comfortable, Lara had never been to America before, and she spent the whole ride glued to the window, remarking at just about everything. Her vim picked him up, and the driver shot him the odd wink. Presumably assuming he was in for a fun weekend with his young wife. A thought that Zeke repeatedly had to delete from his mind. With the journey winding up he started to unwind and finally began to enjoy himself as they opened and emptied the complimentary champagne by the time they pulled up at the hotel.

Zeke's bubble burst as he planted his feet on the ground and looked up at their final destination. It was the same hotel he'd stayed in on his previous trip, and an uneasy feeling of dread and déjà vu washed over him. As fantastic a place as it was, he didn't remember leaving it before, which made him wonder if it held memories that he didn't.

Sensing his hesitation, Lara grabbed his hand and tugged him towards the door,

"Come on, old man," she joked. "New York won't explore itself!" As his shoulder did its best to remain attached to his body. He realised she was right and followed her keenly up the steps and into the lobby. There were possibilities abound, and he realised he was no longer alone. Her enthusiasm and lust for life were infectious as they spread over him. For the first time in months, he felt like he might be able to enjoy himself.

The day whistled passed as they sampled everything New York had to offer, and he was exhausted when they returned to the hotel. The gala would take place in the building, so although they didn't have far to go, the hour was now late, and they didn't have long to prepare.

They had been given a luxury suite at the hotel's summit, rooms with adjoining doors. So long as the door was unlocked, Lara was free to enter his, and she did so, having freshly showered. She knocked and entered wearing just a towel. She carried with her a suitcase and laid it down on the bed.

"What's that?" he asked.

"We're going to a gala, Ezequiel. We can't have you dressed like that!" He opened the case to find an immaculately pressed dinner jacket combo.

"How do you know this will fit?"

"Perhaps I've already sized you up?" she looked at him, and he at her. The voltage of the tempo in the room increased for a moment before she said, "Cassie messaged me your deets! She said you'd try and turn up in jeans and a tee-shirt."

"What's wrong with that?

"As great as they were, I'm not sure New York's finest appreciates *The Clash* as much as you do." Zeke shrugged,

"You'd be surprised." Lara strolled slowly out of the room, stopping short before she shut the door. She shot him a look and said,

"Get dressed. We don't have long!"

Zeke dressed, donned his jacket, and stood staring at himself in the mirror. It reminded him of a scene from *Casino Royale*. It wasn't dissimilar, he just hoped it wouldn't follow the same course! As he surveyed himself in the mirror, he smiled, he'd scrubbed up well, and he realised it had been some time since he'd had occasion to dress as such. By the time he was dressed, it was almost eight. Zeke stepped onto the balcony lit and drew from his cigarette. Lara was fun, but the day had been long, and he was flagging. Time was catching up with him, his back hurt, and he felt thoroughly uninspired. The devil on his shoulder began to tell him to disappear and leave Lara to enjoy the party independently. But before listening to the devil to his right, he turned to his left and saw Lara emerge onto her balcony. There she was, in a beautiful black dress complete with elbow-length white gloves. Stood in the cool wind against the skyline of the New York backdrop. Her hair moved like a steady flame, and her rose-red lips shone out, twinkling at him like they were the Polestar itself. It was like the opening scene from a graphic novel. She was iridescent, and he found himself breathless.

She moved to the edge of her balcony and reached across to him. With her arms dangling over the sheer drop, she beckoned to him and drew him over. She reached over dangerously and straightened his bow tie,

"Come on now," she said. "It's rude to keep a lady waiting."

18

The lift ride to the lobby may well have been to the centre of the Earth, there was a silence, but it wasn't awkward. Lara looked absolutely stunning, and Zeke did his best to keep his eyes front and fixed on the door. Beyond her looks and anything superficial, there was a connection between them. It was very unusual for him to feel this way about someone he barely knew. They'd met just a few weeks ago, but it could have been years. He felt as though he could trust her with anything. Perhaps their souls had met before? The elevator dropped fast, was he falling too?

The lift finally arrived, and the door pinged open slowly revealing the awaiting banquet. They stepped out arm in arm, and this was fun. It was like an upper-class version of his youth. Zeke was excited for the night ahead. His companion was intelligent, mischievous, and very entertaining, deadly combinations in a lady.

The gala couldn't have been more ostentatious if it tried. The wealth of riches here was more significant than the GDP of several third-world countries combined. There were almost as many servers as there were guests and many in attendance. The centre table featured a banquet buffet that Marie Claire herself would have been proud of, the bar was open and expensively stocked, and each table featured a bucket of mixed drinks. To top it off, the myriad staff constantly intermingled with trays of either canapes, flutes, or both, and it was rare you found yourself empty glassed or handed.

The party was ostensibly a fundraiser, but that clearly wasn't the whole story. It didn't quite feature New York's A-list, but plenty of heavy hitters were in attendance. Many of whom most likely made their money through expedient ventures.

They stepped from the lift and into the room, Lara took to the occasion like a shark to a bleeding carcass, and she was an expert at casing a room. Zeke followed by her side curiously as she discussed art, literature, music, foreign policy, and even spoke some Latin. No one speaks Latin.

He felt incredibly underqualified to teach this lady anything, but that was presumably the point. Putting a brain and an imagination in a dress that left little to it and accompanying her with a man who was able to manipulate a crowd to his viewpoint and you had a deadly duo. They were a handsome, eloquent, knowledgeable, and lethal couple. Party or not, they would integrate well here tonight, reminding Zeke that there was always an agenda with Marguerite

They mingled, ate from silver trays, and drank extensively from expensive glasses until Zeke decided he'd talked small for as long as possible. He excused himself in the direction of the restroom and grabbed a cold beer from a bucket on his way out. Lara would fair fine without him, dressed the way she was, she would find no shortage of company.

Zeke did his usual and slipped out of a back door into an alley. He sat alone on a curb, sipping from his beer, blowing smoke into the smouldering night. They'd been in New York almost a day, and nothing untoward had happened. Perhaps all his worry had been for nothing. Zeke sat in a vacancy for too long before he finished both his beer and cigarette, stood, and exhaled into the New York skyline. He'd been brooding on his own and rationalised that it was unfair and no fun to leave Lara alone. What was eating at him, why couldn't he just enjoy this? Life had moved very quickly since he'd met Cassie. They'd had their moments together, but they'd barely stopped to catch their breath. The chaos and uncertainty had kept him going, but the truth was when he stepped off the plane in New York all those weeks ago, there was a feeling that his life had become mundane, a loop, he wasn't having fun and, it was nice to have a simple patch of pure enjoyment, but something felt off. Despite their time together, he'd still yet to fall or land since he'd met Cassie. He hoped that a bit of a change and then the birth of his daughter would straighten him out. The incident in New York had been the headline, but he'd been slipping for a while now. Was this all that he wanted? Ought he not be destined for more? He'd escaped the car fire for a reason, and here he was doing nothing with his life.

The party was large, loud, and lurid. There were people everywhere wearing outfits that cost more than his house. He found himself lost and alone in the melee, and without Lara, he didn't want to be there. He hadn't told her he was stepping out, and she was probably looking for him. Zeke walked the floor as often as possible before concluding that it wasn't there. A waiter walked past him with a tray. Zeke grabbed two champagne flutes, sipped at both, and then carried them out of the room to the lift. Perhaps she'd retired to the suites.

With the key card in his mouth and the glasses in his hand, Zeke bent and tapped the card against the door with his lips, turning, he backed into the door and bumped it open with his bum. The glasses fell from his hands as he bustled into the room, mouth agape as he studied the scene. The flutes fell to the floor and shattered along with his peace. His suite was a wreck. His belongings were everywhere, furniture was scattered, and one of Lara's heels lay alone on the floor. The sight of the sole shoe sent a shockwave through him, and without thinking, he grabbed the handle of the adjoining door and dashed inside.

Zeke burst through the door with the passion of a young matador keen to impress the crowd. The room illuminated immediately upon his entry, and his relief at seeing Lara unscathed was swiftly replaced by the events that followed it.

Lara sat on the bed. Her hair was a mess, and tears streamed down her face dragging the magnificent make-up down with them. She looked scared, terrified even, but she was otherwise unhurt. Two men flanked her, one of whom was visibly armed. Zeke took two steps into the room before he heard the unmistakable click of a pistol and halted in his tracks.

"Passion is always our undoing," came a male voice from behind him. Zeke conceded the man was right. He hadn't even looked. He'd run in there like a bull into a china shop, and now he was trapped. But Lara's scared eyes met his, and her fear made them tremble. His passion turned to rage, and he went to step toward her.

"I wouldn't do that if I were you!"

He placed one foot in front of the other before the feeling of cold hard metal pressed up against the back of his skull. Zeke gritted his teeth and closed his eyes. Hoping that when he opened them, this wouldn't be happening.

"There he is! We've been looking for you for some time. Imagine our surprise when we see you here celebrating at a party."

"Who are you? What do you want?" asked Zeke.

"I want to know what happened to my men!" Zeke looked at Lara, as much as he was sangfroid, he had to get her out of here.

"Please," said Zeke, "let her go. She has nothing to with this."

"Do you suppose that line ever works?" he said as he fished through Zeke's pocket, removing his wallet. "Mr Olsen huh? Nice to finally put a name to a face."

Zeke could feel the breath of the man behind him on his neck, he had yet to get a look at him, and annoyingly it seemed a pure coincidence. They must have recognised him from an image or CCTV, but now they knew his name, date of birth and home address. This was bad!

"So, Mr Olsen, I'll ask again. What happened to my men?"

"I don't know!" The man behind him must have signalled to one of his henchmen beside Lara, and he stepped forward and backhanded her hard across the face. She let out a small yelp before collapsing on the bed.

As Zeke watched the scene unfold, watches and clocks worldwide must have cooperated in slowing down time. He'd been in the room less than two minutes, and it had been the longest two of his life. Lara slowly sat back up, beheld Zeke, and looked petrified, she looked at him for help, guidance, or hope. He wasn't sure he had any.

"Once more, Mr Olsen, what happened to my men?"

"I don't know what you're talking about. Whoever it is you are after; you've got the wrong guy!"

Before he'd even finished the end of his sentence, the man hit Lara harder across the face. She fell back to the bed once more but remained still this time.

Seeing her abused for the second time was the last for Zeke as a fire lit in his heart. He was tired, but an immortal spirit lived in his frail body. He'd run in like a bull in a china shop, and now it was time to do as a bull does.

With the pistol still pressed against his skull, he threw his head back with the speed of a wild animal, giving its possessor no time to react. The butt of the gun snacked against the head of the man behind him, and when no shot was fired, Zeke ran for the man who'd hit Lara and took him down as ruthlessly as a horse hoof tramples roses. Zeke fought back hard with the man on top of him, both hands wrapped around the pistol as they jostled for control. The room and everything in it became a blur, like being trapped on a merry-go-round that kept gaining speed, spinning further and further out of control. Until it reached terminal velocity and finally, the gun fell into someone's possession, a shot was fired, and everything went dark!

"Zeke, can you hear me? Zeke, are you okay?"

He opened his eyes slowly and looked up at the darkness that hung above him. The first thing he remembered was feeling cold, and the second was the smell of perfume. He knew immediately that it was Lara's scent and it provided instant comfort.

He sat up gradually and did his best to acquaint himself with his surroundings. He appeared to be lying on the floor in a dirty, wet back street. Lara's face featured the marks from her assault, so there was no way this was a dream!

"Oh my gosh, Zeke. You're okay; you're okay!"

"Lara," he managed. "What am I doing on the floor?"

"I don't know," she replied.

"What do you mean?" Zeke replied jovially. "One of us must know how we got here. I'm lying on an alley floor, you're hovering over me like you thought I was dead, and I'm pretty sure that is a rat." Lara shook her head as if she was none the wiser. "But the hotel…that happened, right?" She nodded. "And you're, okay?"

"I could do with some ice?" she said, gesturing to her face. Zeke reached up at his own,

"Hmmm, me too," he said. He paused for a moment to allow his senses to return. It was beyond the realms of surrealism. The altercation in the Hotel hadn't been a dream, and neither it seemed was this. They found themselves in a New York back street, complete with a building with a metal fire escaped that reached almost to the floor. The road was littered with bins, and there was rubbish everywhere. If you looked hard enough, you could see the eyes of rats in every dark recess.

"Right, well," he said, standing. "That was some party!" Lara laughed nervously. He glanced over at her and noticed she carried one of their backpacks. "What's in there?" he inquired.

"Everything essential, wallets, passports, change of clothes."

"Good thinking," he said.

"Zeke, I didn't pack it. You were wearing it when I woke up!"

"So—"

"Yes," she replied. "The last thing I remember is being struck. However we got away. Whatever got us here, it was you!" She moved towards him faster than he could react and threw her frame around his.

"Oh my gosh, Zeke. I was so scared."

"It's okay," he said as confidently as possible as he placed his arm around her. He rubbed Lara on the back comfortingly for a moment and tried his best to piece together what was happening. He hadn't managed to look at the man behind him, but his words loomed in Zeke's mind. They'd recognised his face at the party but only knew his name from his driving licence. They were clearly part of the same organisation he'd tangled with initially, but why did they think he worked for someone. He'd never been exposed to anything remotely like this in his years. He was conflicted in his emotions. He felt powerless and powerful, scared, and excited. It was rare that he felt anything, and part of him loved the departure from being numb. But he knew for sure that they needed to leave New York, whoever these people were, they had his home address, although for some reason something in his mind told him not to worry about it!

Zeke removed himself from Lara's embrace, looked at her frankly and said, "Come on, let's go! We need to get out of here!" He took her by the hand and led her away, but she stopped his movement and said,

"Shouldn't we go to the police? Who were those men, Zeke?" The interruption was inconvenient, but he figured she deserved answers, not that he had any.

"I have no idea," he replied. "About any of it, but I don't think the police will help us."

"Zeke," she said, "I'm not going anywhere until you start talking! I just got kidnapped from a party by three men with guns! This is insane. Please talk to me?" Zeke put his head in his hands and paused for a moment.

"Okay," he said. "After I left the gallery last time, I was attacked. I don't remember what happened. I know that I had an Interpol agent turn up at my fucking house asking me questions about murder. But that's it!"

Lara looked at him, "Zeke, that's crazy. What do you mean you don't remember?"

"Lara, I was in the alleyway, and then I was on the aeroplane. I feel like I'm losing my fucking mind.

"I guess it's possible that the men who died were connected to the ones that attacked us, and for some reason, everyone seems to think I either did it or know who did. But I know fucking nothing!"

"So, tonight?" He shook his head.

"I remember the man hitting you again and then wrestling one of them. After that, it's just you, me, and the alleyway."

"Hey," she said, taking his hand softly. "Calm down, okay. You saved our lives tonight. That's gotta count?"

"But what if I did something—"

"Hey," she said, grabbing him by the face. "Those men had guns. They hit me twice. If anything happened to them, they got what they fucking deserved! I don't know how you got us out of there, though."

"Viking spirit."

She grinned,

"You're right about one thing, though," she said, looking around. "We definitely need to get out of here!"

The rest of the evening that followed was low-key in comparison. They were both shaken, battered, and bruised. Lara had been mollified surprisingly easily despite the enormity of what had happened especially since he'd just told her something he'd not even admitted to his wife or best friend.

Zeke found them a cheap, anonymous motel nearby and paid with cash. They made up fun, fake names, then filled the evening, sharing a room, draining a minibar, eating from a vending machine, and watching American sitcoms. Zeke wasn't sure if it was a coping mechanism for Lara or if she was genuinely okay. But amazingly, she seemed unphased by what had happened tonight. It had been an evening to remember for all the wrong reasons. Weapons might be commonplace here, but a pistol was rarely seen in the UK. They'd seen a few tonight! She would have every right to be freaking out.

They shared a room, bolted the door as tightly as possible, and spent the rest of the evening nursing wounds, drinking whiskey and eating peanuts from the minibar.

Zeke felt a little like Clarence and Alabama, battered and united in their motel room. Only Alabama and Clarence were in love. Zeke and Lara weren't, were they?

"So, you don't remember anything from the last trip to New York?" Lara asked.

"Well, I remember some of it obviously, just nothing after the alleyway."

"That must be pretty scary?"

"It isn't, but it is. I don't know if what happened was scary. I might have just wandered around New York, but if something bad happened, I don't remember."

"I can see how that would screw with you a bit."

Zeke nodded, "I mean, I'm alive. I assumed I took a hit, got knocked out, suffered a memory loss, and then came home. Now, suddenly, Interpol is involved, as are New York gangsters. What next? One minute I'm smoking. The next, my whole life has changed. I seem to be wrapped up in the most extreme situation I've ever been in; I'm just sorry that you got caught up in this. We shouldn't have come here."

Lara turned to look at him. They sat side by side on the bed as a lousy cable show played in the background. She placed her hand softly on his and said, "Hey, you weren't to know, plus whatever happened, I'm lucky I was with you."

"How do you figure?" asked Zeke.

"Zeke," she said earnestly, "I was unconscious. I didn't walk out of that hotel room. I don't know what happened with the men, but you must have carried me out when we left. We wouldn't have got away were it not for you."

Zeke felt the sensation of her hand on his and noted a look in her eye. Tensions were running high, and it had been an emotional night. Her hand on his skin drew his attention to her and their eyes met. Zeke noticed the emerald green in her eyes, and they sparkled at him like gems. As she returned his gaze, he got the sense that she felt safe in his company, and the feeling was reciprocated. As though he protected her physically as she did him mentally. Everything around them faded away, and his nerves throbbed like plucked violins. There was an anxious anticipation as their faces drew closer until they were inches apart. He could feel the quiver of her breath against the skin of his face. Their lips inched ever closer until they were mere millimetres away and they prepared to meet, but just as they did there was a knock at the door that thrust them back into reality.

"Pizza delivery!"

The distraction tore them apart, dousing the fire. Zeke stood to get to the door. He grabbed the pie and paid the driver, but before he shut the door, he said.

"I'll get us some more ice!" Before disappearing out of the door.

Having filled the bucket with ice, Zeke loitered near the machine as he puffed away on his cigarette. What was he doing? They nearly kissed! He would have kissed her were it not for the interruption. It would have been a mistake for both, like pouring oil on troubled waters. A night such as this wreaks havoc with one's emotions, they didn't need ice, but he needed to cool off.

Now that he was alone, his brain entertained itself, and it did its best to return to the hotel room. There had been three men. At least two were armed. Lara was unconscious, and he was on the floor. If it were the cliffhanger to the end of a television episode, assumptions would be made as to the hero's likely demise. But just as before he remembered nothing past a certain point. He remembered being on the floor, and that was it! A shot had been fired, but the top suites are notoriously well soundproof. No one appeared to be looking for them, provided they weren't detained before boarding their hastily rebooked return flights. They would be back home within twenty-four hours. Presently they were in the clear, but it made no sense, nothing did. Why did they think he worked for someone? Something was happening to him. This couldn't be a coincidence; the universe is rarely so lazy. Everything happens for a reason. But it was hard to reason when he had no memory or explanation for what had happened on either occasion. Once, you can chalk it up to accident, tiredness, or trauma, but twice, it didn't add up. A mistake repeated more than once is usually a decision. Were these his choices? In his mind, he told himself he wasn't capable of violence of any sort. The blackouts were gone, but of the parts he did remember, he recalled the pure hot rage that flew through him when the man hit Lara. Even the idea of someone laying hands on her again burned into his brain like the shadow of unseen evil. But surely as angry as he had been, there was no way he could take down three armed thugs?

By the time he'd returned to the motel room, Lara was fast asleep, sprawled out and snoring. Despite the mess, she was as elegant as ever, asleep like a saint. She was safe, and given what had almost transpired earlier, he was glad she was no longer awake. He crept into the room and covered her with a blanket. She moved slightly but didn't stir, and it was as he watched her lying on the bed in a heap, that he cast his mind back to the hotel room earlier. Almost as if he remembered something, just before it all went south, and everything went dark, when she was lying on the bed motionless, he could have sworn he saw her blink. Could she have been awake? Had she seen what happened? Zeke dismissed the thought quickly. His memory was the last thing he would trust right now. There's no way she would have kept quiet if she'd seen what had happened. Having tucked her in, Zeke bolted the door, took up residence in the armchair opposite it and began to wait.

When morning came Zeke awoke to find Lara dressed and ready to go. He was stiff from his night in the chair, his head pounded from the whiskey and combined with the lack of sleep her words were as meaningless as the syllables of an unknown tongue. He looked her hard in the eyes and watched as her lips moved away in front of him, motionless until she whacked him on the shoulder.

"Come on, Rip Van Winkel," she said. "Taxi's on its way." Zeke nodded, stood wearily, and dragged himself into the bathroom. He ran the tap and emptied himself as he leant against the wall—the way Lara was made him wonder if he'd imagined last night, he knew he hadn't, but he wished he had. He certainly wasn't keen to bring it up. He washed and packed what little he had quickly, and they departed the hotel in the direction of JFK.

Aside from the usual tension that is airport security and their unique way of making even the most genial person feel like they might be doing something wrong, the flight took off without a hitch or delay. As soon as the wheels went up, Zeke settled down and relaxed, keen to be departing New York. He smiled to himself as he inserted his headphones. What another crazy adventure, he thought to himself as he drifted into oblivion, unaware of what was to welcome him upon return.

19

Their eleventh-hour flight landed at Heathrow late in the evening. The plane taxied to a hangar before anyone was allowed to disembark, and it was then that Zeke realised something was wrong. His life felt surreal as he was escorted from the plane by a team of law enforcement dressed in black. The passengers and crew looked on in shock, and panic spread like wildfire. Everyone assumed they had been on board with a drug smuggler or a terrorist. The team in black hauled him along the aisle and towards the open door. Zeke stepped out onto the stairs Agent Jones greeted him. After a chaotic night accompanied by a long flight, the sight of the man's face was the last thing he needed.

Jones read him his Miranda rights. It was all noise to him—he heard something about perverting the course of justice before being removed to a waiting car, leaving him with nothing but a parting shot toward Lara stood in the doorway. Her half-veiled eyes met his. He'd saved her, and now she was powerless to help him.

Zeke was then escorted down the steps to the waiting car which was the polar opposite of the limousine that had greeted them in New York. The next few hours would go on to be uncomfortable, the rest of the night even more so.

He and Lara were at least out of New York, but this was far from the homecoming he had pictured. What did he think was going to happen? He should have known.

The next sixteen hours passed in virtual silence. Barely a word was uttered. For some, that might be torture. But it was a blessing after everything that had happened. It afforded Zeke time for quiet contemplation without worrying about distressing others. So much had changed in the last weeks, that he barely recognised his own life anymore. The craziness had lifted his ennui, but something as dark and deep as night still lurked, and he knew not what it was. From an academic point of view, Zeke was hopeless. But he was perceptive, intuitive, and generally one of the more intelligent people in any room. Nevertheless, he couldn't see why this was happening. His brain was fried, and his senses were numb, but as he sat alone in the dim light of the dingy cell, the words of Sir Arthur Conan Doyle rattled around in his brain.

"When you have eliminated all which is impossible, then whatever remains, however improbable, must be the truth."

He'd grown up loving *Sherlock Holmes*, but he wasn't sure even the great detective could solve this one! What was the truth? It was improbable that he'd killed anyone, but he couldn't eliminate anything without memory. Not knowing who'd killed them was killing him.

Zeke was woken at dawn and led wearily to an interrogation room. He had barely slept, he was in pain, longed for home and had no concept of time whatsoever. Despite his mischievous youth, a night spent in a police cell was a first, one he was keen never to repeat.

Having been seated opposite the mirror everyone knows to be both reflective and introspective, Zeke slumped over, placed his head on the solid metal desk and proceeded to wait.

Phwaaack

Came the noise of a dossier thrown forcefully down on the table. Zeke sat and looked up. Jones stood enthused as he lauded himself over him. He took a sip from the cup in his hand before taking a seat.

"Mr Olsen, it seems that bodies pile up wherever you go." Zeke leaned forward and looked at him,

"I don't know what you are talking about!"

"Okay, then let me spell it out for you. Zeke Olsen goes to New York, and three men are murdered in the same place you were attacked. Three men who were all known gang members. Then not two weeks later, you make another trip to New York, and three more bodies were found in a dumpster not far from where you were staying. Coincidence?"

"Look," Zeke said wearily, "I know how this must look to you. But I have nothing to do with any of this. I'm just about to have a baby. Do you think I would jeopardise that to kill some thugs for no reason?"

"There's always a reason Mr Olsen! Plus, we believe the other three bodies found are also connected to the same gang. I've done some digging, your employer, well, she flies close to the sun, Mr Olsen, she's seen her share of malfeasance. We've also looked at your financials. You're a well-paid man. So, Mr Olsen, you tell me how this looks?" Zeke paused and thought for a minute.

"Agent Jones, I am a middle-aged art dealer. I deal in art, whatever else goes on I have no idea. I live in a small village in Hampshire, and before last month I hadn't been to New York in more than thirty years. I work in art, not martial art."

"I follow the evidence Mr Olsen, and right now, that is all leading back to you. Six murders! In my line of work, we call that serial. That's multiple life terms!" Zeke chuckled. This was insane. "Something funny, Mr Olsen?"

"This is madness," he replied. "You think I'm capable of killing six hardened criminals? Three of which I didn't even know about until just now! I haven't been in a fight since I was twelve. All you have is circumstantial."

"I've met a lot of serial killers, Mr Olsen. Most of them don't have it printed on their forehead. If you weren't involved, then help me out. Tell me what happened. I'll be talking to your colleagues and friends. I'll get what I need one way or another and believe me, I won't stop until I do!"

With that, the door knocked and opened without waiting for a reply. A very formal and rigid lady entered and sat down beside Zeke.

"Don't say another word, Mr Olsen." She then looked over at Jones without raising her hand out toward him. "Mr Olsen, I'm Ms Rathbone, your lawyer." She then looked back at Jones.

"You're lucky I don't go after your badge for this. You know better than to begin without representation!"

The lawyer Ms Rathbone was fierce, frightening, and efficient, and she had him out of custody within hours. Making Zeke very glad she sat on his side of the table and not the other. The link between Zeke and the bodies was tenuous at best. All charges were dropped as soon as the word *lawsuit* was uttered. Zeke thanked the ruthless Rathbone, who disappeared as promptly as she had arrived, and he was finally free to go home.

The last two days had drained him. Zeke's soul needed a refill. Between jetlag, jail, and lack of sleep. He needed a boost. Jail cells are awful, the food worse, and the list of unanswered questions and dead bodies had only grown.

The nagging feeling that he was losing his mind, memory or both was eating away at him. What if he took his child out alone, and the same thing happened? The close calls were getting closer, and he needed a break from everything. It had been less than a month since he'd finished building his house, and he'd barely had time to take a breath before finding himself embroiled in something you only see in the movies. He wasn't sure if it thrilled or terrified him. It had undoubtedly broken the humdrum, but he fancied neither death nor jail, and both had been circling around him like vultures lately.

When Zeke finally returned home it was to an empty house. The plush luxury of his isolated villa was satisfyingly stark compared to jail, and he was glad for some time to unwind in his own company. As he stepped into the foyer and unloaded his luggage, he understood what it must be like for the Vikings to reach Valhalla. He'd been tangled up in battle, which he'd won for now.

Their flight had landed about thirty-six hours ago, but it could have been years. Zeke hadn't eaten, washed, slept, or been in the vicinity of anything even remotely comfortable since. He stripped off in the foyer and threw his clothes in a heap on the floor then left his luggage by the front door, entered the kitchen, poured a large glass of red wine, and raised it in his hands almost in celebration before drinking from it as he made his way up the steps.

He set down the glass on the bedside table, plugged his phone into the socket by the wall and made straight for the bathroom. Using his voice, he commanded that the house play him some upbeat ska music and then stepped into the walk-in shower.

Having bled the hot tank dry, he waved the shower away, grabbed a large fluffy white towel and engorged himself in it. He moved back into the bedroom and picked up his phone and glass of wine before settling down on the bed.

Zeke took another large sip of wine before looking at his phone. Since his incarceration, he'd had no communication with anyone, and he knew there would be many messages and even more questions.

Cassie would be the easiest to deal with; Karan would dish out a lecture, presumably, in the form of a proverb, Marguerite had sent a lawyer, so she couldn't be too angry, and then there was Lara! They would have questioned her, too, they'd said very little to each other on the flight and although it wasn't an awkward silence, he had no idea what she was thinking. Zeke lay back on his large bed, taking victory sips of wine when a cold shudder encased him. Hopefully, this would be the end of it? I mean, surely this wasn't likely to happen again. Or should he concede that he might need help? For all he knew, something insidious was manifesting inside him, and here he was sipping wine. Cassie would be fine, but what if she wasn't? At what point did his mercurial charm outweigh its worth? There was also the possibility that he was suffering from disease or mental illness, there were so many things he ought to be doing but for now, just for a moment, all he wanted was a bit of normality back.

Zeke looked around him, at everything he had, that he'd achieved. This should be his dream, yet he was driving too fast, drinking too much, staying up too late, and taking too many drugs. Zeke had been normalising it, rationalising it to himself, but what was causing it? Why couldn't he just be happy with enough? He was always pursuing more, and it seemed that eventually, more would leave him with less.

Zeke did his best to dispel the notion and put the whole month out of his mind as he raised the glass to his lips for another sip, but something stopped him mid-motion, and he paused in thought. It was akin to the feeling when a word is stuck on the tip of your tongue, almost there, and you can't quite picture it. As he grappled with it, a violent memory shot through his brain. It was bright, electric, and caustic, graphic images lept from his subconscious to his conscious mind, and he convulsed. The violent movement saw him drop the glass from his hand, and he watched it fall it spiralled, spinning, spurting red liquid everywhere until finally it hit the floor and shattered. The carpets were new and very pale; the red wine spread out and soaked into the pile, leaving the floor looking like a crime scene.

Zeke sat up and looked at his hands, both were visibly shaking, and he felt sick. The image that had just flashed through his mind was like a third person POV game, which he was playing but not controlling. Like an out-of-body experience, he watched himself beat a man repeatedly as he lay on the ground. Blood oozed from his head and pooled in the surrounding area. Zeke took another look at the red wine on the carpet, the mental and physical images collided, and he felt as though he would be sick.

Panicked, Zeke leapt from the bed and, with no regard for the shattered glass, ran across the floor back towards the bathroom and proceeded to run his hands under the tap, washing them repeatedly. Blood was on them, and he had to get it off.

"You are an idiot!"

Zeke turned away from the mirror to see Cassie standing in the bedroom doorway. He'd been oblivious to her presence and would have been startled was he not glad to see her. Her words and company calmed him down, and as he looked at her, he realised he'd cut his feet as he fled from the bed. It had made a trail of wine and blood across the carpet, a path of blood from bed to bathroom.

"I think they're clean!" Zeke looked down at his hands which were now bright red from the heat. He shut the tap off, wiped them dry on his sides, and greeted her.

"I think you're right."

"The floor certainly isn't!" Zeke took a sideways glance out of the bathroom and realised what he had done.

"Oops!"

"And to think I'd missed you," she joked. Zeke went to move from the bathroom to embrace her, but Cassie put her hand out to cool his motion. "Uh uh, no!" she said authoritatively. "Don't you dare step out of that room. Not until I've sorted those feet! I mean, was it not enough to spill the wine? Did you have to tread it around the place?" Zeke looked down at the floor once more. It looked like someone had dragged a corpse across it, the sight of which caused another momentary mental image. A brief flash, alleyways and blood, bloody alleyways.

"Are you okay?" she asked, concerned. "You look a little pale?" Zeke nodded unconvincingly. "Been a pretty fucked up couple of days!"

"You don't say, and you've ruined the bedroom carpet! Hey, it doesn't matter, so what if it's new? You stay there, sit. I'll get the first aid kit."

Zeke flipped down the toilet lid and took a seat. Cassie, having returned, bent to the floor, and examined his feet, "How?" she began, "You know what? I'm not even going to ask."

"Thanks," he said as he looked down at her from above.

"I'm only doing this, so you don't get more blood on the carpet."

From his vantage point, he could see straight down Cassie's top. He caught sight of her breasts as she bandaged his feet and watched in a trance every time she moved.

"There, all done," she proclaimed, standing back up. Just don't step on the glass again, please?" Zeke nodded,

"You know I could see down your top from there?"

"Yeah," she replied, "I could see up your towel, so believe me. I noticed!"

Zeke raised himself from the toilet seat and moved to within a breath of her. He went to speak, but she placed her finger on his lip sensually. The blood left his brain as he let another organ do his thinking. He grabbed Cassie by the ponytail and raised her gently but firmly from the floor. Their lips locked as they staggered out of the en suite together and across the room, one pulse racing the other as they came together. He set her down, and Cassie pulled him on the bed, climbed on, threw her legs over, and straddled him. Zeke could sense the extra weight she now carried as her thighs pinned him to the mattress, he felt almost helpless, serving only to turn him on more. He ripped a hand free, reached up to her shirt, and tore it open. Her chest heaved as her bare breasts were exposed and she exhaled in surprise, and he realised how long it had been since he'd really seen her. Zeke reached up to grab at her bosom, and as he did, she ripped the towel from around his waist. Her dominance drew him in further as she slowly wrapped her hands around his throat. With one hand still firmly cupping her breast, he raised the other from the bed and reached up and grabbed her face tenderly, he could feel her heat, and she was warm and wet to his touch. The sensation titillated him, and he held her face for as long as he could stand it until the feeling of her writhing on top of him was too much. Zeke summoned all his strength to turn and flip her in one go. He entered her softly at first, but as he felt her warmth on his, he was overcome by carnal desire as together they pushed up against the headboard and went at it like honeymooning rabbits.

With Cassie underneath him still, Zeke wrapped his hands around her neck to pull her in tighter, but as he moved position, he caught sight of the shattered glass and blood-red floor. The crimson mess met his mind. Then like a wave crashing and breaking on the rocks, an image flashed through his cognizance. Suddenly he was on his knees in the alleyway, kneeling and pressing down hard on the man beneath him, his hands wrapped firmly around his throat. His victim struggled back, but his grip was fixed, and his attempts were futile. The man opened his mouth and forced up some last words.

"Zeke, Zeke!"

The words were familiar as they entered his mind, Zeke looked down and saw his hands clamped tightly around Cassie's neck. Her face was reddening, and he loosened his grip.

"Hey," said Cassie as she slapped at his arm. Zeke loosened his grasp and removed his hands, there was a slight red mark from where he'd been holding her. Cassie glared at him, before seizing her opportunity. In his moment of hesitancy, she climbed back on top of him, leant into him and clamped down hard. Biting his lower lip between her teeth she leaned away from him pulling it towards her. Zeke moved forwards as she bit down on his mouth and a small amount of blood began to form. He sat as far forward as he could before she let go, and he fell back against the bed. Cassie licked her lips, opened her mouth, and motioned toward the mark on her neck.

"You're going to pay for that!" she said.

20

Zeke prised himself carefully out from underneath Cassie's still sleeping arm. Under cover of the invading moonlight, he tiptoed carefully across the room, keen to avoid further injuring his feet. Reaching the bathroom without incident, he closed the door behind him softly, and flipped on the light.

The mirrored medicine cabinet that sat just to the left of the toilet was slightly ajar. Zeke caught sight of it in his periphery, finished up his business and paused to reflect. As the mirror stared back at him, he wasn't sure he liked what he saw. He had two ugly cuts healing on his head, and he was beginning to look old and tired. His complexion had hardly changed at all in the last fifteen years, yet suddenly life was catching up with him. Perhaps it was a visual representation of his recent sins? Whatever it was, he didn't like it. For a moment earlier he'd felt the same fury he'd experienced in New York with Lara, but it came with a calming feeling of euphoria. There was a sense that he'd been doing something good; was that what happened in New York? Only he wasn't in New York, and for a moment he'd been strangling his wife, not a lowlife thug. Could he have killed her? Even if he had killed anyone in New York, he was defending himself against lowlifes who deserved to die. The thought that he could potentially have just done the same to his innocent wife was terrifying! Was his mind playing tricks on him? Or, rather, was he playing tricks on his mind?

Zeke stared into the mirror darkly, knowing all too well what lurked behind it. Opening the door he took in the assortment of packets, tubes, and blister packs. There were countless different names for each, yet one in common was written on all of them. He had uppers, downers, pain medicines, anxiety pills, and anti-depressant medication. You name it. They named him. Was this how it happened? Was overmedication causing the problem or was it him? No doubt each one came with various side effects, he used them all far too liberally. It was not inconceivable that this was causing his issues. He was having such vivid flashbacks that bordered on hallucinations. It was such a sudden onset, but he'd been living this lifestyle for years. Looking back on his reflection he was forced to concede that he'd been going too far, too hard, too much lately. There was a constant itch that needed scratching with one vice or another and recent events had shown that he wasn't invincible despite what he chose to believe. Zeke took one last look at the stockpile and closed the cabinet door. For all his flaws, Ray was a good and knowledgeable chemist. Zeke made a mental note to visit him, he'd be able to shed some light on matters of medication. He took a final glance at the new and simultaneously old version of himself before turning off the light and returning to bed.

21

Zeke hadn't seen much of Marguerite since the original trip to New York and not at all since he'd been arrested, and he was mildly anxious about returning to work. They had known one another for over ten years now, and if there was anything he knew for sure about Marguerite, it was that she spoke with nothing but absolute candour. He was convinced that there was some degree of misdemeanour within the financial aspects of her business, and she would probably not want an organisation such as Interpol delving too deep into her affairs. She knew to expect the unexpected with Zeke, which had drawn him to her in the first place, but he knew in himself that he was becoming a liability and couldn't help but wonder how much would also be too much for her.

Marguerite had come into Zeke's life shortly after he met Cassie. For reasons unknown, she had entered his bar one afternoon to use the facilities. It had been a long day, the two of them had got to talking, and Zeke had welcomed the distraction. If there were a way to describe Zeke, it would be a mash of creativity, brilliance, and a bit of a mess, and it hadn't taken Marguerite long to pick up on that. She had seen someone whom she resonated with, could mould into something new, and she'd invited him up to Soho to see her flagship store. He was to be wined and dined before a proposition landed on the table. Zeke had garnered from what he saw and heard, that some off-the-books dealings were probably involved. But it had been exciting, a lucrative offer and not the type of opportunity one regularly turns down.

For Zeke life had stagnated, the small fortune he had once accrued was dwindling, and a feeling of listlessness and ennui was building up within him. The bar work was enough to keep him occupied without being overtaxing, and the monotony of routine was just small enough to stop him from going completely insane, but he deeply craved more.

He needed a blend of mental, physical, and pleasurable stimulation to get by, and the banality of getting up, going to work, eating, and going to bed just to repeat it the next day was eating away at him. He craved stimuli and excitement; life was as dull as constantly served Champagne. So, when the offer to work with the mysterious Marguerite came along, it was too good to refuse.

Marguerite was a tall, enigmatic lady, she was mid-sixties, and although the lines on her face had been exacerbated from years of cigarette smoke, she wore her age with grace. She was eloquent and well-spoken but was not beyond telling someone to *fuck off* on occasion. Marguerite came from old money and carried herself with elegance and refinement. But you could sense she had seen her share of darkness and hardship, which, combined with her wealth and connections, meant she was not someone with whom you would seek to tangle.

Marguerite took a shine to Zeke the moment they met. There was a glimmer in his eye like a message carved on his forehead that only she could read. Marguerite needed someone like Zeke, and Zeke needed a new life. It had brought him and Cassie this far, and he was eternally grateful to her despite the recent events. That said, despite their time together, he knew that he wasn't beyond becoming extraneous, and he wasn't keen to find out what came if he outlived his usefulness.

Zeke awoke to find Cassie gone. It was late in the afternoon, and he must have slept for about fourteen hours. He fumbled about the nightstand, located his phone, and went through what he'd missed. There was a message from Marguerite,

Take the rest of the week off!

Pithy as always, and slightly relieving given that he needed to get his head together. There was a text from Cassie, a simple winking emoji, and a dozen missed calls from Karan, followed by a message that said, *Call me.*

Just as he set the phone down, it started to buzz, and the image of Karan appeared on the screen, Zeke stared at it for a while, but he knew he couldn't keep dodging his friend.

"Hey man, what's up?"

"What's up? You're seriously gonna 'what's up' me?"

"Sorry, it's been a bit hectic. I only got back from prison yesterday afternoon."

"You see, that's exactly the problem! That is not a normal thing to say to a friend!"

"My bad," said Zeke. "I know, I know. I shouldn't have left, but you know me. I can't turn down a free party in New York?"

"Dude, that's not funny. Your arrest made national newspapers."

"That's quite cool, though."

"Zeke," Karan quipped, "we're not kids anymore. You're having a child. You can't keep living like this. I love you, man, but something must change. I'm starting to wonder if I even know you anymore!"

"I know. You're right." Zeke went to continue but then stopped himself. Almost as though he could sense his hesitancy, Karan asked.

"Is there anything else? You know you can tell me anything?"

"No, I think I just need to take it easy."

"Zeke, they arrested you in connection with murder! Murder Zeke!"

"Oh, come on. You and I know both know I had nothing to do with that?"

"So, what happened this time?"

"Lara and I partied a little too hard; things got a bit out of hand, that's all!"

"Oh god, you didn't, did you?"

"No! Of course not. I wouldn't do that to Cassie."

"Well, you'd better not. You need that woman."

"I know. I know!"

"Okay, remember, I've known you since uni. I know how you were with the ladies."

"We're old now, man. I've grown up."

"Some of us have!"

"Yeah, yeah. I hear you."

"Hey, look, we've got Ray coming over for dinner. Bring Cass. It's been a while?"

"Thanks, I would. But I think I owe it to her to stay here for a bit. Work gave me the week off. We should probably get the nursery sorted."

"Fair, you're lucky the week off is all they gave you. Okay, I'm going to check in with Cassie. All I want to hear about is baby preparations."

"Yes, mum."

"Oh, and pick a damn name!"

Karan hung up, and Zeke put the phone down on the side. He stretched himself out across the enormous bed and smiled. He was a fucking idiot! There had been so many times in his life, that he'd prayed to be where he was now. He had everything he wanted! Messing it all up would be beyond stupid.

Zeke opened the door to his study and set the tepid coffee down on his desk. He sat and waited for his computer to boot up. He looked out of the bay window and across the field. A small layer of frost lingered on the woodpile, which reminded him how remote they were. As he stared, he thought it was curious that the axe was missing. Cassie wouldn't have been chopping wood. Maybe he'd left it in the garage? It wasn't likely someone would steal it around here. The light from the computer screen illuminated his brain and distracted his thoughts. He sipped on his coffee as he opened the web browser. As he typed into the search engine, his recently closed tabs sprang open, and he realised how lapse his internet security was. Zeke opened the settings, cleared his history just to be safe and then ticked the option to sign out of all his accounts. There was a nagging sensation about everything that was going on. He'd seen too many films where people's computers had given them away. He had nothing to hide, or at least he thought he didn't, but he was in the middle of a crisis of confidence, and paranoia was starting to creep in. Was it possible someone was doing this to him? The notion sent a shiver down his spine, but you find yourself left with the improbable in the absence of any rational explanation. This Interpol guy had a real hard-on for him, and he just didn't know why. It was ludicrous even to think about it, but was he being set up?

A notification pinged up from one of the open tabs and provided an immediate welcome distraction. Zeke clicked the tab to discover that he had a new friend request. Given his disdain and general lack of use of social media, this was a rare and ironically intriguing experience. So, he opened the tab to find a friend request from Lara Richards. Something which would prove very useful in the coming months.

22

Agent Jones was on borrowed time as he looked down at the crime scene photos scattered on his desk. He'd been allotted a space in the doldrums of the station and the promise of full cooperation of the staff. And while they'd followed through on giving him an area to work, their cooperation hadn't been exactly enthusiastic. The dingy room and seclusion didn't bother him. The lack of collaboration did. Good or bad, criminals or not, people were dead, and writing it off as a turf war between gangs was a lazy way of saying, "Good, we don't care." He knew that his methods of operation hindered help, but he didn't have time to be diplomatic. Jones fit the antisocial, work-obsessed detective archetype perfectly. He was famously alone and had seen many personal relationships deteriorate due to his relentless pursuits. He was born and raised in Boston and had been Boston PD until the rules broke him, or vice versa. He got results wherever he went, but usually the wrong way. His detective prowess and ability to profile made him a good fit for the FBI until he wasn't. Their loss was Interpol's gain, and so long as he was stationed alone and brought results, his superiors were happy.

He now worked out of Interpol's headquarters in Lyon, and his brash persona went largely unnoticed among his French counterparts. At Interpol, he rarely dealt with serial killers, so when a case like this fell into his lap, he grasped it with both hands. To Jones, these killings were a blessing in disguise. He was convinced that the deaths were all connected. Unfortunately, he was only given a finite amount of time to pursue it. The high-profile arrest of an affluent art dealer making national news had hindered his cause, it had drawn no results thus cutting time and patience in half. He was sure he would find something and was convinced that he had his man. But all he really had was grainy crime scene photos, no witnesses, and a paucity of time. Not for the first time in his life, he found himself hopelessly staring at nothing after business hours and on his own.

Jones knew in his heart he was right about Zeke Olsen. But knowing and proving were very different things. He'd dealt with many a calculated sociopath over the years, and they were notoriously hard to catch. They hid in plain sight, looking and moving like everyone else. He'd tangled with many, some he'd caught, but most fooled the world around them so well, that they had left him looking foolish.

The killings in New York fell under his purview, and it had seemed like a gift at first. If he could solve this case, it would be his redemption. He had been given a month to investigate it initially, but the faux pas at Heathrow looked to have cut that short, and he was rapidly running out of time. This Olsen guy was either a genius taunting him or a lucky fool. He knew in his gut that he was right but so far that meant nothing. As much as he had full access to the resources of the Metropolitan police force, their patience, too, was running thin. He'd been unable to charge his only suspect, he had no evidence on him, and absolutely no sympathisers in his outlandish theory that a middle-aged art dealer had the blood of six gangsters on his hands. In a few days, he would return to Lyon and the case would be dropped as gang-related violence, a win-win for local police. No one wanted a new serial killer, but everyone needed an excuse to facilitate warrants for various known drug dens.

The NYPD had run very basic forensics. It was an alleyway, and there were fingerprints everywhere. The scene had essentially been contaminated before anyone even arrived.

There were no witnesses, DNA, CCTV, murder weapons, or motive. Zeke's fingerprints were on the rear fire door, but interior footage showed him exiting through it. It put him at the scene, but that was it. All he had to go on was the crime scene images, and as dogged as he was, even he was starting to concede he might be at a dead end.

Jones eyed the congealed coffee on his desk. A layer of film had formed on the top and ran across both edges of the white polystyrene cup. As he looked at it, he wasn't sure what angered him more, the cup or the fact that anyone dared call the swill inside of it coffee. The congealed liquid stared back at him, and he clenched his fists. The hour was late, and the building was almost vacant. Then, in a burst of frustration, he stood and shoved over the desk. As it fell, the limited items scattered, and the stack of pictures flew into the air before drifting slowly to the floor. Sitting back down, Jones slumped in the chair and placed his head in his hands. Just for once, he'd like for something to go his way. He grabbed his coat from the chair and threw it over his shoulders, but as he moved, an image on the floor caught his eye. Looking at one of the pictures from a different angle, he saw a mark on the face of one of the corpses that he hadn't spotted earlier. He stooped, seized the picture from the floor and rotated it a few times before grabbing a magnifier from his strewn belongings. It was hard to make out through the grainy image, but the face of one of the dead men featured what appeared to be a very distinctive imprint. One he was sure he'd seen before. Where had he seen it? Then, like hearing the blast of a military trumpet, it hit him. He knew exactly what it reminded him of.

Jones clapped his hands together, removed his phone from his pocket, and began to dial.

23

"So, I hear that Zeke got arrested?" said Ray grinning.

"Wait, what?" said Ivan pausing as he raised his soup spoon to his lips.

"You haven't heard? Damn thing made the middle section of national papers, brought Heathrow to a standstill."

"Oh, that is juicy," said Ivan.

"Ivan, ignore him," moaned Karan. "Rumours of Zeke's demise have been greatly exaggerated. It did not bring the nation's largest airport to a standstill!"

"He did get arrested, though," interjected Ray, "and it was in the paper."

"Really?" mused Ivan, "Well, now I'm intrigued. He's never vapid that man, is he?" He finally swallowed the soup and lowered the spoon back to the bowl as the three of them sat around the dining table near the indoor pool. "So, when were you going to tell me about this?" asked Ivan. "I must say this is quite some news for our sleepy little village."

"Well, you would need to be here for me to tell you.

"I'm here now!" Ivan retorted. "Anyway, since when has my absence been a problem. Look around you," he said, motioning to the steadily heating pool. "We don't pay for all this on a college lecturer's salary."

"Here, here," said Ray raising his glass. "To the finer things in life."

"Oh, shut up," said Karan. "You can't talk. You're only here because you haven't got a marriage to ruin."

"Not yet," said Ivan, winking at Ray. "Our man has a date later, some hot stuff he picked up at your man Olsen's office party."

"Really?" said Karan shaking his head. "Who?"

"A gentleman never tells, do they, Ray?" said Ivan.

"Don't encourage him," he said to his husband. "And you," he said, turning to Ray, "Grow up." Ray sneered, and Ivan laughed. "Hey, look, we're Zeke's friends, alright. You both came to the man's wedding. Anyway, have you met this guy, Jones? I looked him up. He's been fired from almost every agency he's worked for due to his crazy theories and relentless pursuits. The guy is unhinged."

"They'd make a good couple if you ask me," joked Ray.

"He has a point," interjected Ivan. I can't remember the last time I saw Zeke sober. He was out of it when we picked him up. Whatever is eating at that man, he's overdoing it."

"He is not! Plus, you don't get to have an insight. You gain a kilo every time you come back from a business trip and don't tell me it comes from eating tofu!"

"I dunno," said Ray. "I was poking inside the medicine cabinet at the party. There are more pills in there than I have at work."

"What were you doing going through the medicine cabinet."

"You missed a good party, though, Ivan," said Ray.

"Don't change the subject," berated Karan. Ray shrugged at him,

"Curious?"

"Aright, okay, look. We all have our problems," said Karan. "And clearly so does this Jones guy, huh. He arrested Zeke, and he let him go. End of story, we can't let this turn into some witch hunt!"

"Does it not make you wonder, though?" asked Ray. "Guy goes to New York and comes back with a head wound. He goes to New York again a week later and returns with another. It's a bit of a coincidence. Don't you think? Zeke took a woman from work with him the second time. I hear the pair had adjoining rooms, and they wrecked both." Karan and Ivan paused for a moment in thought, "Anyway, speaking of girls," said Ray as he pushed his chair away from the table. "I gotta be going." He stood and tipped the rest of his wine down his throat. "Ivan," he said, sticking out a hand. "Always a pleasure." Ivan reciprocated, and Karan went to stand. "No, no," said Ray placing his hands on his friends' shoulders. "Don't get up, old man!"

Karan rolled his eyes and turned to look at his friend behind him. "You smell like many wine bottles. You aren't driving again, are you?"

"Ah, it's only across the village. I'll be fine."

"I really wish you—"

"Oh, don't be such a spoilsport," interrupted Ivan. "A cab will take forever. We can't have our man being late."

"Alright," said Karan crossing his arms. "But you know how I feel about this. One of these days—"

"I'll be fine sour puss," Ray said, pressing his friend playfully into the chair.

"Okay, shall I see you out?" asked Karan.

"No, I know the way, basically my second home," he said, winking down at Karan. Ray sauntered passed the table, grabbed his coat, and threw it over his shoulder. As he moved into the hallway, he yelled. "Karan wants a dog! I'll see you at the weekend!" His voice echoed off the marble floor as he disappeared drunkenly into the night.

24

"Where was it the Magna Carta was signed?"

"I believe it was Runnymede, sir."

"And did it take them this long?"

The technician looked over his shoulder and sighed, "I'm going as fast as possible. You know I was in the middle of a date when you called me?" Jones didn't reply. Instead, he pushed his hands into the neck of the seated man. "Price you pay for being the best and the *quickest*."

"Look, I can do this quickly, or I can do it properly?"

Jones sighed and sat back down at the desk. He looked at his watch; it was almost two a.m. It had taken over an hour to get someone in to analyse the pictures, and even if he got what he needed, he would then need to find a judge to get a warrant, all of which took time. Time, he didn't have.

The digital copies of the images had been forwarded from New York, but the CSI's work had been lackadaisical, and he needed someone with the know-how to clear up and make a high-resolution zoom. Jones was confident that the marks on the cheek of the victim were familiar, and if they were, it ought to be enough to get him a warrant. Time marched on, however, and he needed a clear image. This man he'd pulled from his evening was among the best in his field, and it irritated Jones to think he might be dragging his heels to spite him for calling him out at this hour.

Finally, after what felt like decades in the dingy computer room, the technician wheeled his chair away from the desk and pointed at the screen.

"Ta fucking da," he said. "Can I go now?"

Jones paused as he stared at the image in front of him, "But first, tell me what that looks like." The man moved back towards the screen and squinted slightly.

"I dunno, that's your job."

"But if you had to guess?"

"I don't know, maybe initials."

"Yess," Jones exclaimed, grabbing the man enthusiastically by the shoulder, "those look like fucking initials."

Having been let go, the man stood, nodded awkwardly, grabbed his coat, and slammed the door behind him. Alone in the room, Jones picked up his phone and started to dial.

"Get me a judge. I need a warrant!

"Yes, I know what time it is. Trust me. They'll want to hear this. We might have just caught ourselves a serial killer!"

25

The events of back-to-back New York trips loomed large in Zeke's mind, and so was his memory of them, or lack thereof. Like a hangman waiting. But a few weeks had passed, and so far, nothing further had come of it. He'd tapered back on pills and alcohol, and life was very much back at a steady pace. They'd had friends over, attended baby scans and antenatal classes, Cassie was getting ready to take maternity leave, and crucially Zeke's head was clearer than ever. The time off had been a blessing.

Cassie had worked at the university hospital ever since she'd graduated, but after she gave birth, she would eventually open her own practice, and it had given them time to check out office spaces. As much as Cassie was keen to help people with psychological problems, they didn't want them coming to their home for obvious reasons.

Christmas was now firmly on the horizon. The weather was brisk, and people huddled together in the street for warmth. The air seemed to contain a greater chill than normal, a sensation that warmed Zeke's heart. The extra time they had together pre-Christmas was brilliant. Their day of looking at business parks and commercial units had brought them to the edge of Winchester, and now that the sun had set on the day, it was a perfect time to see the markets. The Winchester Christmas market was set on the Cathedral grounds, and it loomed large over it in the setting sun. Cinnamon was in the air—a smell that predominantly appears at this time of year. Adults and children alike shared in the same activities and sensations, a sight that fuelled their festive fire. They could ice skate, he could eat sticky treats washed down with mulled wine, and most importantly, they might have some fun.

"Hey, look," said Cassie pointing at a small jeweller just off the high street.

"I already married you," he replied.

"No, silly! Your ring, drop it in. They look old school. You like old school."

Zeke nodded, conceding that he did like old school.

"Cass, there's gotta be one closer to home?"

"I'm just saying. You keep putting it off. That band is not gonna last much longer. Then *when* you lose it all, you'll have the added dissatisfaction of knowing that you should have listened to your beautiful wife."

Zeke grinned. "Alright," he conceded. He left Cassie in the street and ducked inside. "Two minutes," he said. "Then it's you, me, and an ice rink." She smiled slightly as he dashed off.

The small door opened and clattered against the bell above it. Zeke stood in child-like wonder as he surveyed the old-fashioned cabinets and waited to be greeted. It wasn't long before he was met by a small older man, who beheld the heirloom in awe as Zeke explained the project to him. The short white-haired man was delighted at the task but wasn't sure if he would have it done before Christmas, but he would endeavour to do his best. He gave Zeke a receipt and a business card with his personal number on it before Zeke rejoined Cassie in the street.

"Where's the receipt?"

"It's in my pocket."

"Gimme," she said, stretching out her hand.

"Hey, I can look after my own receipt," he said. "Look, I'm putting it in my wallet right now."

Zeke tucked his wallet away carefully and grabbed Cassie's arm playfully. "You owe me an ice skate, Mrs Olsen." She looked at him and smiled.

"Okay," she replied as she winked at him, "just don't be upset when you're beaten by a pasty English girl."

"An English rose, and I wouldn't want to lose to anyone else." Their eyes met, and the familiar feeling of joy fell over him causing him to smile, a grin which continued and walked with them down the cobbled street towards the festivities.

It was around eight when the taxi dropped them back at their house. Cassie entered, citing a need to pee, and Zeke fumbled some cash from his wallet and paid the driver. While waiting for his change, he felt his phone vibrate in his pocket. It had done so various times on the ride home, but he had yet to check it.

Zeke opened the message as he waited and read the text on the screen.

Zeke, it's Lara. We need to talk, meet me at the Park Tavern at 9?

Zeke had done his best to put both Lara and New York out of sight and mind. But he knew in his heart that he needed to see Lara. They had yet to speak since they returned, and not only did he owe her his time, but he was also curious about what she knew or had said. Presumably, she'd told no one about the men in the hotel room. But it was a loose end, which he should have addressed sooner. From his interrogation with Jones, he'd garnered that the men who kidnapped her died, and someone had moved the bodies into a dumpster. Even amid his existential turmoil, it seemed unlikely that it could have been him, which indicated some form of clean-up crew, and a large-scale operation. The thought was insidious and made him shudder. It was like being trapped in the middle of a gangster movie.

"Hey, can you wait a sec?" he said to the driver. The cabbie nodded, and Zeke sprinted back into the house.

"Cass, I've gotta run. The alarm is going off at the gallery. I'll be back as soon as I can."

He didn't delay for a response before returning to the waiting car. Zeke got in, closed the door, tilted his head back and shut his eyes. As the car pulled away, he thought about what was happening. Why had he just lied to Cassie? Should he have reached out to Lara sooner? He needed to know what she'd said regarding the trip, and now he considered it, not knowing was eating at him. He pulled out his phone and considered calling her, but as he did so, a cold thought washed over him, and he realised how idiotic it was to use it at all. Anyone could be listening! He flicked back to the text and typed a simple,

I'm on my way message.

Before locking it and putting it back in his pocket, Zeke turned and looked back at his house as the taxi moved down the country road. He thought he saw a vehicle leaving the driveway, but he was too far away to tell for sure.

Zeke arrived at the tavern slightly late and entered in a hurry. He stepped in from the cold, and the warmth greeted him immediately. The room was crowded, something he would usually dislike, but anonymity seemed vital these days, and a busy room afforded him that much. His eyes darted about the chamber, so many blank faces featuring empty conversations. He spotted Lara alone at a booth and made his way over. As he passed the bar, he paused, turned towards the lady behind it and ordered himself a double vodka before continuing.

The walk from the bar to the table was as long as it was short, Lara spotted him on approach and their eyes met. The noise was overwhelming, making speech impossible. He continued to hold her gaze as he walked, allowing him to figure out what he might say to her. What would he say? Zeke was nervous as he arrived, taking a sip as he removed the chair, allowing the liquid to sink before he sat. She looked up and acknowledged him. As he gazed back at her eyes, he searched for answers, but none were forthcoming. Instead, they sparkled back with a sprinkling of conflict. If he had to guess, her gorgeous green eyes said that she looked both excited and terrified, and as emotions go, there isn't always much of a gap between them.

She was elegantly dressed, and it reminded him of the moment he saw her from across the balcony in New York. She was resplendent then and now. Her makeup highlighted the contours of her jaw, and Zeke watched on spellbound as her mouth moved up and down. He knew she spoke but heard no words. Between his stare and the ambient noise, he caught himself watching her lips rise and fall, rise, and fall. Finally, the silence broke, and one word crashed against his skull.

"Wait, did you just say Interpol?"

"Yes, Zeke. What do you think this is all about? I had that agent turn up at my house today."

"Who was he?"

"Same guy from the airport."

"What did you tell him?"

"Nothing, the guy's an arsehole!" Zeke laughed. He knew he liked Lara.

"What about the hotel?"

"Zeke, I told him nothing other than to get out and come back with a warrant if he wanted to discuss anything else."

"Thanks."

"Don't thank me just yet, Zeke. I mean, what the hell?" Zeke reached for his drink, but she stretched her hand out and cooled his motion. "Honestly," she said, "I'm kind of afraid to ask." Zeke nodded. "Are you in trouble?" Zeke shook his head. "Did I do the right thing?" she asked.

"Of course, you did," he replied, placing his other hand on top of hers.

"But I lied, Zeke! At the airport, I told him we got drunk, left the party, got lost, and checked into a random motel. That's not what happened, is it?" Zeke shook his head. "What do we do? I don't want this man ruining my life or yours!"

"Do you trust me?" Zeke asked as he patted her hand. She nodded. "Then don't worry, I didn't do anything. He's just a dog chasing his tail. He'll get tired soon."

"I have so many other questions, though. And I'm not going back to New York with you soon!"

Zeke chuckled heartily, "Trust me," he said reminiscing about the notion of a crew of angry gangsters waiting for him there. "I have no intention of ever going back to New York." Zeke raised his glass to his lips, emptied the remnants into his mouth, pounded the cup on the table and said, "Drink?" Lara nodded, so he picked up the empties, returned to the bar and ordered.

Zeke paid for the drinks, lifted the cups, and began to turn back around. But as he did so, Lara ghosted passed him, touched him lightly on the shoulder and said, "It will have to be quick. I need to go soon." The contact caught him by surprise, and as she passed, he caught the scent of her perfume. It was the same one from the night in the hotel. The aroma triggered something in his brain, and as he looked across the bar, he caught sight of himself in the mirror behind it. The room faded to black, and the Zeke that stared back at him had a gun in his hand and blood all over his face. He remembered the man hitting Lara and her body lying stricken on the bed, his hands clenched as he thought about it, and he grabbed one of the glasses so tightly that it shattered in his hand, spilling liquid all over the bar. Zeke looked down at his cut and bloodied hands, then at the bar and the drink he had spilt. Except it wasn't wine, the bar was covered in blood that pooled and then trickled over the edge down to the floor and gathered around his feet. He looked back in the mirror and saw three men dead on the ground behind him, a smoking gun in his hand.

"Zeke."

The words startled him, and he dripped a small amount of the recently poured drink onto the bar.

"You, okay?" she asked. "You seem jittery!" Zeke looked down at the dribble of liquid on the bar. At his clean, unharmed hands, then at the mirror behind it.

He nodded, "Yes," he replied with a laugh. "I've been drinking since four."

"That will do it," she said. "I'm just popping to the loo. Did you hear me? I can only stay for one more." Zeke nodded, waited until she departed, and cautiously carried the drinks back to the booth. As soon as she was out of sight, he allowed his grin to drop, what on earth was that? It had been a while since he'd had an incident, and he thought it was over.

When Lara returned, her appearance had changed slightly. Her hair was down. She'd freshened her makeup and looked incredible. In the time she'd been gone, he'd had time to reflect on just how great she was. The events in New York had been mental, even for him. Yet here they were, cool as you like having a drink.

"You know, you're pretty rare, Lara."

"Thanks," she said with a smile, "you're not so bad yourself."

Their eyes met, and a comfortable silence ensued. Lost in the peace, Zeke recalled the moment their lips nearly met and as he looked at her now, he almost wished they had. Not wishing to dwell, he broke it by asking, "So," he said, breaching the quiet, "big date tonight?" Lara blushed.

"Yes," she said with a smile. "But hey Zeke, since you're here, there is something else I need to talk to you about." As she spoke, a notification lit up her phone on the table, and from where he was, Zeke could decipher the time.

"Shit," he said. He downed his drink, pushed back his chair, and grabbed his coat. "Sorry, Lara. I told Cassie I wouldn't be long." He stood and tapped her slightly awkwardly on the shoulder. Lara opened her mouth to speak again, but Zeke was already in motion.

"I gotta go," he repeated as he moved across the bar.

It was gone midnight when Zeke snuck drunkenly into the house. Dark clouds had filled the sky on the ride home, an ominous sign. The alarm had been set, and the place was unusually dark and quiet. Zeke typed in the code to deactivate it and proceeded to call out Cassie's name, primarily in vain.

"Cassie," he yelled into an empty house. "Cass, you here?" The house was silent as he moved through it. Zeke ran his hand along the wall, found the kitchen light and illuminated the room. The light entered his eyes, and when it did, he noticed a note that sat neatly on the middle of the kitchen table.

26

Most of Zeke's problems in life had come from the constant pursuit of happiness. A mercurial youth became an enigmatic adult who always sought out the next thing that would take away the pain. He had flirted with addiction his whole life, and in many ways, he thought that stability was what he needed. The journey towards the coveted peace had been arduous, but it kept him going. Yet now that it had finally arrived, he seemed to be no closer to inner peace, and he was beginning to question if it was ever what he needed.

Zeke sat in his kitchen and stared at the note in his hand. Cassie had a single sibling, a younger sister by the name of Suzie, and Suzie was a liability. She was one of those who would get her life on track, only to derail in the most spectacular ways. Zeke could empathise to a degree, and perhaps it was why Cassie was always so patient with him. Regardless, whenever Suzie had a *problem*, everyone had to know about it, and Cassie would always be dragged in. The note was pithy, Zeke supposed that Cassie was growing tired of being summoned, and with the proximity to Christmas and the impending birth of their child, the timing was poor.

Zeke read the note in his hand. Cassie would be gone for a few days, maybe longer. Suzie's sudden demands usually irritated him, but he was grateful for some alone time. He'd been triggered again by something in the bar, and it was becoming apparent that he wasn't okay. He had a lot to figure out. Everyone had questions, and so did he. But he was the one who should have answers, yet he knew less than anyone. It was as though he'd blinked for a moment too long, and suddenly everything in life was different. It was surreal, like a nightmare from which he could not stir. There were so many things out of his control, including his mind, and he feared losing everything.

Zeke closed his eyes and set his head down against the kitchen table. Its surface was cool against his skin, and for a moment, he wished he could shoot back in time to before he left for New York. Perhaps if he'd never set foot on that plane, things might just be different. Why did he always have to be so self-destructive?

When he awoke, the kitchen was cold and dark, the lights and heating had gone off on the timer, and his neck hurt from the angle he'd slept on the table.

Zeke sat up, stretched, stood, and poured himself a glass of water. Drink drunk, he shoved his hand into his pocket and removed his phone. There was a solitary message from Lara, which he opened quickly and read.

Good to see you tonight. I hope I didn't get you in trouble with the wife. X Lara.

Forgetting entirely about the time, he pulled up the keypad and typed. The 'X' at the end of the message drew him in, and he remembered that Lara wanted to tell him something before he left.

All is good here. The wife has gone to see her sister. Fell asleep on the kitchen table. I hope the date went well.

Zeke hit send and realised he had forgotten to ask. He went to send another message before realising the time. He went to move the phone away from his face, but he saw the familiar dots that meant the recipient was typing. Zeke looked up at the clock on the kitchen wall, the small light from his phone provided just enough illumination, and he saw that it was just after three. Sensing that she was already up, he started to type once more.

Oh, what was it you wanted to ask me?

Zeke then deliberated before adding an *x* before he hit send. The return dots then flashed away at him for a while as he remained transfixed until the reply appeared on his phone.

I can't talk now. Get another drink sometime? It's late. Go back to sleep on the table. : p xx Lara

Zeke stared at the words for a moment before deciding better to reply. It was late, and her words were playful, almost flirtatious. Zeke shook his head, keen to forget about the questions that nagged. He put his phone away and opened the fridge, grabbed two beers, and made his way to the front door.

Outside it was as cold as the white rose waking at daybreak. The barefoot walk across the stones was almost excruciating as the cold panged at his feet. Zeke arrived at his annexe, unlocked the door, and looked at the sky. A small amount of sleet fell from the heavens, and he closed his eyes and prayed for snow. Once inside, he grabbed a blanket and wrapped it around himself. He then threw his body down on the sofa and his legs up on the table simultaneously. Zeke sipped from the beer and flicked through the channels, as he let his mind slowly drift away.

27

Zeke entered the flat and set his bag and keys down on the table by the door. He moved across the foyer, into the kitchen, opened the fridge and wrestled the top off a beer. They were due to complete its sale this weekend. He'd been in London with Marguerite all week, juggling both was difficult, and it had been long.

"Zeeeeeeekkkke," came the voice from down the hallway. "Zeke!"

He set his drink on the counter as he heard footsteps bounding towards him. Cassie appeared suddenly at the kitchen door and looked him up and down like a dog who'd missed its owner. She threw her arms around his neck and clung to him dearly. He just about had time to brace himself for her weight before she lassoed her body around him. He staggered backwards slightly and fell against the countertop. Cassie clamped her lips around his passionately, removed herself and stood expectantly before him, before she waved a small piece of white plastic that was in her hand.

"Zeke, look!" she said proudly, as she held the plastic aloft. "Look at it, Zeke."

Zeke looked down at her hand, then back up to her face. He took another look down before opening his mouth.

"Okay," he said, "three questions. First, did you pee on that? Second, was it around my neck? And third, oh my gosh, what does it say?"

The words left his mouth rhetorically. In the year that they'd been trying to conceive, he not only knew what the stick was, but in all probability, he probably also knew the brand from sight. The likelihood that Cassie had brought another negative test to his attention was slim, which could only mean one thing! They were having a baby. She nodded to confirm what he was thinking, and the reality of the situation hit him. In truth, he'd been reluctant at first. The fear of projecting his trauma onto a child was a genuine concern. But the longer they went without being able to conceive, the more he coveted it. But as reality stared him in the face in the shape of a white piece of plastic, he didn't know what to make of it, or how to feel. The flat was packed, and the barn was almost finished, the timing was right, but something seemed off.

He took the stick from her hand tenderly and raised it to his eyes as if by looking at it himself would either confirm or deny it. The happy little face that indicated 'pregnant' stared back at him, and he wondered how many people in history had been less than pleased to see the happy face.

Zeke handed the stick back to her and asked, "Are you certain?" She nodded.

"How many times?" he asked. Cassie reached into her pocket, retrieved, fanned out various test kits, and waved them in front of him as though she wafted herself with an old-fashioned hand fan.

The movement drew a wry smile from Zeke, and he relaxed slightly.

"Well, then, my lady, no beer for you?" he said, casually picking up the bottle and sipping from it. "So, this is real?"

Cassie nodded. "We're having a baby," she said.

"We're having a baby," he repeated. "We're having a baby!" Zeke took another long sip from his drink to hide the fact that he was speechless. As he drank, her words repeated themselves in his brain. He was happy, but he wasn't. What if he created a monster? What if he was incapable of love? He set his drink down with his feelings and grabbed Cassie softly by the face. He kissed her firmly, and she purred tenderly as he held her in his arms.

"You taste like beer," she whispered. Zeke smiled and nodded. Their eyes met, and she said, "So, who should we call first?"

28

Zeke awoke the following day to a haze. The television was still on but displayed nothing but a blue screen. He blinked as he tried to shake away a head that felt like it was full of sand. As he stirred, he became aware of the eerie feeling when you know you're not alone in a room. With slight trepidation, he rose and put his arm over the back of the sofa, turned and looked at the door. "Marguerite?" he said.

She appeared like an apparition, just hovering near the door. Was she really there? Was he dreaming? Zeke rubbed hard at his eyes with both hands and took another look. "Holy fuck, Marguerite, you're actually here? What's going on?"

"The door was open," she replied.

"That doesn't mean you can just come in."

"Well then, young man, that should teach you to lock doors."

Zeke shuffled up on the sofa awkwardly, and she took this to be an acceptance and moved slowly into the room. She approached the couch, sat elegantly, and removed a cigarette from her purse before she stuck the pack out towards Zeke. He grabbed one, and she lit it,

"How long were you standing there? he asked, trying to comprehend the situation.

"Young man," she replied earnestly. "I'm sorry to barge in on you, but we don't have much time." Zeke looked at her curiously as his mind scrambled. He went to speak again, but Marguerite reached out and touched his arm. "Please," she said, "just hear me out."

"Okay," said Zeke, still acclimatising to the situation.

"Young man," she said, "there is no easy way to say this. So, I'm going to come right out with it."

Zeke nodded. He was anxious and excited. Whatever was coming was either good or bad. She paused for a second to compose herself, and a deep feeling of dread formed in the pit of his stomach. He'd never known her to mince her words, meaning whatever it was, it couldn't be good.

"Those men in New York," she began.

"Which time?" Zeke asked.

"The first time," she replied. "I had a hand in that!"

"You what?" asked Zeke. He stood from the sofa, and the rush of blood and nicotine flooded his brain. "You had me attacked?"

"It's not what you think."

"Then what is it?" he demanded as he began to rage.

"It was just business," she said, "I needed to sully the name of that gallery. None of the rest of this was supposed to happen!"

Zeke stopped pacing and rubbed hard at his face. He took a long drag of his cigarette as he considered what was said.

"How could—"

"Look," she said, interrupting. "We don't have time to argue. I never meant any harm to come to you. Plus, you know there's more to our work than meets the eye!"

"Marguerite," he stammered.

"No Zeke, please listen to me. I have a source in the police. He tells me that Jones is coming here with a search warrant. He thinks he has grounds for your arrest for murder!"

"Murder?" cried Zeke. "And you think—"

"I don't know, Zeke. I'm just here to help. I got you mixed up in this, and I'm sorry. I can help you if you let me?"

"Marguerite, I didn't kill anyone!" He looked at her sternly, "Tell me, you believe me?"

She stubbed her cigarette out on an empty bottle and stood, "Look, whatever happens, I can help you. But you have to tell me the truth."

"I am telling the truth."

"So, what did happen?" Zeke sat back down and exhaled. He paused in thought and then said.

"Honestly, I don't remember."

"But what happened after the men came up to you."

"I don't remember."

"What do you remember?"

"I left the gallery, lit a cigarette, put some music on, and the next thing I know, I'm sat on the plane."

"Oh, Zeke," she said. "I'm sorry. I really am. They were just supposed to scare you. I thought if something like that happened outside their prestigious gallery, it would put a dent in their image. I didn't mean for it to come to this!"

"You know they were thugs, right?"

"Well, it had to look real."

"You're a piece of work, Marguerite, you know that?" She nodded.

"Zeke," she said pensively. "Do I even ask about last time?" He shook his head solemnly.

"Please don't tell me you had anything to do with that?" They shared a stifled laugh.

"Look," she said, "I have to go. It won't look good if I'm here when they arrive." Zeke nodded.

"Do you know what he's after?"

"No," she said. "Do you?" Zeke shook his head. "Well, I'd think if I were you. If he finds what he wants, there won't be much I can do."

"Thanks," he replied. Marguerite turned to go, but as she reached the door, he said, "Why are you helping me?"

"You did what you had to do?"

29

Zeke sat in his car with the engine running. He'd been motionless on the drive for a good thirty minutes, staring at the exit in the mirror behind him. The burble of the V6 engine was the only sound. It was loud but still couldn't drown out his thoughts. Marguerite's admission to guilt was a curious one, he valued and probably needed her assistance, but couldn't help but wonder how much she was involved in this.

A million different ideas had come and gone, but all of them revolved around running away. He might make it, find a country with no extradition, and live alone on some remote beach or farm. It sounded peaceful, but he'd always be running, alone and looking over his shoulder. Every move, purchase, and interaction would have to be calculated. That was no way to live. It did sound better than jail, but he couldn't leave, not now. In just a few weeks, he was having a daughter, all those nightmares he'd had about making a monster out of his child. Either way, she'd have a criminal for a father. Better to be one that hadn't run away!

He switched the engine off and rested his head against the steering wheel. He was desperate to wake up. This couldn't be happening. Could it? It didn't seem likely that this man could get a warrant for nothing, but what did Zeke have that could warrant a search, or worse, his arrest? What if he was arrested and went to jail for something he didn't remember? He didn't have the propensity to kill, did he? However he looked at it, the problem was that there were only so many possibilities. The first being that this was a huge mistake, the second was that he was being framed, and the third wasn't worth considering. It seemed unlikely, but maybe he was drugged. It was gang-related; after all, was he an unwitting patsy? But that seemed improbable. Why would anyone want to frame him?

The third possibility was that he'd killed all three men in the alley. Then he'd gone back to New York with Lara, only to repeat the trick in a hotel room. For that to be true, it would mean he had the blood of six men on his hands. Was it possible he'd been killing people in his lost time? It just couldn't be accurate, but at the same time, what if it was? He also couldn't help but wonder what Marguerite had meant when she said that he did what he had to do. What did he do? It was like he was the star of his reality show, except everyone had a script except him.

Zeke moved his head and glanced down at his hands. Was he going crazy? They had been wrapped tightly around the steering wheel and had begun to turn white. As he pulled them away, they began to shake. He was tired and confused, and the gap between what was real and what wasn't had shortened significantly to the point he could see both with the same glance. He'd been pushing his body to the limit with drugs and alcohol. Was it really any surprise that he was cracking up?

Zeke turned the key once more and restarted the engine, whatever was coming he figured he could at least have one more drive. Maybe none of this was happening? He glanced down at the ignition as the engine started up, put the car in reverse and looked into the rear-view mirror just in time to see the steady stream of blue lights flow into his property.

30

Zeke stood alone at the altar. He waited nervously as he watched the room. The area was small and packed, intimate, and crowded simultaneously. He shifted his glance to the faces, a smile here, a nod there. He made as much contact as possible before looking down at his feet. Zeke took a deep breath with his eyes closed and felt his chest move back and forward. His knees were weak, and a cold sweat had appeared on his neck. Here stood the man who was never afraid, yet this room full of people seemed terrifying to him. The fervour hit his brain and made him feel like running. But just as his mind said *flee*, he opened his eyes and saw Cassie enter the room. She was elegance itself, enrobed in a bright red dress. He hadn't seen it before, but he had known it would be anything but white. Cassie smiled at him across the room and slowly made her way toward him. As she did, Zeke looked at the crowd of people. He barely recognised any of them; Cassie's guests outnumbered his four to one, and none of them were familiar.

He stood exposed on his own at the front, and her walk down the aisle seemed to take forever. Zeke knew this was her day, what she wanted, so he swallowed his pride. At this moment, he had never seen Cassie look as beautiful as she did, an acknowledgement accompanied by the familiar sinking feeling. Would anything ever be as good as it was right now? Would he live up to the expectations, or would she?

Zeke distracted himself with the faces as he waited for her. His eyes met Karan's, and they lit up as they collided. His friend smiled at him, then nodded towards Cassie and winked.

Of all the things in life Zeke could do without, Karan wasn't one. The smile from a friend refilled his vim, and he calmed down.

All eyes turned towards Cassie as she made her way to the altar, a small gasp emitted from the crowd as she appeared and relieved Zeke from the spotlight.

Cassie arrived resplendent in red, they had forgone most traditions, and she came alone, took his arm, and walked the small distance to the waiting minister. They'd decided to save money and use their in-progress barn conversion as the venue. It didn't take much to transform the lifeless remains into a modern chic setting. It was warm, and as the sunlight floated through one of the gaps in the beams, it hit Cassie's face and illuminated her like a spotlight.

As they arrived, he relinquished her arm. Zeke looked down at her dress, the room around him and the heartfelt looks cast upon them, saving the mental image as best he could. Then he noticed the tag hanging from the side of Cassie's dress, and it caused him to smile. She turned to him, their eyes met, and she blushed. Tears fell from the eyes of those in attendance, and this was it. Years in the making and months in planning all came down to this as the ceremony began. The rest of the room faded to black, almost as if by magic. Nothing and no one else mattered. It was just the two of them, and the rest of the world was a void. He took one last look as he closed his eyes. From behind his eyelids, he heard the minister open his mouth.

"Mr Olsen," he began. "Mr Olsen?"

The words were accompanied by a harsh knock, like the sound of knuckles rapping on glass.

Zeke opened his eyes and looked through the misty passenger window. His eyes met those of Agent Jones, and his heart sank. Oh, for just a few more minutes in that moment! Several uniformed officers had accompanied the agent, and his courtyard looked like the opening scene of a daytime crime drama. The knocking at the window continued, and muffled words permeated the condensed glass. The garbled words reached his brain, and Zeke reluctantly wound down the window.

"Mr Olsen, please step out of the vehicle and put your hands behind your head."

The scene was a farce, and it seemed unnecessary. But Zeke had learnt the hard way in the past that anything other than contrition only exacerbated law enforcement. As ordered, Zeke rolled the window up slowly, opened the driver's door, stepped out and placed his hands behind his head. The officers who had been sequestered from the local station seemed to be in two minds, and everyone retained their places, awaiting further instructions.

Zeke stood awkwardly against the car breathing in fresh country air as he was frisked. Jones, who had worn a permeant grin since arriving, spun him around and proudly produced a piece of paper that detailed the extent of his warrant. As Zeke took it in his hands to read, Jones continued.

"Mr Olsen, this is a warrant to search your premises and your person. Your cooperation in the matter would be much appreciated."

Jones eyed Zeke up as he read, like a hawk sizing up its prey. From the other side of the paper, he saw Jones' gaze meet Zeke's hands, and the grin fell from his face. As the agent eyed up the empty space on his finger where the ring usually sat, it suddenly hit him. Zeke had spent weeks desperately trying to figure this out, but the ring was his ever-present. If they suspected him of foul play, the engraved, cracked metal ring featured many a hiding place for evidence that wouldn't easily be washed away.

Jones span him round and then patted him down. As he looked over the roof of his car towards his house, he saw swathes of officers entering his property. The feeling of losing control was awful. It reminded him of being a child. His house, person, car, and even his freedom were being violated, and he didn't like it.

Zeke sat on his sofa, blanket around his shoulders as he sipped at his coffee. The morning had come and gone in a blur, and he'd been forced to sit and watch on as everything he held dear was opened, emptied, probed, sifted through, and tipped out. The scant consolation, though, was that the face of Jones would turn sour at every dead end, and if it was indeed the ring they were after, it wasn't here.

He was safe for now. Yet as he thought about that, the feeling of losing control reappeared. If they wanted the ring, there was no way he could stop them from getting it. The morning spent watching his house turned upside down offered plenty of time for contemplation. If the three dead men were the ones that had come for him, he might have fought back. He'd had blood on him at the time that didn't appear to be his. He assumed it was, but what if it wasn't? Even if he'd simply thrown a return punch, it was conceivable that DNA or blood had lodged itself into the ring, it was riddled with places to hide, and he imagined that modern forensics would have no problem analysing it. If the ring directly connected him with one of the deceased, it not only invalidated his story but would surely be enough to warrant a criminal charge. If the blood of a dead man he claimed not to know was found on his ring, he was in severe trouble, yet he still had no idea what happened!

After four long, excruciating hours, the search was finally over. Zeke's clean, modern house looked like it had been ransacked, but they were walking away empty-handed. It provided temporary relief until Jones stepped forward with a picture he'd removed from the mantelpiece. It was of him and Cassie on their honeymoon. His arm was around her shoulder, with his hand dangling slightly above her breast.

"Where's this ring, Mr Olsen?" Jones demanded.
"It's at the jeweller's."
"That's awfully convenient!"
"It needed repair."
"And fire cleanses all sins, doesn't it?" Jones leaned in and whispered to him, "Even if the DNA is gone, if I can get a match from that monogram, then so are you." Jones then stepped back away from Zeke and said. "Which one?"
"Erm, it was one in Winchester, just off the high street," Zeke replied, trying to push Jones's words out of his mind.
"The name, Mr Olsen?" Zeke stood and moved towards his coat,
"Give me a second," he said reluctantly as he removed his wallet. I have the receipt in here somewhere."
"What compelled you to take it to the jewellers?"
"It's over forty years old, Mr Jones," he replied as he fished about in his wallet. Zeke found the card and handed it out to Jones, who almost physically ripped it from his hands. Curiously though, the card had been alone in the wallet and

not with the receipt. "I'm sorry, detective, I seem to have misplaced the receipt."

Jones studied the card and handed it back to him, "And your certain it's here?" Zeke nodded. "Because if you deliberately give me false information, that's obstruction of justice!"

"Oh, it's there," replied Zeke, slightly remorsefully.

Jones signalled to his men to wrap it up, and the local officers trudged out of his house, each looking at him slightly apologetically. Jones followed them out, pausing at the front door.

"I'll be back," he said menacingly before getting in his car.

Zeke shut the front door and slumped to the floor. That had been excruciating. What had become apparent, though, was the ring was what they were after and, indeed, was all the connection they really had. Zeke was conflicted, was this a let-off, or would he be back? Did he deserve this? Had he done it? What would they find on the ring? Because it was a mystery even to him. He was so close to the arrival of his infant daughter. To miss that now would be horrendous, but what could he do?

31

Zeke climbed into the car, started the engine, and then floored the accelerator. The wheels spun on the gravel drive as he pulled away at speed, leaving a cloud of shingle behind him. It might be one of the last times he would drive his car. He would make the most of it! Of all the places he could be going in what might be his last hours of freedom, he never thought it would be this. But he needed answers, had to know what was possible and what wasn't. Still, if something was going on, if he had committed a crime, or if there was something wrong with his memory, then there had to be a reason or at very least an explanation.

Zeke drove as fast as he could without drawing too much attention to himself. He was genuinely nervous and frequently had to dab at the layer of sweat that accumulated on his brow. In light of all the flashbacks and hours of unaccounted time, he'd boldly decided to go cold turkey on his medications, the effects of which he was now feeling. His body ached, he was nauseous, fatigue squeezed hard against his eyeballs, and his mood was wildly inconsistent. Life had turned a shade of sepia, he was listless, and his back hurt, but none of that mattered. Zeke looked at his watch. It was just after five in the evening. He hoped who he was after would be home just as he prayed that the jeweller had been out.

Zeke arrived in the small village and parked in the square opposite the apartment. There was no car outside, meaning he was probably early. Zeke sat as patiently as possible, eagerly watching the front door until finally, the man he was waiting for arrived. Zeke gave it ten minutes, took a deep breath, exited his car, and walked over to the green front door.

Ignoring the video doorbell, he knocked his leather-clad hands firmly against the wooden frame.

"Zeke," exclaimed Ray, unable to hide his surprise as he opened the door. "What are you doing here? Is everything alright? How's Cassie?"

"Can I come in?" Zeke asked ignoring Ray's platitudes. He didn't answer any questions or wait for a reply as he blustered past Ray and into the house.

Zeke sat down in the living room as he waited for Ray. When he arrived, he paused in the doorway and asked,

"Uh, you want a drink, Zeke? Beer? Whiskey?"

"Coffee would be good, Ray."

Ray nodded before departing. In the distance, Zeke could hear cups clinking. In the moments he had alone, he had a chance to survey the area of Ray's apartment. The living room was a mess, there were numerous dirty glasses on the side, open books, and magazines on the floor, as well as the remnants of last night's take-out. But he didn't have long alone before Ray returned, sporting the world's fastest made cup of coffee.

"Here," he said, holding it out towards him. Zeke took the piping hot cup and held it cautiously. "Erm, do you want me to take your coat and gloves?" asked Ray.

"No, I won't be staying long, Ray."

"Okay, you don't mind if I do?" Ray asked, motioning towards the decanter on the side.

"Your house Ray."

Ray poured himself a large glass of whiskey, sat across from Zeke and crossed his legs. There was a moment of silence before Zeke opened his mouth to speak.

"How much are we talking, Zeke?"

"A lot," was the reply.

"Well, I mean, it's possible. I would need specifics, though, Zeke."

"But you're a chemist, Ray. This is your job!"

"I know, but there are so many possible interactions. I mean, come on, I know you're taking some things off the books, and drinking a lot. But as with everything, side effects depend on the user. You know that's why we have the Yellow Card scheme. So that people can report new interactions."

Zeke nodded ignoring the lecture about alcohol from the man drinking at six p.m., "So memory loss or hallucinations, it's possible?"

"What are we talking about, Zeke?"

"Just answer the question!" he snapped back.

"Yes, Zeke, mixing drugs can be dangerous. You know if you're worried, you really should have come to me sooner. Anyway, look, Zeke, as much as I love talking about work, what's this—"

"Could it be caused by something else? Could someone have given me something, switched medications?"

"Woah, Zeke, slow down. What's happening? What's with the paranoia? You're worrying me!"

Zeke stood and began pacing about the room. "Time Ray, I've been losing whole chunks of time?"

"What do you mean?"

"I mean, I am doing something, and then the next thing I know, several hours have passed."

"Zeke, man, this is serious. This is beyond my realm of expertise. Go and see a doctor. Come on, your wife and friend are both psychologists."

"What are you saying?"

"Well, you went through some trauma in New York, yes? You could be looking at some dissociative amnesia or something similar. But I'm no authority on this."

"So, it's not the drugs?"

"Zeke, I dunno. But you need to get some help." The cogs in Ray's head began to whir, and he paused for a second before continuing. "Wait a minute Zeke, hallucinations? What is it you don't remember? It's not about New York, is it?" Zeke stopped pacing and looked at Ray, he went to speak again, but something stopped. He knew the withdrawal was sinking into a deep feeling of paranoia. But it was more than that. How well did he really know Ray, could he trust him?

"You're right," he said. "Thanks, I should talk to Karan."

"Hey Zeke, you, okay? You don't look so good?"

"Yeah, fine, thanks, Ray, but I gotta go." He stood and was out of the room before Ray could reply. He dashed across the square, got in his car as quickly as possible and set off in the direction of nowhere.

32

Zeke thrashed the Alfa hard, driving until he almost ran out of fuel. He had no idea where he was going, and the reality was he had nowhere to go. But he couldn't just sit home and wait for the police to return.

Cassie was still at her sister's. The contents of the house had been tipped upside down and waiting there would be like waiting for death. Right now, he wasn't on the run. He was just out for a drive.

After what seemed like years of searching, he found a petrol station, filled up, paid cash, and then said to the lady behind the till, "Where is this?"

"You want to know where you are?" she asked. Zeke nodded. "We're about ten miles outside of Guildford."

"Thanks."

"Are you okay, sir? You look a little pale."

"Just tired." The woman eyed him suspiciously as he paid up, got in the car, and drove off in a hurry. It felt as though everyone knew what was happening except him, and he didn't like it.

He continued his drive until he found a remote layby and pulled over. A harsh wind almost ripped the door from his hand as he opened it, and the air was brisk as it whipped against his face. As he relieved himself, he took a moment to settle. All these fears had been ripping him apart. He was Zeke Olsen! He just needed to take a deep breath and remember who he was. He wasn't that far from London. Suzie lived there! He could get Cassie, and they could abscond together. He had enough money tucked away. They could get the first flight from Heathrow and just put it all behind him. It was an exciting but stupid notion. At what point would he have to tell Cassie that their impromptu holiday was a getaway? Would she even be allowed to fly; would she freak out? He'd already been arrested at Heathrow once.

Zeke wiped his hands clean and got back in the car. As he did, he realised that he was running from himself. Something had happened in New York, and there was only so long he could keep convincing himself that he had nothing to do with it. What wasn't he remembering, and why?

Back in his seat, he placed his head against his steering wheel and shut his eyes. As he thought about it, he realised that certain things had triggered what he now assumed to be memories rather than hallucinations. Especially anything that had a connection with New York. If his brain was disassociating, he needed to associate it with something. Think, Zeke, think! As he sat in the car, the CD skipped and played a song that reminded him of a party from years ago, and then it hit him. When he'd stepped into that alleyway, he'd played a specific track right before it all went black. He knew enough to know that music was very powerful and could trigger all kinds of memories and emotions. It was worth a shot!

Zeke hurriedly reached across to his bag and fetched his MP3 player. If he could remember what happened, then maybe he could defend himself. If he knew what happened then, he had a chance. As the device powered up, he connected to the aux cable, pressed play on *Drain You* by Nirvana, turned it up loud, closed his eyes and let the music flow through him.

As the music sank deeper into him, he returned to that night and allowed his brain to open. He sat and listened to the track over and over until finally, it clicked.

Zeke sat upright. He was startled by what he'd seen but was not afraid. Not anymore. It was almost as if he was now ready for the truth. He opened his eyes and faced the memories of what had happened those nights as they painted themselves across his hippocampus.

Zeke opened the car door and fell to his knees; the very real visceral assault was overwhelming, and he heaved hard, bringing up the limited contents of his stomach all over the dirty ground. When he was finally done, he wiped his mouth, sat back against the side of the vehicle, and stared at his hands. These hands had caused so much damage! The disassociation hadn't been shielding him from any misery he'd suffered. It had been protecting him from the trauma he'd caused!

Yet as he sat against the car and the wind whistled through his hair, he looked at his hands again, turning them as he did so. It was then he realised it wasn't damage that they had caused it was quite the opposite!

As he remembered the night in the alleyway, he recalled that fate had presented him with an opportunity, and he seized it with both fists. It wasn't his intention at first, but instinct took over and he realised that these men were volatile, dangerous and had no place on this planet. The next person they attacked could have been weak, or frail. They might not have been so lucky, and he knew in his heart then and there that his conscience couldn't live with that. The police would be unlikely to do anything. It was only a matter of time before they caused serious harm, and there was no way he was letting them leave alive!

33

Zeke hadn't always had a wild streak; before the car accident, he was very much a diplomat's son. Mild-mannered, polite, and well-behaved. But with a lack of guardianship, a consistent authority figure, or any real consequence to his actions, all that began to change. In the years that followed, the institutionalised learning system and its lack of real responsibility for him formed a rebellion inside of him. Two loving adults no longer governed him but rather myriad teachers, tutors, and prefects. His actions resulted in punishment, but never a disappointment.

He'd learnt how to be a man from many different sources, creating an eclectic mix. He'd often wondered just how different his life would be if his parents hadn't chosen the wrong moment to enter the roundabout. Suppose adolescence had been waking up to kisses and breakfast in bed in the morning rather than a fist in the gut. It was a moot thought; destiny had taken him, made him this way, and he never really understood until now.

Zeke had spent so much of his life trying to outrun his thoughts, feelings, and his brain. Numbing his senses and hiding from who and what he was. He'd spent many nights with friends he hardly knew and others completely alone. Always searching, but never finding answers! Vice after vice, but one seldom found answers at the bottom of an empty bottle.

What he enjoyed was more! More speed, more thrills, more drugs, alcohol, or adrenaline. But when all you need is more, there is never enough. It was a road he had been walking for some time without knowing why.

Meeting Cassie changed that for a while. It quietened the longing, settled him down, and filled him up. She was both calm and exciting, his sail and his anchor. They shared a mysterious connection, and for a long while, that had been enough, or so he thought.

But taking a life had been instinctive. Perhaps he simply wasn't born to sit behind a desk. The trauma he'd suffered as a child had been so intense, so deep. But even suffering has its meaning, and there is beauty in meaning. Zeke realised that no high was capable of matching the lows he had experienced. He was numb, and killing evil people was the only thing he'd ever experienced that came close to replicating the beauty of meaning.

So far, he had rid the world of six sinners, and ridding the planet of some of its stains had been a drug like no other. It replaced the need for anything else, and suddenly he understood, his whole life made sense. But as much as this completed him there was no way Cassie could ever understand, could she? He had killed men, all of whom had years of blood on their hands, the system might catch up with them, but they would never get what they deserved. But he could ensure that they would by eking out a small amount of justice. As much as he loved his life with Cassie, Karan, Ivan, Ray, and their soon-to-be daughter, it would never be enough, not on its own. It would just be a loop, parties, gatherings, trips, weddings, and celebrations. He had money, he was a *success*, but otherwise, he would leave no mark on the world. For all the years he could spend on the planet, he'd be forgotten overnight. When you realise how quickly people forget the dead, you stop trying to impress the living.

Zeke got back into the car, lit a cigarette, and blew the smoke out around him. There was a catharsis to accepting what he was capable of and what he had done. Zeke liked control and the memory loss had left him feeling powerless. But now it was back, he knew a power like no other, a feeling no vice could replace. Knowing he could dedicate his life to a noble cause was everything he'd ever needed. Regardless of what happened in the remaining hours, he could hold his head high. The world was a slightly safer place thanks to him. It was a start, and hopefully, would have time to continue it anonymously.

He started the engine, turned the car around and set off towards home. He was clear in his mind now, and whatever occurred next would happen for a reason, it all would.

Snow began to fall as Zeke drove home. The sight of it always cheered him up, and by the time he'd made it back, the yard had a covering of a few centimetres, and there were no tracks in it. No one had come or gone recently. He clicked the remote door opener, parked the car in the garage, and then exited hastily to take in the rarity of snow. It was falling faster now, and the sight of it against the flashing fairy lights set his heart a glow. Zeke opened his mouth and held it to the sky, allowing some flakes to enter. They landed on his tongue, melting as he closed his eyes.

Some like to relax in the sun, but Zeke basked in the cold. His retained freedom was curious. Unless the jeweller had been unobtainable, he was surprised that no one had been back. He gleaned some renewed hope that he might be in the clear because there was, of course, the possibility that work might have begun on the repair, and that would surely wash away any evidence of his sins.

Zeke removed a lounger from the garage and sat in the yard, watching the twinkle of lights as the snow began to land on him. Whatever happened, he needed a plan. He'd been sloppy in New York. Even if Jones drew a blank today, he struck Zeke as the relentless type and not one he could make disappear. Killing street thugs, murderers, and rapists was one thing, but not everyone deserved to die. And in the case of Agent Jones, his only crime was being too good at his job.

Sitting on a sun lounger in the snow, he removed another cigarette and puffed away. He'd been in hiding for nearly forty years now—the reasons for why he'd been the way he was his whole life became clear in those moments. He finally knew who he was, what he was, and what he could do. It's not every day one discovers their true purpose!

34

Ray had known Zeke for almost eight years, and in that time, they'd frequented each other's dwellings, and attended parties, venues, and weddings. But in all those years, Zeke had never shown up at his house unannounced and certainly never alone.

He'd spent the time since Zeke's departure drinking and trawling through internet news about the deaths in New York. He'd seen Zeke in many forms, up, down, sad, happy, high, drunk, weird. But he'd never seen him act the way he had today. Ray had an analytical mind, and Zeke had unsettled him earlier. He had never really been able to place the man, and yet today he felt like he was finally figuring him out. The strange feelings he harboured about Zeke had only been exacerbated.

In the preceding weeks, Agent Jones had questioned most of Zeke's friends and acquaintances, he even came to Ray's house, which frustrated him even more. The questions were largely perfunctory, but the one that remained in his mind was whether Zeke wore any jewellery. He'd dismissed it then, but now that he gave it some thought, Zeke only ever wore one piece of jewellery, it was usually ubiquitous—and thus conspicuous in its absence today. Ray wasn't quite sure what it meant or what it had to do with the murders, but he knew a few people that might. So, he picked up the phone and began to dial. Either way, he hoped that the call he'd made earlier would bring him some answers.

"Hello, Kam's Chinese takeaway how can I help you?" came the accented voice.

"Oh, sorry," replied Ray, slightly confused. "I think I might have called the wrong number!"

"Gotcha!"

"Ivan?"

"Hey Ray, I got you good there. Didn't I?"

"Ivan, what are you doing with my phone? Give me that!"

Ray heard a slight commotion in the background before Karan's voice finally beamed down the receiver.

"Sorry about that, Ray. Ivan's just being silly. What's up?"

"Um, to be honest, it's about Zeke?"

"Zeke, what now? Look, I told him he needed to get his shit together. What's he done?"

"Nothing really."

"Well then, what is it, Ray?" Karan asked.

"Did that Interpol guy get in touch with you?"

"Sure, yeah, he came round a few days ago and asked a plethora of ridiculous questions. Why?"

"Did you ask you about Zeke's ring?" Karan paused for a moment. "Well, did he?"

"Erm yeah, I think so, Ray. What's this all about?"

"Well, he came round here tonight?"

"Who, the Interpol guy?"

"No, Zeke, look, he wasn't wearing it!"

"Ray, have you been drinking?"

"Yes, Karan, but that's not—"

"Look, Ray," Karan interjected. "Please tell me you didn't ring me to ask about Zeke's jewellery?"

"He wasn't wearing it, Karan!"

"Good god Miss Marple. Cassie said they dropped it in a Jewellers when they were in Winchester. Mystery solved, okay?"

"But—"

"Ray, it's late. Ivan is here. Give me a ring in the morning if you need to solve any more of Zeke's accessory issues, okay?"

And like that, he hung up, leaving Ray alone in a room with nothing but his thoughts and his drink. The remnants of which he downed before setting the tumbler down on the counter. He stared at it for a moment before angrily flicking it across the room. It made hard contact with the wall, denting the plaster before splintering into a million tiny shards that spread themselves all over the kitchen floor.

Annoyed that his outburst required further work, Ray moved across the room and picked up the larger pieces. As he stooped and scooped the glass, one of the shards sliced across the palm of his hand. So sharp was it that he felt nothing until the flow of blood oozed from his hand and dripped quickly onto the floor.

"Fuck," he yelled in anguish as he threw what he'd already collected back down. He was expecting company soon, and the cut was an inconvenience. It all was. He had a bad feeling about Zeke and couldn't shake it.

35

Zeke spent every second that he wasn't incarcerated indulging in simple pleasures. It was getting on for nine, and still, no one had come for him. The snow fell in droves, and he'd been out in it for as long as his body temperature could handle. He'd even made a small snowman and set him on guard outside the front door. If simple pleasures were to be stripped away from him, then now was the moment to seize what was left of the day.

Having accomplished everything he could think of that wouldn't be possible in prison, he disrobed, stepped into the walk-in wet room, waved on the shower, and then cranked the heat up as high as it would go. The warm water hit his cool skin, and as the opposing feelings met, he thought about his moment of catharsis.

Everyone must go through life thinking about *what-if* moments? What if I had to drag someone from a burning building? Could I? Or would I freeze? Or what if an intruder came in the night? What do I do if I get attacked by three street thugs? Zeke had his answers. He'd been there. He'd done it, and now that he remembered, he was glad. That was the overriding emotion, elation. Whatever happened next, he would hold his head high. It was a simple moment of chance, followed by another. Almost like tests, but the world contained six fewer monsters because of him.

Zeke stepped out of the shower, rubbed his hand over the mirror, and wiped away the steam. As he reflected, he recalled the last night that he and Cassie connected. He wished she were here right now just as he was pleased she was not. Looking at his new image, he opened the cupboard and reflected upon its contents. It had been days since he touched anything inside it, and he felt sharper, more aware, as though he'd found a former clarity, with the bonus of never having known such a thing. Zeke reached inside and scooped all the packets into the sink before. He then popped each tablet into the toilet individually as he flushed them away. As painstaking as it was, he realised these had all been going in him, numbing him, controlling him, stopping him from being who he really was. They needed to go.

Emptying the pills was a lengthy task, but with each pack, he flushed. He felt anew. Then as the last drugs entered the liquid and he watched the water spin around the bowl, a sense of pride and confidence came over him. The steam had dissipated from the room. He could see clearly now.

Zeke was still in the bathroom when the inevitable happened. The doorbell chime drifted through the house like an icy wave, and a feeling of tragedy overcame him. He looked at his watch. It was getting late. Still better late than early morning. He grabbed a robe and slippers from behind the bathroom door and slipped into the bedroom. The lights in the yard had gone out, and it was only moonlight that crept through the gap in the curtains. He snuck a glance from the shades and looked down at the ground. The snow had almost stopped, and there were just a single set of tyre tracks in the snow. It seemed unlikely that even someone with the hubris of Jones would have come alone. Surely if he'd found something, then Ahab himself couldn't have been prouder. Zeke ambled down the stairs slowly, knowing full well that each step might be his last.

Zeke's mouth dropped as he opened the door and found himself standing face to face with Lara. The two faced each other in stunned silence until one of them finally opened their mouth to speak.

"Zeke," she said, sounding panicked. "I'm sorry. I know this is irregular, but I didn't know where else to go."

Zeke nodded to her and quickly beckoned her into the lobby. She was dishevelled and inappropriately dressed for the weather, so he ushered her in straight away. As she stepped in, he closed the door behind her, as his mind struggled to comprehend what was happening.

Zeke studied her as she stood in the porchway, her usual lustre was missing, and her fringe hung over a portion of her face covering one of her eyes. She was dressed for the night, a small jacket barely covered her torso, and her legs were bare. Wherever she had come from, she'd left in a hurry. She wrapped her arms around him and embraced him as though he was a long-lost relative. He held her as she held him, and the two stood locked in a moment that could have lasted forever.

Her body was all a-quiver, and it was then that he realised that she was crying. "Lara, what's going on?" It was as though his words soothed her, and the tension dropped from her body. She held on to him for a moment longer before finally relinquishing and taking a step back. The light passed across her face as she did, and he became aware of what she'd been hiding.

He moved towards her, and she hesitated slightly. But something about his motion calmed her, and she allowed him to brush the hair away from her eye.

"Lara!" he exclaimed, "What happened? Who did this?" She shied away from him as he examined the bruise around her cheek. She tried to talk but only spoke more tears. Zeke guided her into the living room, wrapped a blanket around her and had her sit. He stepped away towards the kitchen, but as he did so she said,

"Zeke, don't go!"

"I'm not going anywhere," he said softly, "I'm getting you a warm drink, I'll be back." Lara nodded tentatively.

By the time he'd returned, she had loosened up. He handed her a warm mug of tea and a cold ice pack.

"Thanks," she said, taking both. Pressing the ice against her face. Zeke motioned to leave again, but as he did, she reached out and grabbed his arm, "Please, just stay!"

36

Lara sat and nervously sipped at her tea. She was visibly apprehensive and looked over her shoulder periodically as though something insidious might happen at any moment. It was almost half an hour before she uttered another word, Zeke waited patiently all the while.

"I'm sorry," was the next thing she said. Sat on the second sofa just across from her, Zeke looked at her sincerely and said,

"Hey, stop apologising. You have nothing to apologise for."

"I was going to tell you, Zeke, I tried. He was so sweet and romantic, and I just thought that–"

"Thought what, Lara?"

"It doesn't matter, Zeke. It's impossible anyway."

"Nothing's impossible, Lara," he replied positively.

"Trust me, this is! You'd hate me if I told you all of it!"

"Well, tell me some of it. I think we've established I'm not easily phased." Lara smiled.

"That's fair. Okay, well, don't be angry."

"No anger here."

"It was Ray!"

"Ray?" he replied, surprised. "My Ray, Ray-Ray?" She nodded. "Well fuck, I didn't see this coming! And he did this?" he asked, gesturing to her face with rage.

"You said you wouldn't be angry."

"Oh, trust me, I'm not angry. Not with you anyway."

"He might be coming here, Zeke. You should have seen him. I was terrified." Lara became visibly upset once more, and Zeke shifted slightly closer to her.

"Alright," he said, "talk me through it. You're safe here no matter what!" She paused for a moment and composed herself.

"Well, it started at the pre-Christmas office party. I barely knew you, and you were there with Cassie, Karan, Ivan, and Ray. We got to chatting, and he was kind. He was different, and I know this might sound stupid, but I thought it might get me closer to you." She paused, and Zeke went to speak. "Please just listen," she said, "I know how that sounds, Zeke. But you just have this gravity that pulls people towards you. I don't understand it myself, but I just wanted to be closer to your orbit.

"Anyway, Ray and I exchanged numbers, we went on a few dates, and it was nice. Until it wasn't."

"Then what, Lara?" Zeke asked, desperate to know more about another situation to which he'd been wholly oblivious.

"Well, it was after New York. That's when it changed. At first, I thought it was just jealousy, but it became more than that. He wanted to know what happened, Zeke. He kept asking me questions and making me do things I didn't want to. When I refused, he would get angry." She started crying heavily again, and Zeke shifted seats, so they were side by side. He put his arm around her gingerly to comfort her.

"Hey, hey," he said. "It's not your fault. Okay?"

"But Zeke," she blubbered. "I think he wants to get you in trouble, and he made me help him. I wanted to stop him tonight, but that's when he got angry."

"And that's when he hi—"

She nodded. Cutting Zeke off before he finished his sentence. "I'm so sorry, Zeke. I didn't mean for any of this to happen."

"Hey, look at me. You're safe, and you did nothing wrong."

"But what if you go to prison because of me, Zeke?"

Zeke paused for a moment.

"What do you mean?"

"He has something that he thinks implicates you. He's been trawling through the news and going on about theories for days now." Zeke sighed as he thought to himself. The police, Interpol, were just doing their jobs. He was powerless to stop them, but he could deal with Ray. The thought of him laying hands on Lara upset him, the image even more so as he remembered the thug hitting her in New York. Zeke wondered how many others had befallen the same fate at the hands of Ray, and a wave of primal anger stirred in him.

"Look, you go upstairs. Cassie's away. Take a shower, and I'll dig out some of her clothes for you, and then get some rest."

"What about Ray? I need to tell—"

"I'll cross that bridge when or if it comes to it. Just go upstairs, everything will be fine!" She nodded, hugged him, and stood. "The bedroom is to the right at the top of the stairs, bathroom's en suite," he said, pointing her in the direction.

She nodded and made her way up the stairs. As she reached the halfway point, she stopped and turned back. "Zeke," she said, "I've loved…the times we've spent together." The slight pause between the words 'loved' and 'the' was just big enough to be curious but not enough to drag his mind away from the state of affairs.

Zeke heard Lara enter and use the shower. Once she was in, he set down some of Cassie's clothes on the bed. With it, he left a glass of water that he'd laced with sleeping tablets. He felt terrible about drugging her, but if Ray were to turn up, she would be better off not knowing, not seeing, and not being involved!

"Make yourself comfortable," he yelled through the door, "If you need me, I'll be downstairs." He then departed the room, closed the door behind him, went back down the steps, and prepared himself for what was to come. Zeke knew that the strongest of all warriors were patience and time. The patience he had in abundance, time, however, might not be on his side.

Zeke stepped outside into the snow and took a moment to bask in its magnitude. Growing up, he'd known an abundance of it, and it was one of many things in life you don't appreciate until they are gone. Once outside, he locked the door, made his way across the yard to the garage, opened a single door, pulled out a seat, wrapped himself in a blanket, and prepared to wait.

37

Sitting in the cold darkness of the garage had made the concept of time irrelevant. Zeke didn't know how much time he had, so he didn't care. He had a great vantage point from here and could deal with whatever turned up first. Given the late hour he hoped that Interpol had been unable to locate his ring, and since he had time he didn't expect to have, he would make the most of it. Zeke had always found Ray to be boorish, prosaic even, but never once had he imagined that he had this side to him. It made him question the botched marriages. No one knew what happened. Had they failed at his hands?

Chronic remorse is ultimately futile, but Zeke agonised over everything his mind had missed over the years. He'd been numbing his senses and dwelling on his problems, but always indulging in more of the same behaviour and never seeking to make a change. If you want to change the world, you must first start with yourself. Fate had contrived to bring him this far, and he would make whatever happened next count.

It must have been two hours before headlights emerged on the main road and slowly turned into his driveway. It was a lone car with a set of vintage lights Zeke would recognise anywhere. The compound was dark, including the house. Zeke had shut off all his CCTV, and the only light currently came from the old headlights of Ray's BMW. The car lurched sluggishly up the driveway and approached the open garage door. Ray manoeuvred the car halfway in, shut off the engine and then hauled himself out of the vehicle haphazardly.

Zeke remained blanketed in his seat as Ray approached him with a drunken, brazen swagger. He strolled up to Zeke until they were in a breath of each other, loomed over him and finally stopped.

"Where is she, Zeke?" he demanded. Zeke could almost taste the alcohol on Ray's breath as the words drifted across the short divide. He had a menacing look in his eyes and a rage wrapped around his knuckles. Zeke had never seen Ray like this, and if he were any other man, he might have been afraid.

Zeke didn't utter a word. Instead, he fixed his eyes on Ray. The silence seemed only to anger him more, and he stepped towards Zeke, prodding him on the shoulder, obviously quite unaware of the mistake he was making.

"Zeke, you psycho," he stammered. "You can't hide behind those dead eyes of yours forever. I know what you are, what you've done, and I can prove it."

"What do you want, Ray? What do you think is going to happen here?"

"What's going to happen is you're going to tell me where Lara is, and then you're going to tell me what my silence is worth."

Zeke paused, he could feel the tingle, the excitement, and the anticipation brewing up inside of him. He knew now that Ray was a wicked man, one who was making an unfathomable mistake. Zeke breathed in deep and composed himself before he spoke.

"I tell you what, Ray, you leave Lara and Karan alone, go far, far away from here, sort your life out and never lay your hands on another woman. Then and only then will I consider that none of this ever happened. That's the best offer you're going to get."

"No, no!" he stammered. You don't get to threaten me. You are a murderer. I want Lara, and I want money."

"Last chance Ray."

"No, I've been right about you all along, Olsen. You're a killer, and you belong behind bars." Zeke looked at Ray. Getting a lecture from a woman beating extortionist irritated him, but it was of minor consequence.

"You're right, Ray," he said. "I am a killer. I've killed six men so far. But if you knew this, in coming here you've made a grave error."

"And what's that? I have a failsafe. If I die, the truth about you will come out. You are the one who has everything to lose."

"Maybe, maybe not! But greed, arrogance, ego, that's been you're undoing!" Ray sneered.

"How so? You have just as much to lose if I die?"

"No, Ray, I don't," he said, finally standing from his chair. "Because, when you die here tonight, you'll be gone forever, and your final thought will be that I gave you the chance to walk out of here alive!"

As he stood, the blanket fell from his shoulders, revealing the large spanner that had been in his hands all along. Ray's eyes followed the blanket as it fell. As they met the floor, he realised he was standing on plastic sheeting. His stomach sank as he looked back up just in time to see the spanner hurtling towards his head.

The metal instrument connected with his head before he could even open his mouth. It struck his skull with such a force that he collapsed to the ground in a heap. Blood gurgled from his mouth as the last of his brain activity remained before silence, and Ray was no more.

Zeke hovered over the body. A bloody grin had painted itself across his face, and the feeling of euphoria was immense. Ray was volatile. How long before his anger took a young woman's life? Or his drunk driving wiped out a whole family. He looked down at the body below him and wiped the blood from the spanner with a towel before putting it back in his tool kit. He then took the bloody cloth, placed it over Ray's face and paused in a moment of silence.

Zeke crept alongside the parked car and peered from the edge of the door. Outside all was calm, and there was no one about presently. The snow had continued to fall, and when he looked up, he noticed the fledgling flakes tumbling in the moonlight. The dead body aside, it was picture-perfect!

Zeke knew he had no time to savour the moment. He took Ray's keys from his pocket and began the task of wrapping him in the plastic. He'd wrapped many things at this time of year, a dead body wasn't one of them, and as he did so, he wondered how many more there might be?

Shifting Ray's considerable bulk was no easy task, but epinephrine finally had him wrapped, rolled, and placed in the boot.

Zeke jumped into the car and fired up the engine with adrenaline coursing through his veins. The house was still dark, and leaving the headlights off, he reversed it to the edge of the compound. Before setting off, Zeke adjusted the rear-view mirror, catching a glimpse of himself. There was a vitality to his face that he hadn't seen before. He felt fresh, alive and with purpose. It was like looking back at an entirely different image. He took a final glance back at his house before setting off into the snowy night, unaware that Lara watched on upstairs from the darkness of the bedroom window.

38

Zeke picked up the pace as he jogged home. He'd been out of the house longer than he would have liked, and if Lara awoke, he would be conspicuous in his absence. Not to mention the impending arrest that could befall him at any time, although something in the air told him that fate was on his side.

It had been a long time since he had jogged, and although his body ached, he'd forgotten the lucidity of thought it offered. It was perhaps conceivable that as sloppy as he had been in New York, he might just be afforded some good luck. Jones, it would seem, was alone in his theories, and should the ring have already been altered by the jeweller, there might not be any surviving evidence. He conceived that the monogram might have made an impression on the man's face, but with nothing but poor crime scene photographs, it would never be enough for a conviction. The only issue would be Jones, Zeke would forever be in the man's mind, given that he was spot on in his analysis. Would he ever leave him alone?

As he ran through the night, his feet made fresh imprints in the snow, like a lily in bloom, or the first footsteps on a new planet. Snow was such a keen ally. Any footprints or tyre tracks he left would be gone by morning.

"Ezequiel," he said out loud to himself as he ran. "Ezequiel!" That was his name, "God strengthens, God is strong." Perhaps it was no coincidence; maybe that was his purpose. Was he a reckoner? He could and should have died that day with his parents, and yet he didn't! Had divinity intervened? It had been years since he had been to church. Maybe that ought to change. Zeke wasn't entirely sure what he believed, but he knew he had been reborn! Every step he had taken, every choice made, and all the pain suffered had led him here. If he were to get a second chance, this would no longer be a life wasted.

Disposing of Ray's corpse had been relatively easy. The man was a known drunk driver. His blood alcohol would be well over the limit; he was bold, reckless, and the road was icy. Lara would give a statement to say that he had given chase to her drunk after assaulting her, and he didn't imagine the police would have much interest in an investigation. The subterfuge was simple, the execution far more complicated. Finding a suitable bend in the road was easy, and although it was late, there was still the odd car. The thrill was immense as he unwrapped Ray's body, hauled it into the driver's seat and then pushed it over the edge. The car rolled a few times and hit a tree before a small fire broke out. The flames were bittersweet, they'd wiped away his family, but today they had absolved him of his sins. Fire cleanses everything.

He'd removed the plastic sheet and buried it far away along with his outer layers. It was a loose end but not one he could turn up with at home. If he was arrested for multiple murders, it made little difference. If not, he could retrieve and dispose of it at another time.

Running home after his exertions was an enormous task, but he continued. He was anxious to get back, so he put his head down and focused—one foot before the other, one foot before the other.

Zeke arrived home to a house that was still dark and quiet, his relief was palpable, and he made straight for the garage, closing the door behind him. He stripped down, removed everything he had been wearing, and put it into a bucket of bleach, including the spanner he'd used to kill Ray. He then wiped his naked, tattooed body with caustic wipes that stung horribly. Before he set about making sure there was no evidence anywhere else in the garage. Zeke then hosed himself head to toe using industrial cleaner and sugar scrub. Clean, cleansed and satisfied, he gathered his belongings and braced the icy cold, naked walk back to the house.

Zeke woke early the following day, his body ached, but his mind was fresh. He still had the business card given to him by the man at the jewellers, and he remembered it featured a personal mobile number. He felt cruel dialling at this hour, but this mystery had gone on far too long.

He hastily typed the digits into his phone and began to dial. The phone rang endlessly without going to voicemail, but just as Zeke was about to give up the line connected, and he was met by a soothing male baritone.

"Hello, Winston Smith."

"Good morning, Mr Smith," came Zeke's response. "I hope I didn't wake you. Is this Winston from Winston's Jewellers?!

"Speaking."

"Excellent," replied Zeke. "I'm sorry to bother you, but I was keen to catch you before the holidays. I dropped a ring in for repair not long ago—"

"Oh, yes, Mr Olsen?" came the response. "You know, I got straight on with it. It breaks my heart to see heirlooms fall into such disrepair. It's all done for you."

"You are an angel, sir. Would it be possible to collect it?"

"No, I'm afraid not, Mr Olsen!" Zeke's heart sank. "Your young wife has already been in and picked it up!"

"Oh," was Zeke's response. "My wife?"

"Oh dear," replied the man. "I do hope I haven't spoiled a surprise."

"No, not at all," assured Zeke. "That's excellent news."

"Good to hear it," replied Winston. "I rarely get to work on something like that these days. It was my genuine pleasure. I bet that ring can tell some stories?"

"More than you know," replied Zeke.

"Well, Mr Olsen, was there anything else I can do for you?" Zeke paused for a moment in contemplation.

"You haven't had anyone else come looking for the ring, have you?"

"No, sir, just your wife. Pretty young thing. You've done well for yourself there."

"Yes, she's wonderful," replied Zeke. "Okay, well, you have a delightful Christmas, Mr Smith."

"And to you, Mr Olsen."

Zeke hung up the phone, set it down on the counter, and mused for a moment. Perhaps that was why the receipt was missing? Cassie was constantly bailing him out, even unwittingly so. With the ring repaired and back in his possession, it would leave Jones very little to go on. With a lawyer as adept as Rathbone, there was no way any charges would stick. It had been a close call, but perhaps it would be a great Christmas after all.

39

When Lara finally appeared just after lunch that day, she found Zeke sitting pensively in his study. So consumed was he by his thoughts that her knock on the door startled him and caused him to jump in his seat.

"Hey," she said, moving into the study and setting a hot mug down on his desk. "Whatcha up to? You were so motionless I thought you might be dead!" The word *dead* barely moved him given his late-night exploits. It was ironic because he was quite the opposite. Zeke peeled his eyes from the bay window.

"Snow's gone," he said, turning his eyes towards her. Words to the both of them, knowing that so too were any tyre tracks or footprints. His eyes were drawn to her as he turned and looked at her hair. It was straight and hung delicately over her shoulders like a summer twilight. He'd never noticed how long it was before. She stood before him wearing one of his oversized hoodies that only just fell to the length of her bare legs.

"Nice hoodie!" he said jokingly.

"Sorry," she replied, "it was on the back of the door."

"Keep it," he said. Doing his best not to picture that under it she wore nothing, that and getting it back would always remind him of that. "It suits you. I haven't worn that in years." She moved into the study and perched on his footstool. It was an odd dynamic, he barely knew her, but there was already a large bond between them.

"Did Ray come by?" she asked nervously. Zeke shook his head.

"Dead silent all night. But not even I would have fancied taking the car out on those roads last night!" he replied.

"Zeke Olsen not wanting to drive his car!" she exclaimed. "That's saying something."

"Not wanting to and knowing better are different things. Plus, between you and me, I'm not sure who I love more, Cassie or that car!"

"Well, Zeke Olsen," she said as she stood up. "Your secrets are safe with me." The way she said *secrets* intrigued him, was it a slip of the tongue? But he didn't have long to ponder. Lara reached the door, turned back, looked at him and said, "Thanks!"

"It's my pleasure," said Zeke bashfully. "But all I did was answer the door."

"You've done more than you know," she replied.

"Well, you are welcome!" he said, utterly unaware that she'd watched the previous night's events unfold from the bedroom window.

"Hey," she said, "can you call me a taxi."

"Call a cab?" he laughed. "What century are we in?"

"I don't have my phone on me," she replied ashamedly.

"Of course," Zeke replied, realising that most of her belongings were probably still at Ray's. "I tell you what," he said. "I have nothing to do. Let me finish my drink, and I'll drive you?"

"Drive? Are you sure it's not too icy for you outside?"

"Please," he replied earnestly, "it is never too cold for an Olsen!"

40

After dropping Lara off at work, he found a quiet space and parked the car. She seemed to be in a much better place than she was the previous night. Although he had found it a tad curious that she seemed far less worried about Ray's potential retribution or reappearance. Still, he couldn't dwell. The truth was he had so many mysteries swirling around in his brain, not to mention that his tally of murders now stretched to seven. The last of which was a man he'd known for many years. Oddly enough, the only thing that troubled him was that he hadn't realised sooner. He'd seen Ray for what he really was, and the world was a better place without him. The notion of someone laying hands on his soon-to-be-born daughter made him feel sick to his stomach.

Zeke had been trying to get a hold of Cassie all morning to no avail. He'd even been brave enough to try Suzie directly but got no answer. Zeke hadn't seen her in years, and as much as he needed to speak to his wife, he was relieved that Suzie didn't answer.

Setting his phone down on the vacant passenger seat, he relaxed in contemplation. He could still taste Lara's presence, and there was something about her that he couldn't quite understand. She'd seen more of the real him in the short time they had known each other than anyone else. It hadn't scared her away, and if anything, it seemed to only increase the feelings between them. It scared Zeke to think he might be falling for someone else, but he'd known himself to have his fair share of capricious moments, and her motives were still a mystery. Finding his true self and seeing what both Ray and Marguerite were capable of made him realise that so many people aren't who they appear to be. He had spent a lifetime hiding from himself, how many other people did the same thing? Zeke sat in silent contemplation that was only interrupted by the ringing of his phone. He grabbed it immediately and raised it to his ear.

"Cassie?" he said expectantly.

"No, Zeke, it's your other wife!"

"Karan?" he asked.

"That's the one," he replied in a solemn tone. "I did text you, Zeke. Are you free to talk?"

"Sorry," replied Zeke. "It's been a hectic few days."

"Well, I could really use you about now!"

"Yeah, I'm all yours, pal. What's going on? You sound off!"

"Zeke, it's about Ray! You might want to sit down for this."

Zeke listened intently as his friend began to describe what had happened; his words were laced with sadness and disbelief. Tears could be heard in his voice as he started, and it made Zeke very glad that they weren't face to face. He'd not taken the time to consider this eventuality, but he'd just killed his best friend's friend, a situation he never thought he'd find himself in. Karan was clearly in shock, and he was glad he wasn't there in person. He was in no way prepared to comfort someone on a loss of life that he'd caused.

"Woah, slow down, Karan," he said. "Just take a deep breath. What's happened?"

"Ray," Karan sobbed. "Emergency services found his car last night. Zeke, it had gone off the road."

"Is…is Ray, okay?"

"They found a body in the driver's seat Zeke, it was badly burnt, but they think it's Ray!" Karan paused, "Zeke, this is all my fault!"

"Woah, Karan, this is definitely not your fault. Okay?"

Karan sniffed, "Zeke, Ray was always drinking and driving. I should have done more."

"Karan," he said, "this is not on you, okay? There was no way you could have stopped this from happening."

Silence.

"Karan, where are you?"

"I'm at home, Zeke."

"Is Ivan with you?"

"Not at the moment."

"Okay, look, I have a few things to take care of, then I'll be right over."

"Okay, thanks."

"Just sit tight. I'll be there soon."

Zeke hung up and pushed his head back into the rest. Fuck, he hadn't thought about this! Karan was possibly the best individual he'd ever met, and he didn't deserve this. Karan was the one person he trusted in the world more than anyone, and it was reciprocated. Lying to him had been purgatorial, but Ray was a menace. He would have dragged Karan into some mess eventually, and it was up to Zeke to shield him from that. But still, this was not what he wanted. Everything said ought to be true, but not everything true should always be said. Karan could never know the truth about Ray or him. The man was the embodiment of goodness and altruism. The truth would ruin him.

41

The next few days drifted by peacefully and without event. It made for a pleasant change. Agent Jones hadn't reappeared, and it was curious, annoying even. Zeke needed to know if it was over, but it wasn't as if he could call the police to see if an Interpol agent still suspected him of murder. Especially since he'd recently added to the list. He slept slightly easier, but his gut told him something was off. The man would resurface somehow. He had to be careful.

Ray had little in the way of family or friends, and Karan was listed as next of kin. Which resulted in the poor man being asked to identify the charred remains, adding fuel to his grief. Given the conditions, the fire hadn't burnt for long. The authorities had been able to perform an autopsy and identify him from his dental records. Toxicology confirmed that Ray had been substantially over the blood alcohol limit. Given the lack of any motive, evidence to the contrary, and the conditions the crash was adjudged to have been a drunken accident.

Zeke barely had time to think as the weekend rolled around, which brought Cassie and Ivan back to their respective others in time for Christmas. It was refreshing to have some peace, but Ray's death weighed heavily on Karan's heart. Zeke felt helpless and didn't know how to fix it. Something which bothered him far more than taking a life.

Cassie was due to give birth very soon, and the impending reality was starting to sink in. In truth, he was excited but also fearful. What if his daughter took after him? Can you ever grow up to be normal with a killer for a father? It was a question he could ask of only himself, and he hoped to God that she took the lion's share of her genes from her mother. For his part, he had to do his best to shield her from the world's monsters. If people are moulded rather than made, then she needed to be protected from the horrors of creation, even if that included the real him.

It was Christmas Eve, and the pair sat eating breakfast in the kitchen. Decorations hung from the ceiling, and from where he sat Zeke could see out of the kitchen and across to the living room. The twinkle of the fairy lights held his gaze until Cassie spoke. Her voice danced into his brain like music through mist.

"We still need a name," said Cassie.

"We've got one," Zeke replied. "We're the Olsens."

"No, you idiot, for our baby."

"Shit, you're right, we do. Let's pick one now."

"Right now?" she inquired.

"Sure, why not?" he replied. "No time like the present. Plus, what if something happened to me? This might be our last moment to choose a name together."

"The only thing likely to happen to you over Christmas is me killing you," she joked.

"I'm just saying," Zeke replied. "If we don't pick one now and something does happen to me, you'll regret it for the rest of your life."

"This sounds like blackmail to me," she said.

"Actually," he replied, pointing his spoon at her, "it's extortion."

"Are you okay?" he asked. "You seem different!"

"Good different, or bad different?"

"Sharper, more alert."

"So, good different?"

"Hmm, for now!" she replied.

Zeke shovelled a spoonful of corn flakes into his mouth. He'd barely finished chewing when he said. "What about Kara?" he asked.

Cassie looked up at him suspiciously. "Cara spelt with a '*C*' or a '*K*'?"

"A '*C*'?"

"Good," she said, "because, for a minute there, I thought you wanted to name our daughter after a character from your favourite sci-fi show."

"You know, I hadn't even realised. But, hey that was a very prescient show for its time."

"Hmm," she replied, "you know what? I like it!"

"Yess," he exclaimed, "so, Kara, it is?"

"Cara it is," she said. "With a '*C*'!"

A short silence fell over the kitchen as Zeke continued to trough.

"So," she said, "what do you want to do now?"

Zeke paused for a moment as he hurriedly finished his large mouthful, "I...I," he said between bites, "I'm going to go for a run. Then I was considering midnight mass later!"

"A what?" Cassie said in surprise.

"A run," he repeated, "I run now."

"Midnight mass?"

"Yeah, my mother used to take me every year on Christmas eve. I thought it would be nostalgic and a good way to exorcise demons etc. I also still need to do my wrapping. I've only wrapped one thing so far!"

"You know, if you hadn't said that you still need to do your wrapping this close to Christmas, I'd wonder what you'd done with my husband!" Zeke laughed and finished his bowl of cereal. Once done, he stood and placed the empty bowl on the side.

"I'll use it again later," he added before she said anything. The reality was Zeke hated running. But after his late-night jog, he felt it prudent to keep up appearances. Having set the bowl down, he stooped on his way out and kissed Cassie on the head.

"I love you," he said. Cassie smiled, and he spoke again. "Once I'm back, I'll shower, and we can do whatever you want to do."

"I don't want to go to midnight mass."

"Fair." Zeke moved towards the exit, but as he got to the door, he stopped, turned back, and said, "Oh, hey Cass, I spoke to Winston's. He said you'd picked up the ring?" She looked back at him cluelessly, saying nothing. "You do have it, don't you?" Cassie paused for a moment before replying,

"Shit! Zeke, I'm really sorry. I thought I'd surprise you with it, but I must have left it at Suzie's."

"Okay, not a problem. How did it look?"

"What do you mean?"

"Well, did he do a good job?"

"Duh, of course," she replied. "Sorry, Zeke, I'm a bit forgetful at the moment. Yeah, of course, it looks great. I'll ring Suzie later, make sure she keeps it somewhere safe."

"Okay, sweetie, no hurry, huh," he stepped back into the kitchen and kissed her on the forehead. "Thanks," he said, "I owe you one!"

42

Christmas came and went in a flash, the previous week's snow had been a false dawn, and the day was typically wet and miserable. Not unlike Ray's funeral. Not one of his ex-wives attended, and the affair was small, sombre, and depressing. Karan had yet to shift himself from his funk, and the burden weighed heavy on Zeke. Here he was consoling his best friend over the death of a man who had died at his hands. He felt helpless, there was nothing he could do to help him without either admitting to what he'd done or breaking Karan's illusion of Ray.

The gloom of death exacerbated the bleakness of January, but the early arrival of *Kara Olsen* lifted it just before the end of the month. The coming of new life replaced the darkness caused by the loss of an old one, and there was cause to be thankful once more. Zeke had more than one reason to be grateful. The new year brought about more than just a few resolutions. Not one month ago, he had resigned himself to the fact that he would never see this day, and he thanked the heavens every day that he had a second chance. He'd been sober for months now. He noticed what was happening around him, saw things for how they really were, and more importantly, he had and could hold his baby girl.

Kara's birth overshadowed the fact that there had been a tragedy in the community, and Ray was fast forgotten by most. It had forced Zeke to realise just how ephemeral life was and he was glad not to be in a freefall, but he was conflicted.

Zeke was trapped between what he felt to be his new higher calling, the fear of either losing his family, his control or creating a monster. Taking the lives of the wicked had saved his soul, but like a vampire in need of blood, he lived in fear of relapse and had yet to figure out how to lead a double life. Even if law enforcement never caught up with him, he had a recurring nightmare that either one of his wife or adult daughter would ever find out what he had done. Years of love and happy memories would be shattered in an instant.

Imagine finding out that your father is a serial killer? No matter the reasons, was it something an average person could find possible to understand? Taking the law into your own hands isn't allowed. But justice rarely gets served. In killing Ray, he'd likely put a stop to a man who'd been abusing women for years. Yet if people knew what he'd done or what he was, he would be ostracised, shunned, and ultimately jailed. He was happy where he was, but he knew he needed a plan to move forward. Falling back into old ways that he had left behind wasn't an option, but neither was being exposed. He had a fine line to walk, and he needed to find the path soon.

Kara's arrival saw Cassie take up her maternity leave, and the job at the university hospital was one to which she would not return. It was an exciting time. The house was complete, Zeke had amassed good money, and once they settled as a family, Cassie would open her practice and see clients as and when it suited her. Despite not yet being forty, Zeke had plans for early retirement. With Cassie's help, he'd invested soundly and was well set up for life. The notion of retirement had both terrified and excited him. Who doesn't want to wake up for a day of their choosing every morning? But he had been worried about indulgence with the void of a vocation. Now, however, he would have all the time he needed to fill his own void whilst removing the world of its. As plans go, it fell perfectly into place for him, Cassie being the angel she was, she wanted to help even the most depraved souls. Cassie was good at her job, but not everyone could be saved. But Zeke could free the world from the ones she couldn't!

The notion even crossed his mind that they could work in partnership, a crusade to rid the world of evil, but even he knew the idea to be folly. Despite his good intentions, he could never envision a world where Cassie would be okay with murder. But it mattered not, because as he considered it Zeke remembered a quote by Mark Twain.

'There were two days of vital importance in someone's life. The day they are born, and the day they figure out why.'

Zeke had finally figured out why! He had spent his life plugging gaps, filling the vacuums with drugs, alcohol, and sleeping tablets. Constantly searching, always needing something he couldn't get. Zeke knew he was destined to be more than he was, and when wealth and stability didn't fill that gap, he knew now that he'd fallen into a spiral. Yet here he was, lucid, alive, confident, and strong. He was in no doubt he'd been saved from that fire for a reason, and he knew exactly what that was!

It had been almost a month since Ray's funeral, and Karan was still in deep stages of grief. It pained Zeke to see him so, but there was little he could do. It was a problem he'd caused.

Then as if by magic, Kara was pushing three weeks old, and much of their life revolved around her. Zeke desperately wanted to find more time for his friend Karan, but the life of a new parent was incredibly complicated. So much was already so different, and the events of New York, Interpol, police cells, and even Lara appeared as though it was another lifetime. At times he wanted to question those he knew to make sure it had happened, but it was a subject he'd rather lay to rest.

Kara had her mother's eyes, which pleased him, given that eyes are the route to the soul. Hopefully, it meant she would take after her mother and not him. She had such tiny fingers and even smaller toes. They would grow, as would her mind. She was a blank canvas, and he still had no idea how to paint it. He needed her to see the word for what it was, but not him for who he was. Their values had to match while remaining different. When their eyes met, it was like looking at another version of Cassie, but one that he had created. He held her tight and whispered,

"I will kill anyone who tries to hurt you," he was sure she'd smiled, and from that moment forward, he knew she was his.

Holding her in his arms was the closest he'd ever felt to anything, the most amount of love he'd ever experienced. Zeke had taken some time off work and had barely put her down the whole time. She was so fragile, and the world was so harsh. How could he shield her from that, from him?

The doorbell chimed, shattering his thoughts, and he realised it was far too loud. He would have to alter that lest he kill a visitor for disturbing one of Kara's naps.

"I got it," Zeke whispered loudly through the house. He set Kara down in her bassinet and shuffled to the front door. The grin on his face faded fast as he opened it to be greeted by two uniformed police officers. The sight of them made him want to curse and yell profanity. He thought this was over, but instead, he composed himself and stepped out of the house, leaving the door ajar behind him.

"Mr Olsen?" came the words from one of the officers who stood before him.

"We need to ask you a few questions."

43

Zeke stared at the two officers, momentarily motionless. A thousand thoughts rushed through his brain all at once. His head was telling him one thing and his heart another. He couldn't account for their visit, but on the other hand, could they? He'd vexed vivaciously about any and all loose ends, and there was nothing he could think of that would implicate him in anything beyond lousy timing or bad luck.

The truth was he was a venerable member of the community, and as much as his panic setting told him to flee or do something stupid. Stolid calm was all that was called for here.

"Mr Olsen," the officer repeated after a long pause.

"Yes," he replied, "sorry, officers, what can I do for you?"

"Are you okay? Mr Olsen?"

"No, not really. I have a three-week-old. I don't even know what day it is." The two men laughed. "I'd invite you inside, but she's asleep, and if you wake her, one of you is staying until she's down again!"

"First child?"

"Is it obvious?" Zeke replied. Both men chuckled once more.

"It gets easier."

"Why, do you have a manual?" More laughter.

"Look, Mr Olsen," said the Sergeant. "We're sorry to trouble you at a time like this. We're from the local station and we know it has been difficult for your family and friends recently."

Zeke nodded.

"It's probably nothing, but we're following up on a missing person report."

"A missing person?" The Sergeant nodded.

"We had a call from the sister of Agent Jones. She claims that he has gone missing. We all assumed he'd gone back to France, but no one has seen or heard from him in weeks. Since this is one of the last places he was known to be, we must follow it up."

"Yes, of course," Zeke nodded, "I haven't seen him since the day he had my house ransacked."

"Apologies for that. It would seem his warrant was unwarranted, and he departed shortly after that."

"Well, I'm sorry you've wasted a trip, gentlemen. As I said, the last place I saw him was here."

"And he's not reached out to you at all?" Zeke shook his head. "Okay, well, just keep an eye out. Off the record, word has it. He's got a reputation for his obsessions. If he shows up here, give us a call."

"Will do!" The two officers trudged back across the stones towards their car, leaving Zeke alone in his mind.

44

To compound Karan's misery, he had been left as executor of Ray's will and estate. In some ways, it gave him closure, but it also meant he had the task of dividing up the man's assets, resolving any matters, and sorting through his belongings. It brought about some much-needed catharsis and occupied his vacant time. But Ray was a slob; his filing left much to be desired, he was in debt, and the place was a mess.

Ray, being Ray, came with a proud stoicism, and he'd never confided in Karan about his financial issues. The apartment was his but had been re-mortgaged, there was credit card and loan debt, and the only actual item of value had been the vintage BMW which died along with its owner.

The projection of Ray's life was just that. Meaningless connections and short-term affairs sunk him into pleasure. He gambled he drank, he overspent. The failed marriages had stolen any notion of love, and while he seemed happy, there was clearly a deep sadness in the man. It pained Karan that he'd never reached out for help, all the nights they spent together helped his own loneliness, but he'd been selfish and short-sighted. They clearly both had their problems.

The investigation into the crash was short. The litigation took a little longer, and once Karan was finally allowed access to the property, it took him some time to work up the nerve to go around. He had thought about needing company. Ivan was naturally busy, so he decided to face his grief alone. The key to Ray's apartment weighed heavy on his keychain. As much as he attempted to ignore it, it became like Edgar Allan Poe's *Tell-Tale Heart*, beating louder and louder until he finally accepted he needed to face the inevitable.

The day came and Karan took the short drive across the village to Ray's house and stood outside the familiar green door. He paused before putting the key in the lock. It was unusual not to be greeted. He pushed open the heavy door with a heavier heart and had to fight his way through the accumulation of mail and flyers. He stooped, picked them up, and walked down the hall to the kitchen. Everything was exactly as it had been, except it wasn't. The aura of life was missing and was it not for the musty smell. He would have expected Ray to come bouncing up to him at a minute's notice. Karan knew it wouldn't be long before he stepped into this hallway for the last time, and he wasn't sure if he would ever be ready for that day.

He paused in the kitchen at the end of the hall and looked at the paltry display of photos. There were a few old ones of them together, but it occurred to him that you don't take enough. It's not as if you expect that one day you will unwittingly see someone for the last time.

Karan set the mail down on the kitchen counter and looked around him. Tears had been accumulating in his eyes for some time and soon formed a steady stream. The room had been left in a hurry, and it didn't add up. There was broken glass on the floor and half-eaten food on the side. His friend left the house angry, drunken, and sad, and he'd not been there to help him. The warning signs were there. He only wished he'd paid more attention.

Karan examined the one glass that hadn't been knocked over. It featured red lipstick around the rim, so clearly, this was an all too familiar altercation with a woman. The man never learnt. Karan moved to the window and drew back the drapes to allow what was left of the patient sunlight to enter the room.

Not knowing where to begin, he started by cleaning up. He put all the crockery in the dishwasher and switched it on. Then he removed the pungent bin liner and took it outside. When he returned, he opened a window and began sorting through the mail.

So many of the letters contained bills, final demands, and disconnection notices. It was almost too much. Why hadn't Ray just asked for help? As he set the stack down, he noticed a padded envelope that protruded in the middle. He almost ignored it were it not for the fact it wasn't sent mail. It must have been on the counter all along, and when he flipped it over, he noticed his name hastily scribbled on one side of it. Karan tipped the contents onto the table, and a small jewellery box slid out along with a folded note. None of this made any sense, so he unfolded and flattened the letter on the table and removed his glasses from his pocket and started to read. He'd barely got into the letter when a sharp knock at the door reverberated through the house. Curious to see who it might be, he placed the note down on the table, removed his glasses and set off down the corridor.

"Hey, Karan," came the voice of a female as he opened the door.

"Hi," he replied, surprised, and confused. "Oh, it's you," he said finally. "Have you done something to your hair? I almost didn't recognise you?"

"Nope!"

"Sorry, I'm useless without my glasses these days! Come on in. I could use the company. So, what brings you over here anyway?"

45

Cassie was already gone by the time Zeke woke that morning. She'd found more productivity with her time off than he had. Not that he minded, it gave him plenty of alone time with his daughter, and he liked the silent company. Cassie was hard at work starting the new practice, meaning she came and went a lot. But Kara was a low-maintenance child, and he had the added benefit of being able to tell her his secrets, knowing they were safe with her. She was like a silent, unjudging therapist who appeared to enjoy his stories. It felt odd talking to his infant daughter about murder, but he had no one else to confide in, and it was very therapeutic.

Zeke was midway through telling Kara about the second trip to New York when the now-familiar sound of the doorbell interrupted story-time. Zeke picked up Kara gently, placed her against his chest and moved towards the front door, opening it cautiously. Standing in front of them were a man and woman. From their posture and outfits, they couldn't be anything other than law enforcement. It was a sight that had struck such terror into him before, but it barely phased him. Whatever happened from here on out, he would have to get used to dodging or lying to the police. If only they knew he was doing their jobs for them!

"Detectives," he said boldly, "please come on in."

Having been ushered in, the two plain-clothed officers took a seat on the sofa and gladly accepted the coffee offered.

"So," said Zeke sitting down on the sofa and bouncing Kara gently on his knee. "What is it I can help you with?"

"It's Mr Olsen, isn't it?" Zeke nodded.

"I'm D.I. Bates," said the lady, "and this is my colleague D.S. Sparks. We were actually hoping you could help us." Zeke raised his eyebrow and looked at Kara.

"The police need our help, Kara. Should we help them?"

"She's adorable," said Bates, "How old is she?"

"Ooh, nearly a month now." As Zeke saw the fascination caused by the child in the room, his brain immediately moved to the notion that the infant instantly made him less of a threat. He settled Kara back down and said, "What is it you think I can help you with, I need to feed her soon, so I can't give you much time."

"Well, Mr Olsen, it's about Agent Jones." Zeke must have rolled his eyes, and the female sergeant spoke again.

"I'm sorry. I know what he put you and your family through. I personally can't stand the abuse of power. We're here because we're investigating him."

"Wait a second. What?" asked Zeke, confused.

"I can't go into specifics, Mr Olsen, but not long after he disappeared, we received an anonymous tip-off that he'd been receiving unusual large payments into his bank. When no one could find him, we froze his accounts and found four large unexplained deposits into his account around the time he was digging into you."

"And you think I—"

"No, quite the opposite," interjected Sparks. We think he might have been working with the gang that attacked you in New York. They were known for having ties in Europe. Given the money and his disappearance, we are starting to think that it might have been him! We just wondered if you could shed any light on the situation. Because we're at a dead-end, and as you can imagine, this doesn't look good for us."

"Well, I'll be damned," said Zeke doing his best to feign annoyance. "I'm sorry, detectives, after what he put my family through, I'd love to be able to help you, but I probably know less than you do! Fortunately, I haven't seen or heard from him in months!"

Bates nodded, "We thought it would be a long shot, but here," she said, handing him a card. "Take my number. If he does try to contact you, be sure to call us. We don't want him being a threat to you or your family."

"We can station some officers near your house for a time if you'd like?" said Sparks.

"Oh, no. I appreciate the concern, but that won't be necessary," replied Zeke picturing the notion of having the very people he was trying to elude stationed outside of his house. The two detectives then stood, and Sparks made for the door.

"Bye, cutie," Bates said, wiggling Kara's toes. Zeke went to stand, but she said. "Oh, don't worry, we'll see ourselves out."

46

Kara began to cry, and Zeke realised he had held the long-since empty bottle to her mouth for too long.

"Sorry, angel," he said, removing the container. He soothed her in his arms while considering what had just happened. Just when he thought his life had found some sort of equilibrium, something new came along.

Jones was a prick. There was no doubt about that. The man came close to ruining Zeke's life, but he was only doing his job. His disappearance had been a blessing at first, then a mystery, and now it was downright peculiar. It was feasible, but Jones didn't seem like the corrupt type. Zeke was glad he was gone. But Jones didn't strike him as a crooked cop. His disappearance made Zeke's heart happy, but his brain felt bent out of shape.

As usual, he didn't have time to dwell. They were using a babysitter for the first time today, which unsettled him. In addition, he would see Marguerite at work after recently finding out she was the catalyst for all of this. Not that it mattered. If anything, she'd done him a favour with her actions. But it did now make him question his relationship with her, as well as the extent of her involvement.

The sitter arrived exactly on time, and Zeke reluctantly handed Kara over to her. The girl was local and came highly recommended, but to Zeke, she barely appeared capable of looking after herself. Letting go of Kara's tiny hands was hard. Yet he and Cassie would have to get used to someone else taking care of their child.

After a difficult goodbye, Zeke left the house and headed in the direction of work. He glanced at his hand and still had the sense of something missing. Cassie assured him the ring was safe at Suzie's. She had even offered to post it apparently, but he wouldn't trust Suzie to put his bins out, much less do this, so he decided to wait. Still, the sooner the ring was back in his possession, the happier he would be. If only he'd known on his first flight to New York that the small band of gold would cause so many damn issues.

Zeke hoped that being back to work full time would bring a sense of *normal* back to his life. The last few months had been nonstop tension, chaos, and death. It would be nice to just sit behind a desk for a while, close a few more big deals, and then be free to fulfil his destiny.

Knock, knock.

The gentle tap at his office door restarted time. He looked up from his computer screen to see Marguerite standing in the doorway.

"Hi," she said furtively.

"Hey," said Zeke, greeting her with a smile.

"I hear you've been removed from the no-fly list?" she joked.

"I have indeed." Zeke laughed. A short silence ensued before Marguerite broke it.

"It's good to have you back," she said. "Do I take this to mean you're staying?"

"Of course," he replied. "Where else would I go?"

She shot him a bashful smile before resuming her usual composure.

"How's the baby?"

"Well, you'll have to come round and see for yourself."

"I'd like that."

Another pause.

"You've made an impression with Lara, she said.

"A good one or a bad one?" he asked.

"Good. She's full of praise," Marguerite effused. "We'll have to get you two out in the art world again once she's back."

"Back?" he asked.

"She phoned in sick this morning. I don't think it's serious."

"Oh."

"Anyway, young man, I really must be getting on. Business to attend to. I really am glad you are here. No hard feelings?"

"Not at all," Zeke said with a grin that masked his true emotions. Although he didn't trust her, she could be a formidable opponent. It would be wise to tread carefully.

With that, she disappeared, and Zeke was alone again. Yet he didn't have long with his thoughts before his office phone rang.

"Hello," he said. "Zeke Olsen here."

"Zeke?" The desperate cry resonated in his ear.

"Cassie? What's up? You never call the office."

"Zeke!" she said in a panic. "It's Karan. You need to come quickly. He's been in an accident!"

Zeke paused. This couldn't be happening.

"Zeke," she repeated. "You there?"

"Yes," he said. "Where is he?"

"Can you meet me at the hospital?"

"Of course, it's Karan!" he replied, looking at the clock on his desk. "General, right?"

"Yes."

"I'll be forty minutes max. I'll see you there."

Zeke instantly grabbed his keys and raced out of the door. He ran down the stairs, past the giant fist planet, and into the parking lot.

The hospital was a forty-minute drive on a good day, so Zeke put his foot down. Every time he thought life was levelling out, it seemed to be turning into a nightmare again. Maybe he'd already lived once; perhaps this was hell? He wasn't sure how to deal with life without Karan, and he realised he'd been nowhere near good enough to him lately.

Zeke arrived at the hospital, abandoned the car, and bustled through the main doors. A quick interrogation of the reception staff later, and he was in the lift on his way up to intensive care.

He arrived breathless and sweaty to the sight of a distraught Ivan and a panicked-looking Cassie. You can gauge a lot from a moment and the looks on people's faces. This one told him that it was serious. The fact that the usually absent Ivan was already there was ominous, and he could glean that the prognosis was bleak without even having to open his mouth.

Cassie wrapped her arms around him the moment he arrived. When he got free, he moved across to Ivan, who looked him in the eye and promptly began to sob.

"Ivan, what happened?" he opened his mouth to reply, but all that came were audible sobs. Zeke never knew what to do in these situations, so he stepped toward him and drew him in for a deep hug. Ivan put his head on his shoulder and let it all out. As he rubbed the neck of a man with whom he'd never been quite this intimate before, he thought how odd it felt to be on the other side once again. The death of his parents had been the last major tragedy he hadn't personally perpetrated. Everyone in this room was stricken with grief and sadness. Karan was the last person who deserved something terrible to happen to him, but instead of being sad, he was angry. If he was doing what he was supposed to be doing if he was truly reborn, then why was this happening?

Still trapped in an Ivan hug, Zeke looked over his shoulder and into Cassie's eyes.

"What happened?" he mouthed. But before she could reply, Ivan righted himself and spoke.

"Zeke, it's Karan. He was over at Ray's house…and…and he was sorting things out in the kitchen, he must have slipped and hit his head. Zeke," he lamented. "He's in a coma. They don't know if he's going to make it."

The words registered in Zeke's brain; an icy chill covered his soul, and he was confounded. He was so used to tragedy, pain, death, and loss. But this was Karan, his best friend! He didn't know what to do, to say, or even how to feel.

Zeke did a lot of reading and remembered discovering that the house can be a hazardous place. Every year in the United Kingdom, six thousand people succumb to household accidents that become their final act. The simple erection of a shelf or trimming of a tree can lead to death. Some three million people are forced to visit the emergency department due to domestic incidents. Home could be a dangerous place! And yet, despite that, Zeke's gut had a nagging feeling. Karan was robust and insanely careful. They had known each other for more than ten years, and he couldn't even remember the man breaking a fingernail. He was always the first to reprimand Ray for his drunk driving. He made sure everyone had their seatbelts on before pulling off, he'd never had a speeding ticket, and Zeke had never seen the man engage in any form of DIY. He would be straight on the phone if anything needed changing or fixing. Karan literally put the letter *K* in caution.

When he thought about the timing of everything, the fact that this happened at Ray's and the yet unknown whereabouts of Agent Jones made it even more curious. He had a paucity of facts, and he didn't like it. But Karan didn't have accidents!

"Zeke!"

Cassie's words broke through his chasm of thoughts like a tropical storm.

"Yeah," he said, shaking himself back into the room. Cassie placed her hand on his arm and led him a few yards down the corridor until they were out of Ivan's earshot.

"How are you doing?" she asked.

"How?" he replied. "I don't fucking know. How did this happen?" Cassie shook her head and shrugged her shoulders sadly.

"One of the neighbours heard a noise and rang the police because they thought the place was empty. When they arrived, they kicked the door in and found him face down on the kitchen floor. Looks like he fell from a stool or something?"

"Or something?" he asked. "So, what are they doing about it?" Cassie shrugged.

"Zeke, it was an accident!"

"No," he said, shaking his head. "Karan doesn't have accidents. They need to be out there looking for whoever did this!"

"Zeke honey," she said, taking his hand tenderly. "Everyone has accidents. I know it's hard to accept.

"I don't know what to tell you," she said. "Karan was there on his own. The front door was locked. They took witness statements from the neighbours. But Zeke, they aren't treating this as suspicious."

"Well, why the hell not!" he retorted angrily.

"Hey," she said, squeezing his hand harder. "I know," she said. "I know. It's Karan. We're all devastated, Zeke." Zeke nodded and realised he was probably just in pain. He took a deep breath and said.

"How's Ivan?" he asked, realising just how overwhelmed he'd be if it were Cassie lying there instead.

Cassie sighed, "I dunno. Karan wanted Ivan to go to Ray's with him, but he had to work. The first thing he said to me was that he should have been there."

"Fuck," said Zeke softly. "Cass, how has this happened? His eyes were red and teary. "What can we do? We have to do something. We can't just sit here."

Cassie nodded, "The Doctor told us they need to do an MRI scan before they know the extent of the damage. They just need to wait for the swelling to reduce."

"Wait?" he replied. "Goddammit, it's the twenty-first century. What are we waiting for?" Zeke's voice had been gradually rising with every word he enunciated. He was almost shouting as the *r* left his lips, and the commotion caused some people to stare, including Ivan. Their eyes met, and he felt the fear and sadness that lurked behind them.

Zeke composed himself, walked over to Ivan, and sat beside him. He placed his hand on his shoulder and said, "You want me to return to yours and get you some things?" It was an excellent excuse to leave. He couldn't just sit about. Ivan looked at him plaintively, then nodded.

"Shall I come with you?" Cassie asked as she walked over and joined them.

"No," he said. "You'd best stay here with Ivan. I won't be long."

Ivan raised his hand and limply handed him a house key, "Text me what you need?" Ivan nodded. Zeke took the key from his lifeless hand and put it in his pocket. Cassie walked him as far as the elevator and embraced him tenderly before he stepped back into the empty lift.

"Message me if anything changes," he managed. He caught sight of Cassie nodding as the doors closed.

The lift descended exceptionally slowly, and he hurried back through the lobby and out the main doors when it was down. He didn't feel bad about leaving. Sitting around would achieve nothing. They also had a child still in the care of a teenage babysitter. He needed space to think, and to talk to his daughter.

Zeke didn't stay long at Karan and Ivan's. He was no fool and knew that when head injuries confounded top doctors, it rarely ended well. It was eerie being there without them, and even worse because he knew it as *Karan's*, and it probably wouldn't be for much longer. He tried looking on the sunny side, but even if Karan recovered, there was every chance he'd never be himself again, and he didn't know which was worse! He collected everything Ivan had asked for and some things he hadn't and swiftly departed.

He arrived home in a hurry, paid and thanked the babysitter who was busy tweeting, or texting, took back control of his child and carried her upstairs. He set Kara down in the nursery, grabbed a bag from the guest room and moved into the bedroom to collect some items for Cassie should they spend the night.

Zeke stepped into the bedroom and switched on the light and was caught by total surprise. The bed was bright red and covered in rose petals. Cassie had also clearly attempted to make some swans out of the towels. The swans looked far more like swamp creatures, but a small jewellery box containing an all too familiar ring sat in the middle of the bed. Zeke dropped the items in his hand, bolted across the room, grabbed the ring, and held it aloft. The jubilation at finally having it back in his hands made him forget about the day's tragic events momentarily as he clutched it against his chest. The ring looked fantastic for an overhaul, something about its reappearance didn't quite add up. But Cass was always full of surprises, and it was the only bright spot on an otherwise devastating day.

Zeke sterilised the ring in as many different ways as possible, before sliding it back on his finger. After all the trouble it had caused, there was no risk worth taking. With it dried and polished, he restored it to its rightful place on his finger, looked at it and smiled. He reconciled with himself that in future, any and all personal effects should be removed before engaging in any potentially murderous activity.

Zeke collected the items and put them in the car. As he strapped Kara in and looked at her eyes, he wondered what he'd done to deserve Cassie? She'd given him so much, and now he owed it to her to keep her safe, both from the world and from who he really was.

47

Having spent the night curled up on a hospital bench Zeke arrived late and in pain for work the following day.

He was tired, bleary-eyed, and could easily have taken a day off. But he couldn't sit around hospitals all day; he needed a distraction and to think. Karan's condition hadn't changed overnight. His mind was running like a leaky faucet, and he simply had to get out of there. Something about the sterile, always old-fashioned nature of most hospitals makes you want to leave as soon as possible. The constant lights, sounds, beeps, and drips made it almost impossible for him to contemplate. He felt like he was missing something right in front of him, something or someone who had been there all along, and it was driving him crazy.

He'd hoped by going to work. He might at least speak to Lara. Beyond his infant daughter, she was one person he felt comfortable confiding in some of his darkness. It had been a long time since he'd had any close relationship with any woman besides Cassie. He needed everything Cassie was, yet he felt almost like he could be himself with Lara. They seemed to share some of the same pain or darkness. She had a story that she was yet to tell, she'd been there in New York, and it had washed off her reasonably easily. She'd even lied for him. Perhaps they shared a dark friend.

Zeke entered the gallery, kept his head down and bolted straight for his office. He powered passed the hand fist and ascended the stairs. But as he did, an absence caught his eye. He took a few steps down the spiral stairway and looked deeper. Something that should be there wasn't. It was Lara's office. The room remained, but it was empty, almost as though it had never been occupied. He descended the stairs and stood outside the open space. One of the gallery attendants passed him by, and Zeke almost physically grabbed him.

"Hey," he said, "where's Lara?"

"Ms Richards?" the man replied. "I hear she quit!"

"Quit?" he asked. "Why?" The man shrugged his shoulders.

"I just work here."

"Yea, sorry. Thanks," said Zeke as he let the man go.

As he walked the stairs back to his office, he considered what was happening. He'd found himself wanting a more exciting life, but not like this. It seemed like everything changed daily, and none of it was in his control.

Why had she quit? Why hadn't she said anything? Zeke trudged up the spiral stairs and removed his phone from his pocket. He scrolled to her number and began to dial. But suddenly, a ghostly thought entered his mind, and he quickly cancelled the call. What if she knew something? Was she part of what was going on? A flash of panic shot over Zeke, and he struggled to breathe. He ducked into the nearest bathroom and locked himself in a stall.

Zeke sat with his back to the toilet door. His life was falling apart around him, his friends were disappearing or revealing major character flaws, and he didn't know who to trust. He'd probably been hours away from going to jail for the rest of his life but for the odd disappearance of Agent Jones. As he leaned against the wall, he recalled the feeling he'd had in one of his dreams. The sense of being lost and the absence of people he loved was beginning to terrify him. Was this his punishment or his reward?

The rest of the day went by uneventfully. No one had an accident or died! Zeke managed to distract himself by doing some work. With Marguerite away, the day-to-day affairs were under his control, and he committed fully to the task. When it hit six, he felt the strain and decided to stop for the day. He'd heard little from Cassie, and there was nothing to suggest that Karan's condition had either improved or worsened. No news is good news, as the adage says, but no news is hell!

Zeke had spent some time sniffing through the personnel files during the day and had managed to dig out Lara's address. He'd resisted the urge to call her. But with Cassie presumably still at the hospital, he had nowhere particular to be. Lara's apartment wasn't far from work, so he took the short drive over.

Zeke arrived outside the stark stone building. The rain was lashing down; he was weary and didn't know what he was doing here. The elements battered against him as he held down the buzzer, and his usual stolid self seemed to disappear. The next few moments could be make or break. Getting an answer might not be what he wanted, and getting no answers meant he'd just got soaked for nothing!

Zeke held down the buzzer far longer than was socially acceptable, but her car was outside, so he assumed her to be home. It was a video bell; she would know who it was. Then after what felt like an epoch of depressing the button, it clicked, and he heard the unmistakable tone of Lara's voice.

"Zeke?" Her words flickered slightly, and she sounded scared.

"Can we talk?"

Silence. "It's not a good time right now, Zeke."

"Lara, what's going on?"

"Zeke," she replied, "you're the one person I want to talk to right now and the only one I can't."

"What does that mean? Lara, it's really wet out here. Can I come in?"

"I'm sorry, Zeke."

"Can you at least tell me why you're leaving? Is it me?"

"Kinda, but it's not what you think. Please, Zeke, just go!" she said diffidently. "I just need to get away for a while. Look, I never wanted to hurt you; please just stay away." A pause. "Hopefully, I'll be able to explain one day. Goodbye, Zeke."

"Lara, Lara!" The static of the intercom went quiet, and Zeke realised he was talking to himself.

Upstairs, Lara withdrew her finger from the intercom and slumped to the floor. Once there, she began to cry. Her apartment was sparse, and most of her belongings had been boxed up, a large bag sat near the front door, and a printed boarding pass dated for the end of the week lay on the table near it.

48

Ivan stayed in the hospital as much as he could. Official visitation hours don't necessarily apply when your spouse is clinging to life, and the shock of the incident made him reassess his commitments. He was remorseful at how much time he'd spent away from home. The weight of being a lousy husband added to his pain, and he was almost disconsolate. It was practically an hour's journey back to his house, so he'd checked into a local hotel, cancelled his engagements, and barely moved from Karan's side. Karan had sustained significant trauma to his head, and although Ivan was clinging to hope, the prognosis was bleak. Cassie dedicated as much of her time to running interference. She was good at dealing with these situations both personally and professionally.

Zeke split his time between work, the hospital, and his own head. Despite no evidence to the contrary, he couldn't accept that what had happened to Karan had been an accident. He saw little of Cassie and Kara, and the business with Lara troubled him. Marguerite was out of the country, Ray was dead, Karan was in a coma, and Ivan was a wreck. Everything had changed in the six months since they'd finished the house. Zeke was lost and almost wholly alone; his newfound sleep cycle had been interrupted, and a dark feeling was creeping back into his mind. There had been a small window of time when he thought everything was falling into place, yet here it was completely falling apart.

The following week drifted by without event, something he usually found tiresome. But in the current climate, a week without death, tragedy, or scandal was a relief, and he had the feeling that it was too good to be true.

He felt Lara's absence at work, sepia was seeping in, the lack of death was one thing, but ennui always troubled him. He was restless and could feel anger and rashness stirring inside of him. Life had been moving forward, yet here he was worse than ever. He was almost at rock bottom, and he didn't know which way was up.

Zeke was sitting at his desk staring into thin air when his phone rang.

"Hello."

"Oh, good morning. Is that Mr Olsen?"

"Speaking."

"I'm sorry to trouble you at work, Mr Olsen. I appreciate you might be busy!" Zeke moved the phone from his ear and took note of the number. The incoming call came from the accounting firm he'd hired a few years ago. Numbers were not his strong point, and with all the money that came in and out, he'd felt it prudent to have it handled professionally. The firm and its employees were lifeless but pragmatic. In Zeke's mind, people who lived for numbers saw the world differently.

"No, it's fine!" he replied politely. "What can I do for you?"

"Mr Olsen, my name is Ms Sherrington. I'm the accountant who handles your wife's new business account."

"Yes, Ms Sherrington, I remember you!" he said desperately trying to picture her. "What's up? I'm afraid Cassie is unavailable at the moment."

"Well, actually, Mr Olsen, it's you I need to speak to."

"Go on," he replied, intrigued.

"Well, Mr Olsen, you asked us to ring you if there were any irregularities with the account."

"That I did," he replied, mildly concerned. "There's nothing wrong, is there?"

"It's just a courtesy call, Mr Olsen. But I just wanted to tell you that the account is overdrawn. If you want to avoid fees, you'll need to add funds before the end of the working day."

"Okay, Ms Sherrington, thanks for that," he replied placidly. "I'll sort it out this afternoon."

Zeke set the phone down on his desk and tipped his head back to look at the ceiling. He'd put in excess of one hundred and fifty thousand pounds in that account! Surely this was some kind of mistake? He knew that Cassie had been looking at premises and all the related costs, but the fact was there should have been enough money to buy almost anything. With no personal access to the account, he hastily transferred a large sum into it and did his best to shelve his thoughts. With everything that was going on, he'd speak to Cassie later. It was just money, and he was sure there would be a logical explanation.

49

The weekend rolled around and brought Cassie home with it. Ivan was still camped out near the hospital, Karan's family and friends had descended, and there had been little change in his condition. So much had happened in the space of the last few weeks and months it was impossible to know where to start with anything, and despite having a lot on his mind, Zeke was glad just to have his family back together.

"There are my girls," he said as Cassie walked through the door carrying Kara, he was thrilled to see them. Zeke held them both as tightly and tenderly as he could for as long as possible before letting go. As much as he'd missed Cassie, it was the silent talks with his daughter that he craved. She was like his confessional box, and a catharsis exuded from it.

"How are you?" he asked her sincerely.

"Tired, both of us. But we're okay."

"Karan?" Cassie shook her head soberly.

"It doesn't look good, Zeke."

"But we have hope, right?"

"We do," she said, "we do."

Cassie departed for the stairs, ascended, and set about sorting herself out. Alone with Kara, Zeke took her into the kitchen and set her down safely. Her eyes were open, but she wore a sleepy, tired expression. She had already experienced so much in her short life, and Zeke wondered how much weirder her life might get. Deciding that cooking was an unnecessary effort, he ordered some food on his phone and settled down to do some reading.

The food arrived in time for Cassie's reappearance, and the three of them ate in the kitchen, Pizza was a wise choice for weary hands, and he even allowed himself a beer to wash it down. The sound of chewing filled the room. Zeke looked at Kara. Her eyes were closed and deciding that she would be absent from any potentially awkward conversation, he opened his mouth and asked.

"Hey, Cass? I had the accountant on the phone this week. I gotta ask—"

"Oh my gosh, Zeke," she interrupted. "I'm so sorry. Did I take the account overdrawn?" He nodded. She finished her mouthful, took a sip of her drink, and said.

"I'm sorry, honey. I was buying lots of things for the business. And then I stumbled across a surprise."

"What surprise?" he asked.

"Well, it's a surprise, Zeke," she said. Zeke laughed. "All I can tell you is that it might involve a certain someone's birthday."

"Oh my god," replied Zeke. "It's next month?" With everything going on, his impending fortieth had totally slipped his mind. "That's an expensive birthday," he said.

"It's not every year you turn forty."

"Thank God," he replied. "Thanks, you remember everything." Cassie smiled.

"But," he said, "Cass, that's a business account. Purchases need to be accounted for." Cassie laughed maniacally.

"Since when does Zeke Olsen worry about things like that?" Zeke took a moment to laugh at himself, conceding that it was unlike him. But he'd had a period of reconciliation lately. Doing anything that could attract any unnecessary scrutiny was not okay anymore. Not with the plans he had.

"I'm turning forty," he said casually. "Maybe I'm becoming more sensible. Plus," he said, squeezing Kara's foot softly. "We have a baby now. We have to be there for her."

"You're right," she conceded. "I...I just wanted it to be a surprise, especially given everything that's happened. I figured if I used the joint account, you'd notice."

"I would," he said, laughing.

"Anyway," she continued, "I mean, there is space in the garage." Zeke's ears pricked at the talk of either motor vehicles or machinery.

"Oh, well, in that case," he said jokingly. "Just make sure you get receipts to Sherrington. I'm sure we can write whatever it is off as a business expense. Hey, we can probably even claim some of the tax back."

"There's my husband!" she said, smiling. "All this talk of running, and prudent financial decisions. I was beginning to worry where you'd gone!"

"I'm still here," he smiled. The pizza, beer and jovial conversation were a welcome and much-needed distraction.

"Hey," he said, motioning towards Kara. "We should make the most of this. Think of this moment in thirteen years?"

"Oh gosh," chuckled Cassie. "Imagine if there's more of them?"

"So, when do you reckon you'll start seeing patients?" he asked, trying to hide his impatience and begin his new calling.

"Soon, hopefully," she said, "why? Do you want rid of me already?"

"Of course not," he said, "it would just be nice seeing you do something you love."

"Well, we have to think about Kara, Zeke."

Zeke stood and removed the dirty plates. "What if I retired?" he said, moving towards the dishwasher.

"Then I guess you'd be a househusband. Can you cope with that?" Zeke looked at Kara asleep in her cot.

"I sure can," he said.

"Then go for it. You know I'll always support you."

As he passed her, he stopped, bent, and kissed her head.

"It's so good having you both home."

50

Zeke hadn't been back at work full-time for very long, but he knew he needed to get away from it. Marguerite had offered him some compassionate leave, and he took it gladly. She was still an unknown in his mind, given what had happened in New York. He was learning daily that you never really know anyone. He hadn't even been familiar with himself until lately.

He wasn't much use anyway; he spent the bulk of his days trying to connect dots that he couldn't find. He'd taken his concerns about Karan's accident up to the local police, but as compassionate as they were, it was just an unfortunate accident to them, and he couldn't articulate why he felt the way he did without implicating himself in various crimes. They had done their due diligence to their credit, but there was nothing to suspect foul play. They'd taken evidence from the scene, but there was no forced entry or sign of intruders. The only fingerprints and DNA found were from people who frequented the place. Other than Zeke's hunch, there was nothing, he felt powerless, guilty, and worst of all, he might be wrong. Denial is a strong factor of grief, and there was absolutely no line of inquiry to pursue outside of his gut.

Being powerless bothered him, and despite there being nothing to follow, Zeke figured he would use his time to make some deductions of his own. An investigation is only ever as good as the enthusiasm of those investigating. To the police, it seemed like an accident, looked like an accident, and therefore probably was an accident. They weren't suspicious, and in Zeke's mind, it meant it was unlikely they would find something they weren't looking for. Zeke knew both men well, and he was confident he would spot anything that didn't add up.

Zeke arrived at Ray's flat and stood in front of the taped-up green door. He reminisced about the night he'd come here to see Ray looking for answers. It wasn't that long ago, and yet so much had changed since. Zeke pushed the damaged door open and stepped through the police tape. There was death in the air, and it had become a haunted house of its own making. This would be intense. Either he would find something, or he wouldn't, and he wasn't sure which one he preferred. The place had been largely undisturbed since tragedy befell Karan, and his dried blood remained where he had fallen. Much to his despair, the blood aside, there was little to suggest anything had happened here.

Zeke wandered around, picking things up and putting them down; he observed everything and saw nothing. The flat was a literal dead end, and after hours of prodding, he sat down on a stool in the kitchen and placed his head in his hands to think. He cast his mind back to the night he despatched of Ray, and that was when it hit him. Shortly before Ray arrived, he'd switched off the security cameras! Was it possible Ray had surveillance? Because knowing Ray, it would likely be concealed. When a quick but detailed search of the premises drew a blank, Zeke sat in the living room dejected.

Zeke conceded that he would find nothing here, raised himself and moved down the corridor and back out the front door. It was severely misshapen from forced entry, and shutting it required some effort. But just as he went to yank it closed, his eyes were drawn to the doorbell, and that's when it hit him. How had he been so stupid?

Ray had a video doorbell. The police said no entry had been forced, but that didn't rule out the fact that Karan might have let his attacker in. Crimes of passion were often committed in the heat of the moment. If Karan had opened the door to someone, then they might have rung the bell.

Zeke entered the house, located the computer, and booted it up. To his relief, it wasn't password-protected. Fortune favoured him once more when he was relieved to find that the video files backed up to the computer.

The bell had only been activated four times that day. The first one was the postal service, the second a delivery, the third presumably a door-to-door salesperson, and the fourth he couldn't believe. It didn't quite make sense, but the only other visitor that day had been Lara!

51

Zeke was angry, tired, and the devil inside of him was on a tirade, he was upset and almost heartbroken. The latter two emotions didn't make much sense to him, but Karan had become the closest thing to family he'd ever really known. Lara had seemed to be an ally, a welcome one at that. But why was Lara there that day? His kinship with Lara made his feelings even harder to process, but he had to confront her. Karan was kind, and he would have let her in that day. Can that be someone's fatal flaw? Their altruism? Karan and Ray were close enough that he would have known about Ray and Lara's relationship. Karan would gladly have shared his grief with hers, and as inconceivable as it might seem, it could have resulted in his accident. If recent events had taught him anything, it was that almost no one was above suspicion. Perhaps she had returned to collect her items, Karan didn't know that Ray had abused her, maybe it had come to light and things had become heated.

Zeke knew two things. Lara had been there the day Karan died, and she was mysteriously packing up and leaving. It was suspicious. She had to know more than she was letting on, and his gut told him someone had attacked Karan. Ray said he had a failsafe the night that he died. Maybe Karan had found it when Lara was there? Perhaps he knew the truth? Regardless, it didn't matter. He'd rather go to prison than see something happen to Karan. Many people were not fit to live on the planet; Karan was not one of them! He had to find Lara. She was avoiding him for a reason, and he needed to know why.

Lara was leaving town. That much was true, but she'd yet to leave. She wouldn't return his calls or messages, but the younger generation is naïve regarding social media. Gone are the days when you would put your neighbour's address into your satellite navigation in the event it was stolen. Social media trends and the endless need to validate life with constant updates meant people actively shared their locations online. There is, for the most part, very little you can't garner about someone or their daily routine if you follow them online.

The term *follow* was something of a paradox to Zeke. To *follow* someone in real life is insidious and borderline creepy, but doing it online is now perfectly normal. In Zeke's case, he had followed her to her garage, which was located in a unit on the outskirts of town. She had posted that morning that she would spend most of the day cleaning out her garage, then proceeded to check in there. Garage clusters are usually found few and far between, and with the name, it didn't take Zeke long to track it down. He needed to talk to Lara, he required answers before she left, and he figured the relative privacy of a garage block on a Saturday afternoon would be the perfect place.

Zeke found the block and drove past slowly. Lara's car was parked up near a garage door that was ajar. It was reasonable to assume she was there, so he kept driving.

The sky was darkening as he walked back on foot. He parked a fair distance away to avoid being seen in the vicinity. The sun was packing up for the day, and it was dusk when he arrived. Her car was still outside, and the place was otherwise deserted. He'd dressed as non-descript as possible, left everything he owned in the car save a small torch, and even removed the ring from his finger. He'd taken the house keys off his chain and left them in the car and stashed the car key somewhere safe in its vicinity.

Zeke arrived near the garage and waited. Darkness began to set in, and he paused long enough to ensure no one was around. Throwing his hood up, he crept silently under cover of dusk and slipped himself in the gap in the small opening of the garage door, closing it stealthily behind him, leaving the two of them alone in the enclosed space.

"Zeke," Lara exclaimed with surprise as he entered. She looked uncomfortable, and her voice trembled as she said, "What are you doing here? You can't be here."

"I know you went around to Ray's flat after he died, Lara."

"So," she said.

"What were you doing there?"

"Please, Zeke," she said meekly as she backed away from him. "You just need to go!"

"I'm not leaving until I get answers, Lara! What happened to Karan?"

"Zeke, I'm in danger the longer I stay here, please. Go!"

"Talk to me, dammit, Lara!" He slammed his fist against the wall, and the noise startled her. "From what are you running? What did you do to Karan? Why did you go back to the house?"

"You wouldn't believe me if I told you, Zeke. No one would. I don't even know where to start."

"The beginning Lara. Neither of us is leaving until you talk to me." Tears rolled from Lara's eyes, and she sat on a bench. "I can't win, Zeke. It doesn't matter what I tell you. Either you won't believe me, or you will, and you'll hate me."

"Just tell me, Lara!"

"Okay," she said, then paused. "But just know I've waited my whole life to meet someone like you. I don't know how it's come to this. You deserve better, and I have no idea what happened to Karan?"

"Don't! Just talk, no lies. Tell me, Lara. I'm getting impatient."

"Okay," she replied, bracing herself. "But please don't interrupt. Just listen, promise me that?" Her eyes begged a sincerity, so Zeke nodded and took a seat. The two sat at opposite ends of the dimly lit garage. Lara looked at him and then opened her mouth to speak.

"Ray knew what you'd done, or at least he thought he did. That's when things changed. He became obsessed with the investigation. He desperately wanted something over you. I hated it, and he wasn't after justice. It seemed like pride or jealousy, and he needed money.

"He had me pose as your wife, collect the ring from the jeweller and bring it back to him. But Zeke, I didn't want to. I took it to him that night, but when he told me his plan, I refused to give it to him. That's when he got angry, overpowered me, and took it. After that, I fled straight to you. I tried to tell you, Zeke. Please believe me, everything I've done is for you. That's why you need to trust me when I tell you that you're in danger." Zeke listened. She sounded genuine, but then so had everyone recently.

"This doesn't make sense, Lara. What danger? Cassie collected the ring. Please, don't lie to me, my head is enough of a mess. If you didn't hurt Karan, then who did? If it wasn't you, then who? Jones, Marguerite?

"Think about it, Zeke. What did you think Ray had on you? What else was there? Why would I lie about that?"

"Okay, assume I believe you? You're saying that both my wife and the jeweller lied to me? That even though you gave the ring to Ray it ended up in Cassie's possession. Lara, I thought you and I were friends? How can you lie to me about Cassie like that?" Lara shook her head. As he studied her, he realised that every mention of Cassie's name seemed to disturb her.

"Listen to what you've just said Zeke, think about it. Did the jeweller even meet Cassie?"

"No, you're lying. I thought you would be smarter than to expect me to take your word over that of my wife," he said. "It also still doesn't explain what you were doing at Ray's house that day."

"I went for you, Zeke. I knew he had it there. I couldn't let it fall into the wrong hands."

"Except the house wasn't empty when you got there, was it Lara? What did you do to Karan?" Zeke grew angry and stood. He moved towards her and repeated. "What did you do to Karan?"

"Nothing Zeke, no one answered the door!"

"I need you to start making sense, Lara!" She started to panic, as though something had set her off, and she was almost physically shaking when she said,

"I can't, Zeke. She'll kill me, and I'm scared she'll kill you too. Zeke, just let me go. Please, I'm terrified. The longer I stay here, the more danger we're in." Zeke approached her so that they were face to face.

"What happened at Ray's?"

"I rang the doorbell, but no one answered. So, I walked back to my car, and that was when she confronted me. There was this look in her eyes, and it was petrifying. She told me to leave, get as far away from you as possible and never come back...or else—"

"Or else what, Lara?"

"She'd kill me! Zeke, I'm begging you. You have to believe me; I only got close to Ray to get near to you. I was just trying to make things right. Zeke, I lov—"

"Who's 'she' Lara?"

"You wouldn't believe me if I told you." The misinformation, the lies, the warped mind games were messing with his head. The injury to Karan clouded his judgment, he'd never known grief like this. He felt an anger brewing inside of him; he knew he was emotionally compromised. He wanted to believe Lara, but she was accusing his wife of lying while his best friend was probably dying in a hospital bed. She was holding something back, he could tell; fury overcame Zeke and he stepped toward Lara and lifted her to her feet.

"Tell me," he demanded. Lara looked at him, and he at her. The terror in her eyes was absolute, and he felt that bond for a moment. Was she telling the truth? He was confused, angry, and hurt. Perhaps she was right? In his moment of hesitation, Lara pushed him to the floor and made a desperate attempt to reach the garage door. Fuelled by rage, Zeke sprang to his feet and caught up with her as her hand reached the handle, wrapping his muscular arm around her neck and pulling her back into the room. The pair fell back onto the floor and struggled on the ground, but Zeke's grip was firm, he'd had enough of lies, and there was now little doubt in his mind that innocent people don't run. She was obsessed with him, and Karan must have stumbled upon the truth. She'd silenced him for Zeke's sake, which was a mistake, one that would be her last.

Lara's feet thrashed against the floor as the last of her air gave out, she fought hard, but Zeke's grip was true. She opened her mouth to try and speak but emitted nothing but gasps. It wouldn't be long now. But just as he thought it was done, he felt a sharp pain in his upper thigh. Looking down, he saw that she'd managed to reach out, grab a screwdriver that had fallen on the floor in the commotion and driven it deep into his leg. The pain was immense. As blood gushed from the wound, Lara continued to fight as he struggled to maintain his grip. Zeke dug deep, tightening his grasp as hard as he could. He felt his life force slipping away, his eyes began to close, and opening them became increasingly difficult. He held on for as long as possible until they shut one last time, and everything went black.

52

The ceremony had been short and the day long. The reception was all but over, and people had started to leave. The lights were fading back on, and the pair were alone on the dancefloor, arm in arm. Zeke held Cassie tight as they had one last dance. She nestled deep into his chest, and he glanced down at his new bride. One of the spotlights illuminated the top of her head, and she appeared to him like an angel.

They held each other tight as they danced around the rustic chamber that would one day become their living room. The music faded out, and he could see through a gap in the panels and out into the brush. He remembered acknowledging that it would make for an excellent place for his study. It looked out over the grassland and nature, perfect for his most profound contemplation.

They'd made most of their goodbyes before returning to the dancefloor, and they watched guests depart as they continued to waltz away in silence. It was late, and the room had emptied fast, leaving just a few who remained. Karan, Ivan, and Ray were amongst the last to go, and they joined the dancing duo and hugged each other fondly before departing. Once they were alone, Zeke looked at Cassie and asked, "Should we change before leaving, or do you want to go like this?" Cassie looked down at her red dress, then at his elaborate suit.

"I'm not changing."

"No, you are not," he replied.

"Well," she said, "I suppose we ought to get our monies worth!"

Zeke laughed, "Like this, it is then." He looked at her and smiled, "Are you packed?" She nodded.

"Are you?"

"Ish."

"When does the taxi arrive?"

"I'm pretty sure it's already here!" he said. "One of the benefits of not having any walls is that I can see straight out of the living room."

"It also means we don't have to worry about locking up," Cassie replied. "Should I go wait in the cab?" Zeke nodded.

"What time's our flight?"

"Five-thirty?"

"Eugh, what time is it now?"

"Nearly twelve!"

"I hate you!" she said jokingly.

"It was the cheapest I could get, and a hotel would be a waste of money. Anyway, there's champagne in my bag. We'll take the party to Heathrow." Cassie nodded, kissed him on the cheek, and made her way to the waiting car. He watched her leave before stumbling across the room. He walked uneasily between the beams, made his way across to the garage, and stepped inside to grab their honeymoon luggage.

The door shut suddenly behind him, and he was encased in darkness. He took a step forward, tripping in the shadows. As he fell, he found himself caught in freefall, flailing in an abyss, ever falling, never landing. "Cassie," he called out in the dark.

"Cassie? Cassie!"

Zeke sat upright in a panic. His head spun from the movement. He was lightheaded and exceptionally cold. As he returned to his senses, he looked down at his feet and scuffled away in shock. The movement drew his attention to the wound on his leg, and he did his best to stifle a moan. He looked across and saw Lara's limp, lifeless body, and he was in no doubt she was dead. He moved cautiously to the wall and propped himself up. The motion started the bleeding again, and he knew that if he didn't act soon, he would have no blood left to bleed. Zeke reached out and grabbed a roll of packing tape, wrapping it around the top of his thigh as best he could, the significant tool would have to remain for now, and the pain was relentless.

Bleeding addressed, he slumped his head back against the wall and screamed internally. He hadn't come here with the intention of killing Lara, and the insecurity surrounding what had happened weighed on his mind, as did the loss of another he thought a friend. He'd created a life full of close-knit relationships on purpose, and now he was finding out that he might not know any of them. Lara's words seemed sincere, but her actions said otherwise. He was confused, conflicted, sad, and most of all, he needed to get away from here before he bled to death. Who had Lara meant by *she*? Could it be Marguerite? It was at times like this he was eternally thankful for Cassie because he was learning there was no one else he could trust.

Cleaning up his blood was painful, and so was every time he saw Lara. He really thought that they shared a bond and his heart almost broke at the sight of her. She looked as though she could be sleeping. He never wanted this.

Satisfied that he'd removed any trace of him being there, he tipped over some boxes and scattered enough things around so that should anyone find her body, it might look like a robbery gone wrong. It was a loose end for now, but with her impending departure announced to the world, it could be months before anyone discovered her body.

Having made the sage decision to leave all his personal effects in the car, his main concern now was making it back before passing out.

By the time he got back to his vehicle, Zeke was almost done. He was delirious and confused. He wagered that he had never lost this amount of blood before in his life, and of all the fucked-up things that had happened recently, this was by far the worst. Having retrieved the key, he used the last of his adrenaline to set up a bodged attempt to change a tyre, giving him a tenuous explanation for the screwdriver in his thigh, crawled back into the car, dialled 999, removed and disposed of the tape. Then he sat back as blood poured onto the leather seat. A tear rolled from his eye as he closed them, sat back, waited, and hoped.

53

Zeke opened his eyes and stared up at the hospital ceiling. He wasn't dead. Although was there to be a hell, he reckoned it would look a lot like a hospital. He awoke to see Cassie doting over him, and the look of relief in her eyes when he came around was immeasurable. He sat up gingerly and took note of his infant daughter smiling at him from across the room, and he smiled back. Of all the absurd things he'd done in his life, that was the closest he'd come to losing it, and God was he glad to be alive.

Lara's death shook him. He figured she must have been lying. People will say anything to save themselves. But there was a nagging feeling in the back of his mind. What had she meant? Lara kept saying *she*, and that he was in danger. Of all the fallacies he might have heard or seen, the look of terror in her eyes wasn't one of them. He'd long considered Marguerite to be something of a sociopath. It was a topic that had always intrigued him, and he remembered reading that the majority of those who prospered in business had sociopathic tendencies. It was what enabled them to succeed. Perhaps it had been Marguerite? She sent them back to New York after the initial set-up after all. It would require further investigation, and he certainly couldn't trust her. Aside from Cassie, he didn't think he could trust anyone.

Still, as he looked at the room and saw his small family, he realised that was all he needed, they had let so many people in, and most of them had let them down. He had a family to protect, and the world was full of people who would otherwise do them harm. He'd been spared from so many brushes with death or jail lately, which couldn't be chance. Zeke had spent his whole life seeking his purpose, and if there was a higher power in the world, they couldn't be making his destiny much clearer to him now.

"God strengthens," he muttered to himself. Cassie, who was just out of earshot, realised he was coherent and dashed over.

"What did you say, honey?" He looked at her lovingly and said,

"I was just thanking God I was alive." She hugged him gently and said,

"Give them a thanks from me too."

After she hugged him, she reached into her bag, removed the screwdriver, and presented it to him. "I told them you'd want it back!" He accepted it hesitantly as the memory of Lara's last stand recollected vividly in his mind. He supposed it would at least serve as a painful reminder. "What were you doing anyway? We have breakdown cover for exactly this reason! You could have died!"

"I know, I know," he replied.

"The surgeon said that had it been an inch deeper, you would have bled to death in minutes! You know you'll be off your feet for some time?"

"I know," he said. "Cass, I'm sorry. I've not been the best husband lately."

"No, it's fine," she said, moving towards him gently. "I'm just so glad you're alive." She smiled but then paused solemnly. "Zeke, I have something to tell you." Zeke braced himself. He hoped Lara's body hadn't been found. He didn't like getting news anymore, and he'd changed his mind. No news was all he ever wanted to hear.

Cassie sat next to him and held his hand oh so softly. Her eyes welled up as she looked him straight in his. Her lips quivered, and she paused for a moment before saying,

"Karan didn't make it! he's dead, Zeke!

54

Karan's funeral was a lively affair, as lively as one can be. He was a popular, affable man who would have wanted to go out in style. It felt as though the whole village was in attendance; the entire town mourned.

It took life a few months to settle following the recent events. It had become like a saga of *Midsummer Murders*, and like the show, it was amazing that anyone was still alive. Karan's loss shook Zeke, and he might have even relapsed were it not for his daughter.

Cassie had her practice up and booming. With a leg to heal and a lack of faith in Marguerite, Zeke resigned and spent his days recuperating at home with Kara. She was an avid listener and great confidant, he didn't know what he would do without her, and it gave him greater motivation to begin what he considered to be his life's work. The thought of a creature like Ray treating his daughter the way he had Lara made his blood boil, and he needed the power that it gave him to occupy his grief. Of course, some kinks were to be worked out, but he was useless until the leg injury healed. But it gave him time, and he could fix himself by redeeming the world. He just had to work out how to separate that from his family life. He could never be caught, and they could never find out.

Now that the dust and ashes had settled, the Olsens could finally enjoy the place they built to live. Cassie was busy with her new job, but it didn't matter. It gave him time to plan, time with Kara.

It was early May, and the weather was particularly remarkable. It was just after five, the sun was high in the sky, and the temperature was still in the steady twenties. The weather forecast promised a sunny spell, and he thought it would be an excellent night for their first BBQ in the new house.

He set Kara down in her bouncer, and she supervised as he dragged the patio furniture from the garage and into the yard. He then wheeled the BBQ out and attached it to the gas cylinder. He assumed Cassie would be home soon and knew he had some frozen Angus steaks stashed deep in the 'coffin' freezer. They could eat al fresco and start afresh.

He lit the BBQ, and the flames roared to life. The fire used to trigger him, but as he watched them dance before him, he knew he'd found some peace. Zeke placed Kara in the movable carrier, picked her up and hobbled into the garage. He set her down in her seat on the floor in the middle of the room and moved towards the freezer.

He hadn't even seen it in months, and the memories of another life made him reminisce as he wrapped his fist around the handle. It dawned on him that he hadn't used it since they moved in, and he was surprised Cassie hadn't demanded they get rid of it, given how much she hated it. Before he opened it, he looked back at Kara and smiled.

With his hand wrapped around the lever, Zeke tugged at the freezer door, but it didn't budge. Zeke had considerable strength, yet he'd barely moved the hatch. He reluctantly crouched down to ascertain what was hindering it, and as he ran his eye along the seam, he realised that it hadn't been shut properly. It had been working overtime and was sealed shut with ice. He shuffled across the garage, found a hammer, and then dug around in his toolkit. Ironically, the first thing his hand came across was the six-inch screwdriver that had almost taken his life. The memory of the loss of Lara still haunted him, but it was the perfect instrument to defrost a freezer. He smiled at Kara again, who looked at him curiously before he returned to the freezer with determination.

Using the screwdriver and hammer, he chipped away at the accumulated ice until he broke the seal. Bending down was still painful, so he tossed the hammer onto the floor. But not wanting to leave a pointed instrument that had already nearly killed him lying about; he tucked the screwdriver carefully down the back of his jeans.

Zeke yanked the door open and stared down into the icy abyss. The cold met the room's warmth, and frozen steam filled his gaze rendering him momentarily blind. The top layer of the freezer was covered in built-up ice, it was like looking down at a glacier, and he wasn't sure what he was observing. Zeke rolled his sleeve up and leaned over, reaching deep into the large chest. He ferreted with his hand until it connected with something that wasn't a chunk of ice and wrapped it around the first object he found.

His hand was cold, and his senses numb. He still couldn't see what he was holding, but after years of shaking them, he was in no doubt as to what it was. A shudder shot up his arm and into every fibre of his being as he wrapped his hand around the frozen fingers, his heart told him it couldn't be possible, but his brain was unmistaken. What he held in his hand was that of another.

Zeke recoiled in shock, dropping the arm back into the freezer. He fell to the floor in horror and closed his eyes.

Zeke sat hunched against the appliance. He rocked slowly back and forth as he tried to convince himself this wasn't real. But he wasn't dreaming, there was a body in his freezer, and he had a fair idea of to whom it might belong.

When he finally came to terms with what was happening, he stood up slowly, turned about and gradually looked down into the freezer.

With the large door left wide open, the surrounding heat had crept in and pervaded the unit. The ice was thawing fast, and Zeke's fears were confirmed when his eyes met the cold dead ones of what was once Agent Jones! He placed his hands on the edge of the freezer and gripped it hard. His head began to spin, and he felt as though he was going to be sick. As much as he didn't want to believe it, there was only one possible explanation, the penny dropped in his head, and suddenly everything made sense.

Zeke barely had time to process his thoughts when he realised that he and Kara were no longer alone. A presence had ghosted into the room. He felt it in his soul. A scent accompanied it he would recognise anywhere, and he turned about on the spot very slowly.

55

Cassie stood between Zeke and the door, Kara in the middle, an innocent bystander as the standoff began. The woman opposite him looked like his wife, smelt like his wife, and even moved like her, but this was not her. Cassie had crept into the garage like a poet hidden, and stood menacingly in the doorway, the cold dead look in her eyes serving only to confirm what he already knew.

The silence was almost eternal, as though she was waiting for him to catch up. He'd been so blind, and the whole thing made sense. It was Cassie all along! She'd killed Jones and faked his disappearance. He'd been in their freezer for months. It explained the missing money, her absences, and even their connection. Everything he'd chalked up to fate had actually been his wife.

A knot formed deep in the pit of his stomach, and the crushing feeling of nausea descended upon him once more, he suddenly felt extremely heavy, and he gripped the edge of the freezer for stability.

He looked at Cassie as she looked at him, she had yet to say a word, and the quiet was deathly. Then without warning, she moved into the room towards him. Zeke braced himself as she approached, squashing himself up against the freezer as much as he physically could. His mind jumped back to the look on Lara's face as Cassie moved toward him, and suddenly he understood because he was fucking terrified. Lara was telling the truth all along, she had picked up the ring from the jewellers. The words of Winston Smith rang out in Zeke's brain as he remembered the comment about his young wife. Lara hadn't lied. The ring had been at Ray's all along.

The room span, nothing made sense. The last fifteen years of Zeke's life as he knew it, had been one big lie. Everything was unravelling all around him, and he knew not how to stop it. He'd killed Lara, and she was the only person he'd ever met who really understood him. An emotional pain hit him, one that he'd never experienced before. Lara saw him for what he was. She saw his darkness as a good thing. Karan's injury had evoked yet more new emotions. His paucity of evidence, coupled with his rage, had seen him act rashly. There was so much pain, anger, and confusion rushing through him. He didn't know where to start! It also meant that if Lara hadn't killed Karan, there was only one other possibility.

"It was you, wasn't it? You killed Karan," he said, voice trembling. He was somewhere between angry, terrified, and heartbroken. He'd seen none of this coming.

Cassie closed in on him, ignoring his words completely. Zeke shut his eyes and braced himself. His leg was a hindrance, and given how prepared she probably was, he wasn't sure he could take her on. He opened his eyes as Cassie approached him and looked at Kara. This wasn't how it was supposed to happen.

Cassie arrived at the freezer and stopped. She reached out slowly with her hand towards his face.

"Hey," she said as she stroked his cheek gently. "It's okay. It's okay." Zeke slowly recoiled his head away from her hand and looked her up and down. What the fuck was happening?

"You see?" she asked, motioning towards the freezer. "We're the same, you and I!"

Zeke followed her gaze and looked down at the body in the chest, "No," he said, shaking his head. "No, we're not."

For so long, he had been terrified of what would happen if she found out what he was capable of, what she would do or say if she found out he was a killer. But she already knew, and she was the same, but as much as she was, she wasn't! This woman had no soul or remorse; Jones was an innocent man. Lara had been in love with him, and Karan was exceptional, and she'd seen them all killed. Zeke didn't know what he was, but killing depraved souls saved him. He wasn't a remorseless killer.

"No," he said once more with conviction. "We're nothing alike." Cassie ran the tip of her finger sensually down his body to his belt. She wrapped her finger around it and slowly pulled him towards her. With her head inches from his, she whispered in his ear.

"I know what you've done, Mr Olsen." She then took her hand and grabbed his face, twisting it harshly back towards the freezer. "You did this," she said. "His death is on your hands as much as mine. Between you being a careless junkie, letting your girlfriend pick up the ring, and leading this man here. You caused this, if it wasn't for you, he wouldn't be dead. I did this for us. He would have ruined our family Zeke."

"And Karan, Lara?" he asked mournfully.

"You killed Lara."

"Because you set me up," he yelled passionately. "You knew I'd be angry, and you knew that I would trust you over anyone else. How could you do that to me?"

"I didn't make you do anything. No, I just made you see what had to be done. Even if you were sloppy again! Lara knew too much, and it's a shame. Pretty young thing, I think she liked you."

"Don't," he said. "And don't act like we're a team on this. I don't kill innocent people!"

"Lara was innocent, and you killed her! I did that to show you, so you could see who you really are.

"Oh, and I know what happened with Ray. Where do you think I was that night? I saw you playing the knight in shining armour. You know she watched you from upstairs."

Zeke shook his head repeatedly, "No!" he said, "This isn't real. This can't be happening." Zeke took his hand and removed hers from his face. "And Karan?" he asked.

"He knew what you were, Zeke. He figured it out. Tell me, how good a friend do you think he was? Enough to lie for you. You murdered Ray. Do you really think he wouldn't have gone to the police?"

"It doesn't matter!"

"Really, then answer me this, Zeke, what would you have done if he'd woken up and decided to talk to the police?"

"Nothing Cassie!" he yelled. "He was our friend. I couldn't have killed him."

"You're weak," she said.

"He was innocent, Cass!"

"Don't be so naïve!" she scolded. "No one in this life is innocent."

"You can't just kill people because they pose a threat to you, Cassie."

"Oh," she said, "like the men in New York?"

"It's so different. They were violent thugs. Who knows how many people they had hurt?"

"And Ray? Didn't you bludgeon him to death?"

"Ray was a piece of shit, Cassie."

The crushing reality that was unfolding around him made zero and perfect sense all at once. If he'd had spent his marriage paying attention, he might have picked up on it sooner. The signs had been there all along. They were too perfect, and he'd never understood why until now. They were precisely the same and completely different. Zeke looked over at Kara once more, then back at Cassie.

All the fears he'd had about Cassie finding out who he was, hoping she would understand if she did. Never once had he pictured this. His wife was a monster, a calculated one at that. Ever since they'd met, she'd been at least three steps ahead of him. She'd manipulated him, knew his every move, every thought, and every inclination. She'd probably even orchestrated the night they met. He felt powerless and stupid. He thought he'd been given a second chance at life, one where he could do some good. And now, once more, he was staring down the barrel of the gun. He never thought everything he treasured would be taken from him by the one he loved.

"You can't kill innocent people, Cassie!" he repeated, "None of the people you killed deserved to die!"

"Zeke," she said, "spin it however you like. I'm a killer, and so are you.

"I see you, and you see me. Don't you see? It's you, me, and our daughter, us against the world. That's the way it has to be, Zeke. We're family, and we stick together."

Zeke considered it, maybe she was right. Perhaps they weren't so different after all. I mean, who was he really kidding? Killing made him feel good. It took away his pain and his urges. Was he being virtuous? Or just doing what he wanted? It almost made sense, she almost convinced him. But as he looked into her eyes, he realised that there was no remorse, no love, no consequence. How many other people had she killed? If he failed to acquiesce now, she would probably kill him, and if not now, then when? This wasn't the love he thought he would have, but realistically he had no other choice but to concede, she'd won.

Zeke smiled at her and nodded; a sign that drew Cassie closer to him.

"You're right," he said. Cassie grinned back at him and opened her arms.

"Come here," she gestured. Zeke moved away from the freezer and stepped towards her. Their bodies collided as she wrapped her arms around him. "I love you," she whispered to him tenderly. He held her tight and squeezed her hard. Despite what she said, she couldn't be trusted, there was no way they were both walking out of here, and he knew it. He held on tight, knowing it would probably be the last time he did. He took a long look at Kara, and she returned his gaze. She ought to see her parents together one last time.

"I love you too," he replied. They stood together arm in arm like they had at the end of the wedding and danced their final song. It was just the two of them and for a moment nothing else mattered. He felt the warmth of her skin against his as he held on to her for dear life. As they waltzed, he looked over Cassie's shoulders and smiled at Kara. Cassie leaned into him, opened her mouth, and whispered. "I mean, Zeke, who really gets to decide who lives and who dies? Who deems one life worthy of living and another not?"

Zeke didn't reply. Instead, he took one final look at his daughter and then back to Cassie. He moved his head so that he could look her straight in the eye, then he bent forward and kissed her tenderly on the forehead, moved his mouth to her ear and whispered,

"I do!"

As he uttered the word *do*, he reached behind him and silently withdrew the screwdriver from the back of his trousers. He moved it between them stealthily before driving it into Cassie's inner thigh with force.

A look of shock appeared on Cassie's face as she let out a gasp. The warm arterial blood gushed from her leg like a bloody waterfall as he removed the tool and let it fall to the floor. As it dropped with the dripping blood, he realised how poetic it all was. Were it not for Lara, he never would have had it.

He held Cassie tight as the blood painted them red with its heat. She looked at him, and their eyes met. Her face began to pale and wizen as she slowly drained of life. Tears streamed from his eyes and fell onto her hair as he stroked it with his hand. This was far from how he wanted it to be. It was miles from the picture-perfect BBQ he'd painted in his head for this evening. But even if they'd walked out of the garage together that night, no one would ever be safe from her, not him, and definitely not Kara. She was everything he'd been trying to rid the world of to make it better for his infant daughter, and there was no way he was letting her leave this garage alive.

Cassie had outthought, outmanoeuvred, and out-bluffed everyone and everything her entire life. She fooled him for years, but for once, the look on her face was of pure surprise. In the last fifteen minutes, he'd learnt more than he had in fifteen years. Zeke was clear in his mind now, and he knew what he had to do. One thing mattered, one thing only, and she was sitting a few feet away in her chair. She was his life, his purpose, his Tabula Rasa, a blank slate; together, they could make the world a better place.

As he gently lowered Cassie to the floor, he realised that their common ground was what set them apart. He'd chosen her because they were similar. A moment ago, he thought it was a mistake, but when he looked at his daughter, he realised this was exactly what was supposed to happen. Fate had brought them here, he could raise her in his image, gone was the dread of her discovering who he really was, they would do this together. As Cassie had said, it would be the two of them versus the world.

As warm blood leaked from her like a burst dam, their eyes locked, and he knew that she'd realised she was about to die. Zeke lowered her to the ground slowly. He held on to her dearly as they sunk, until finally, bloodied and still holding on to each other; they lay on the floor. Side by side, with her head on his shoulder just as they had done in this exact spot in the field all those years ago. She didn't fight or protest. She just held him as she let go. It was like the dimming of a switch, the fading of a song, or the lights coming on at the end of their dance. Her time was up.

Cassie lay on her back in a vast pool of blood. He kissed her one last time before he drew her eyelids to close. Then he shuffled away, lay with his back to the cabinets, and drew his legs up to his chest. Zeke then put his head in his hands, and he began to cry.

The pond of blood trickled out from the middle towards the edges of the garage, it encircled Cassie, and she lay there like a bloodied, fallen angel. The tears from his eyes had dropped to his lap and mixed in with the blood that was all over him. It had taken less than five minutes for life to depart her, but it seemed like an eternity.

Zeke looked up and saw Kara waving her limbs at him from across the garage. She was still silent despite having been caught in a tidal wave of blood, and seeing her soaked, his attention shifted, and he hurriedly crawled across the floor towards her leaving a bloody trail as he went.

"Kara!" he called out. "Kara, I'm coming."

He reached the other side and picked her up immediately. She'd seen enough horrors for today. She smiled as he swung her softly in her seat. He reached the door and opened it. The sun beamed in signalling a new dawn, and they stepped out together into the sunshine closing it behind them.

Zeke sat down on a lounger and placed his daughter in her seat on the chair next to him. He grabbed a cold drink from the cooler, opened it, and took a sip. Then he opened the lid on the BBQ, heat radiated out from within, and he turned across to Kara and said, "I think it's ready."

Her eyes met his, and he saw the reflection of the flames dance in her pupils. Her face was covered in her mother's blood, but she just beheld him with wonder and curiosity. Then her look shifted from him as she turned slightly and motioned towards the garage.

"You're right," he said, "there's no time to relax." He stood, picked her back up and started back towards the garage.

"We have much work to do, you and I!"

Thank you very much for reading, as an independent author I very much appreciate and depend on reviews (both good and bad) so, if you enjoyed the book (or didn't) and you are able to then a review would be very much appreciated.

John

Printed in Great Britain
by Amazon